Murder at the Petroglyphs

by

Patricia Smith Wood

Aakenbaaken & Kent

Murder at the Petroglyphs

Copyright 2019 by Patricia Smith Wood, all rights reserved.

No part of this book may be used or reproduced in any manner whatsoever without written permission except in the case of brief quotations for use in articles and reviews.

aakenbaakeneditor@gmail.com

This is a work of fiction. Names, characters, places and incidents are either the product of the author's imagination or are used fictitiously. Any resemblance of the fictional characters to actual persons living or dead is entirely coincidental.

Cover design by Lila Romero

ISBN: 978-1-938436-96-3

Dedicated

To my Mom and Dad

To Mom for instilling in me the joy of reading;
To Dad for teaching me how to write a story

1

Thursday Evening

Tonight the spirits of the Ancient Ones walk among the sacred rocks.

On his first day as a new ranger at Petroglyphs National Monument, Nick Ellis heard people talk about the spirits. He hadn't believed them until he experienced it for himself one night under the full moon. It rattled him so much he considered transferring. Free-roaming spirits had not been part of the job description.

But when he learned about this sacred space and how important it remained for the Pueblo Indians in the area, his initial fear drained away. It was replaced with a sense of peace and respect for what the place represented, and the ancient culture who had created the symbols.

Petroglyphs National Monument on the far west side of the bustling city of Albuquerque, New Mexico is a popular tourist destination, and even locals love hiking the area. Tonight, after the last visitor left, Nick spent half an hour making sure the trails concealed no lingering tourists. Next, he walked toward the small amphitheater to check for items left behind by the day's guests.

His pulse quickened when he heard a sound, and he stopped short. He took a deep breath and pulled out his flashlight. A young coyote stood on the low wall, gazing at him. Nick exhaled quietly, and the animal turned away. Then, with graceful ease, it leaped from the low wall and left as silently as it arrived.

Nick pointed the flashlight toward the right corner and let it play across the floor at the bottom. It illuminated a pile of clothing.

Oh, great. Somebody forgot their jacket and backpack.

He stepped closer, and the flashlight fell from his hands. A body lay on the floor of the amphitheater.

And Nick, for the second time in his career, considered asking for a transfer.

2

Friday Morning

"You never cease to amaze me." Ginger Vaughn stared at her childhood friend and shook her head. She leaned against the office doorframe, waiting for a response.

Harrie McKinsey looked up from the manuscript in front of her and peered over her reading glasses. "What did I do this time?"

Ginger sat in the chair facing Harrie's desk. "I just got a call from Mark Goodrum. He wanted to confirm 'our plans' to meet him and the other guys on Saturday to watch them fly their drones."

"So?" Harrie pushed back a stray lock of her long auburn hair and grinned at Ginger.

"That's all you can say? When were you planning to tell me about this, and why are 'we' going out to the West Mesa to see a bunch of amateur radio operators fly toy airplanes?"

Harrie blew out a breath. "First, you know perfectly well they are NOT 'toy airplanes.' Second, we discussed this at the club meeting last week. You and I were both interested in the slide show Mark put on about drone flying. We wondered how so many hams in the area became intrigued with them."

"Well, sure. But I don't remember my saying I actually wanted to go out in the desert, in the hot sun, wind blowing my hair into a tangled mess, and observe these guys at play. For crying out loud. It's almost June. We should be doing indoor things."

Harrie sat back in her chair and watched Ginger, who hadn't yet looked her in the eye—an unusual situation for her best friend. "What's going on with you?"

Ginger said, "I've no idea what you mean."

Harrie sat without speaking, staring at this woman she knew almost as well as herself.

When Ginger looked up and met Harrie's gaze, she sighed. "Damn, you're good."

Harrie grinned. "True. But you're always up for an adventure. And you've never held back from outdoor activities—in May, or

June, or even July. So what's holding you back this time?"

"It's just that—well—Steve and the boys decided drones are the next big thing. It isn't enough we're all licensed amateur radio operators. Oh, no. They want to explore other ways to spend large amounts of money and weekends not doing their chores."

"I knew it," Harrie said. "I could tell something had you annoyed."

Ginger frowned. "Don't rub it in, Short Stuff. And stop grinning at me, you silly goose."

"Don't tell me you've burned through your inheritance already?"

Ginger looked confused. "What . . . ?"

Harrie shook her head. "It occurs to me you and Steve worked hard all your lives to provide a lovely home, take care of your handsome, talented twins, and build a great life for yourselves. While the bequests we all received from your good friend and my ex-husband were unexpected, I realize you guys were already prepared to send the boys to college and take care of your own retirements."

"So what's your point?"

"Look." Harrie carefully chose her words. "Can't you see? Now is a great time for Steve and the boys to strike out and find things to do together. Before long both Rob and Chris will graduate high school. Next they'll be gone to college and after that . . . ." she shrugged.

Ginger's eyes welled with tears. "Exactly." She brushed at her eyes. "I've thought about that a lot. I also wonder if perhaps we should set up a trust fund for the twins. That would be the best use of Nicos Constantine's money. But Steve seems to feel we should focus on having fun with them while we can."

Harrie said, "What's wrong with that? You've covered all the bases. You might as well live it up and make lots of great family memories."

Ginger sighed. "You always say exactly what I need to hear, don't you?"

"It's easy. I can get inside your head and read what you're thinking."

"That's a little creepy."

Harrie stood and walked around the desk. "Hey let's go grab some lunch and talk about getting the whole gang together for this drone thing."

Ginger sighed, and a big smile played across her face. "Sure, why not? I always give in to whatever wild-haired scheme you come up with. But I beg you, promise me one thing."

"What's that?" Harrie said.

"It hasn't been long since our last adventure."

"So?"

Ginger sighed. "So, I'm begging you. Please, please, please. This time, will you promise you won't get us involved in another murder?"

Harrie picked up her handbag from the credenza and grinned at Ginger. "Sweetie, I never make promises I can't keep."

3

Saturday Morning

Early Saturday morning Ginger drove to Harrie's house, collected her friend, and headed to The Village Inn for a breakfast of coffee and pancakes. By the time they got back in the car, Ginger once again displayed her bright smile and eager attitude.

"I'm glad I encouraged Steve and the boys to take his SUV and go on ahead. This is fun." She maneuvered her yellow VW out of the restaurant parking lot and eased into traffic.

Harrie adjusted her seat belt. "It's great. I wasn't looking forward to the long drive alone." She looked out her window. "But I'm disappointed DJ had to work today. I swear, there's always something going on at the FBI, and my husband ends up in the big middle."

"I know," Ginger said. "But look at it this way. Now Steve will have the pleasure of introducing DJ to the hobby later, and that'll make them both happy. They have such fun futzing around together."

"I guess," Harrie muttered. "Anyway, I'll admit today I'd rather navigate than drive."

Ginger shot her a glance. "Since when don't you like to drive?"

"I didn't say that. I love to drive." She paused, the slightest beat too long, before continuing. "It's just that . . . I want to pay particular attention to the scenery. Besides, I have the directions right here on my phone, and that's what I can contribute."

Ginger frowned. "Uh huh. Sure." She turned her head for a quick glance at Harrie. "You're up to something."

Harrie sighed. "Woman, you're impossible. Why do you always think I'm up to something?"

"Hmmm, let's think this through." Ginger tilted her head in mock concentration. "Do you suppose it's because . . . you ARE always up to something?"

But Harrie didn't take the bait. "You'd better turn left at Montgomery. We need to end up going westbound on Montano, all the way to Unser."

"How convenient. It's lucky for you I need to concentrate on the traffic. For your information, this isn't over. I'll find out eventually what's going on."

Harrie again changed the subject. "What's up with this town and its habit of giving one street two different names?"

Ginger shrugged. "You mean like Montgomery becoming Montano?"

Harrie nodded. "Yeah, and like Comanche turning into Griegos. Why the need to change the names?"

"The way I heard it . . . " Ginger went into her mom/educator mode.

Harrie released the breath she'd been holding. Relief flowed through her like warm milk. She focused on Ginger's explanation.

". . . it all happened after World War II or thereabouts. For years, Albuquerque extended only a little past the railroad tracks. When they chose the site for the University back in 1889, there was nothing much beyond it. University Boulevard was just a dirt road for several years. East of the University, it was mostly mesa. In the Thirties and Forties, they had built houses toward the mountains all along Central Avenue, mostly close to the University. After World War II the town grew quickly. More homes and businesses were built. The builders named the streets, and they rarely paid any attention to how those streets might eventually come together."

Harrie said. "How do you know all this stuff?"

Ginger shrugged. "Blame it on my youth. As a young teacher, I became obsessed with teaching my seventh grade students the history of our state and this city. I suppose because I was so enchanted with it, I tried to instill the love of history in them."

"Well you are an inspiration to us all. I feel downright disloyal for not having information like that at my fingertips."

They continued chatting throughout the rest of the trip, and Ginger didn't mention her suspicions. Harrie counted herself lucky for the reprieve. She needed more time before being grilled. Thinking about last night's dream wasn't a good idea.

They arrived at the George J. Maloof Airpark by 7:30 AM. Already knots of people gathered around the owners of model airplanes, radio controlled cars, and drones.

Harrie spotted their friend Mark, and the other hams from the radio club who surrounded him. They, too, were eager to see the drones after hearing Mark's talk.

Steve and the boys stood close by, observing the process of setting up and readying the equipment. Ginger and Harrie joined them.

"So what have you learned so far?" Ginger slipped her arm through Steve's.

Steve grinned. "I definitely want one."

Ginger shook her head and turned to Harrie. "Didn't I tell you? Can I read these guys or what?"

Harrie nodded. "Definitely."

Rob, oldest of Ginger and Steve's identical twin sons by three minutes, grabbed his mother and lifted her off the ground. "Mom! Drones are V Lit!" He set her down with a flourish.

Ginger tugged at her shirttail. "Robert James Vaughn, knock that off. You're too old to keep picking me up all the time! You're gonna pull a muscle or something."

Chris, the other twin, gleefully laughed at his brother. "You dork. Stop showing off."

Rob lunged at his brother, who expected the move and ducked just out of reach. Then they took off running.

Steve sighed. "I wish I had their energy and flexibility."

Harrie said, "Okay, I give up. What did Rob just say?"

Steve and Ginger grinned. Steve said, "I'm not surprised you don't know. We only found out last week. It's some of the latest teen slang."

Harrie frowned. "It's like a foreign language. Where do they get this stuff?"

"Who knows," Ginger said. "But the translation for us old folks is this: V stands for very, and Lit means 'hot' or 'cool' or whatever we used to say when something was the very best."

"Great," Harrie said. "I think I'll wait until they speak English again before I try conversing with them."

A buzzing sound, like that of a very large bee, brought Harrie's attention back to the group surrounding Mark Goodrum. She saw a white object with red stripes decorating the four arm-like protrusions at the top. Mark had assembled the drone on a picnic table nearby. It lifted off from there as they watched. The machine sported four sets of whirring blades attached to the four arms.

Under the belly of the drone ascending above her, Harrie saw a tiny video camera.

"She's a beauty, isn't she?" Mark, controls in his hands, stood beside her and grinned at his complex machine.

"It certainly is," Harrie said. "What do you call these things?"

"This one," Mark said, "is a Quad-coptor Drone." He described all the wonderful features of his amazing machine.

The crowd gathered around them as Mark explained the features and abilities of the drone. Everyone focused on it flying overhead, and Harrie found she'd lost interest. She drifted away from the group.

Enjoying the calm, lovely morning and panoramic scenery filled Harrie with peace. The Sandia Mountains—and the city of Albuquerque sitting at their base—offered a spectacular view. She wandered a bit south of the drone field and reveled in the relative quietness. Something about the desert air seemed to isolate sound. She closed her eyes and almost imagined she stood miles away from the crowd.

At first her closed eyes saw only the imprint of the mountain view and the city she'd been staring at. In seconds, a similar but different scene replaced it in her mind's eye.

She drew in her breath, realizing this came from her dream last night. A crumpled body lay in a heap inside a circular structure, which seemed open to the air.

Harrie didn't know where it was or what had happened. But she knew, with cold certainty, that this dream would haunt her—like all the others—until she discovered the answer.

4

Saturday Morning

Harrie opened her eyes. *Clear your mind,* she ordered herself. *This is no time to remember your crazy dream.*

She turned back to the ham radio group. They were now farther north and west. No one seemed to notice she wasn't among them. Then she spied Ginger, standing apart from the rest of the crowd, scanning the area. Ginger waved, and Harrie watched her friend jog down the hill toward her.

Harrie hurried to rejoin her. "Where's the drone now?" she asked, as they closed the distance between them.

Ginger caught her breath before she responded. "Mark just landed it." She said, "You scared me, Short Stuff. I looked around, and you were gone."

Harrie patted her on the back. "I'm fine. You know I'm always exploring. It never occurred to me you'd worry."

Ginger pushed her long black hair away from her eyes. "I suppose I should have known. You can't stand still, can you?"

They walked slowly to join the crowd of amateur radio operators.

"So," Harrie said, "has Steve convinced you to get a drone for the family?"

Ginger grinned. "It was a done deal before you and I arrived. He's already planning a trip to the hobby store, and the boys are beside themselves with glee."

When they reached the group, Harrie noticed a new member she hadn't met. "Who's the young guy talking to Mark?"

Ginger grabbed Harrie's arm. "Come on. He's a friend of Mark's."

She pulled Harrie along and stopped beside the two men. "Mark," Ginger said. "Harrie hasn't met Nick."

Harrie flinched and hoped no one noticed. Nick, or more precisely Nicos, was the name of Harrie's first husband. It irritated her when she still reacted to the name. But that small rush of adrenaline annoyed her the most. Flight or fright syndrome. Harrie pushed all that out of her mind and smiled at Mark and his young friend.

Mark said, "Harrie, this is Nick Ellis. He's also a drone enthusiast."

"Nice to meet you Nick," Harrie said, as she shook his hand. He seemed so young, and bore no resemblance at all to the roguish Nicos Constantine, a point in his favor.

Ginger spoke up. "Nick's been telling us about his job. He's a ranger at Petroglyphs National Monument."

"How interesting," Harrie said. "I've lived here all these years, and I've never seen the Petroglyphs."

A shy smile creased Nick Ellis's face. "It's beautiful. You must come pay us a visit. The rock carvings are amazing. The site is covered with them."

Harrie nodded to Ginger. "Let's do that soon." She returned her attention to the ranger. "Tell me, Nick. What's the most interesting thing about your job?"

He took in a big breath and shot a glance at Mark. "Well, a few days ago, I would have said just working in such an amazing environment. We see such interesting people. They come from all over the world."

Mark nodded. "Nick told me about something that happened on Thursday night. I think it rattled him."

A chill went up Harrie's spine, as though the wind had turned cold and aimed itself directly at her. She forced herself to ignore it. "What upset you?"

He shook his head. "I guess I wasn't prepared," he said. "Over the past couple of years I've become used to sharing the monument with the spirits of the Ancient Ones. I'm not even freaked out when I feel their presence."

Ginger said, "Are you serious? Do you mean there are ghosts at the Petroglyphs?"

Nick shook his head. "We don't think of them that way. The word 'ghosts'—at least to me—implies a malicious energy, out to scare the living. That's not the way of The Ancient Ones. The Petroglyphs belong to them. It's their ancient land. We're the honored caretakers. Even today, the Pueblo Indians in this area consider it their sacred ground. The Ancient Ones are their ancestors, and they feel the same connection to this site. Everyone, visitors and staff alike, understands they're being allowed to tread on sacred ground. But *we* are the interlopers—not the spirits of The Ancient Ones."

More people had assembled, drones forgotten for the moment, to hear what Nick had to say. The young man realized he had become the center of attention, and he blushed a deep shade of red. "I'm sorry," he said. "I talk too much."

A chorus of "No" greeted him, and Harrie said, "Please go on, Nick. This is so interesting. I knew nothing of these Ancient Ones you mentioned."

Nick nodded. He seemed to relax a bit. "Well, like I said, I'm no longer nervous in their presence. It comforts me to know they still watch over the land and care for it. That's why I was so upset two nights ago when I had the duty to close up."

A familiar, queasy feeling came over Harrie. She swallowed hard and took a long breath. Her attention drifted from Nick's story to her dream from two nights ago. She doubted a connection, and yet . . . .

She had missed the first few sentences of what happened Thursday and forced herself to pay attention.

". . . but the coyote jumped over the wall, and I thought he was my big scare for the night. The flashlight played across the floor, and what I thought was a pile of clothes, turned out to be a body."

Several of the group reacted. Ginger turned to Harrie, who put her hand to her mouth.

Ginger leaned over and whispered, "What's wrong?"

Harrie waved her away and shook her head. "Just listen," she responded in a whisper.

Ginger pulled Harrie a small distance away from the group. "What do you mean?"

Several seconds went by before Harrie whispered, "That's what I wasn't ready to tell you." She turned her back to the group, and Ginger leaned in closer to hear her.

"I saw that body. I had another one of 'those' dreams, and I know I saw this body he's talking about."

Ginger stared at her friend.

Harrie grabbed her hand and squeezed it. "What do I do now?"

5

Saturday Morning

"Well, for now," Ginger said "I'd recommend you keep your mouth shut."

Harrie nodded. "But this should be a major story. Did you hear anything on the news yesterday?"

Ginger shook her head. "No, but that doesn't mean anything. I sometimes get busy and don't bother watching the news. Anyway, it's always so depressing, who needs it?"

"We'd better get back and see what else he's saying."

"Right."

They strolled back and melted into the edge of the group surrounding Nick and Mark.

Mark looked up and said, "Harrie, has DJ said anything to you about this body Nick discovered?"

Harrie's heart slammed into her chest. Her reaction surprised her as much as his question. Time seemed to stop. In reality, she knew only a few awkward seconds had passed.

She took a breath. "No, but why would he?"

Mark grinned at her. "Don't forget. I graduated from the FBI Citizens Academy. They taught us the FBI has jurisdiction on most federal lands. I figured they were brought in on something like finding a body at a National Monument."

Harrie's heart resumed its normal pace. She shrugged. "I'm not sure that always applies. Anyway, DJ wouldn't discuss something like that with me. These guys are very tight-lipped. What happens at the FBI—stays at the FBI. They certainly don't discuss current cases with their families."

Mark scratched his chin. "Hmm," he said. "I guess it makes sense." His eyes brightened, and his grin returned. "But what if you became involved in the case?"

Harrie frowned. "I'm not following you."

"Well," Mark said, "weren't you involved with a murder case not too long ago? Steve mentioned something at the meeting last week. He said it also involved DJ."

Harrie and Ginger looked at each other. Harrie bit her lower lip. "That was different. I got involved in an incident . . . ." She stopped and started over. "To be more precise, Ginger and I became involved in an investigation of a disappearance. We discovered it had a connection to one of DJ's cases. It was pure coincidence."

Ginger grinned. "We've stumbled into other murders over the past few years. Those were also connected to the FBI."

She stopped and held up both hands to forestall Harrie's inevitable reaction. "But those were flukes—nothing but flukes."

Mark's eyebrows raised. "Were you in the wrong place at the right time?"

Ginger said, "Let's say Harrie has a talent for finding trouble." She put her arm around Harrie's shoulders and gave her a look that said, "Stay cool."

Harrie nodded and blew out the breath she didn't even realize she'd been holding. "That's me, all right."

They stood around, chatting with the hams, watching the drones take off and land. Ginger stood with Steve and the boys, watching drones, while Harrie talked to Nick. She asked for his email address and provided a scrap of paper from her purse to write on.

By now, other drone enthusiasts had arrived, and at least four of the units were buzzing overhead. Not even the discovery of a body could keep attention on earthly matters when flying machines were present.

Harrie and Ginger eased away from the crowd again. None of the group took notice. The aerial display seemed to completely captivate Steve and the boys.

Ginger said, "We need to talk. I'll tell Steve we're leaving—if I can get his attention long enough."

Harrie noticed Nick Ellis now involved in getting his own drone ready for flight. She tucked away the paper on which he had jotted his email address. Maybe they could meet somewhere for coffee. She had a lot of questions but didn't want an audience around when she asked them.

6

Saturday Morning

DJ Scott checked his watch. Almost noon. Maybe he could get home before Harrie returned from her drone adventure.

He signed off on the 302 report he'd prepared and checked it one more time before uploading it to the system. Satisfied, he printed out a copy for his working file and attached it in the folder.

The new case was a strange one. At the moment it wasn't an FBI investigation, even though they had received a call from a ranger at the National Monument. For now, the National Park Service and detectives from APD were the lead investigators. That could change if circumstances warranted FBI participation. He hoped it wouldn't. As always, he worried about Harrie.

He knew she'd had a restless night. Over time, he realized her strange dreams caused her to toss and turn in her sleep. He assumed that was the reason for her movements during the early hours this morning. He'd considered waking her but decided against it. It didn't occur to him at the time that this latest homicide might be on her radar. It seemed unlikely, but after the meeting this morning, then reading other reports, his worries increased. Either he had developed his own sensitivity, or he now knew the signs of strange events entering his and Harrie's lives.

On his drive home, DJ listened to the local news. He sighed with relief at hearing no mention of the body found at Petroglyphs National Monument. That meant the shroud of secrecy they'd thrown around the investigation still held— for the moment. He realized that before long, someone, somewhere, would say too much.

He entered their spacious kitchen and noticed their two coffee cups from this morning still sat in the sink. That evidence indicated she hadn't returned yet. Excellent.

Then he saw the big red blinking light on their landline phone. A message. He pressed "play" and waited.

"Hi Sweetheart." Harrie's familiar voice warmed him. Odd she hadn't called him on his cell phone. He'd have to ask her why.

"Ginger and I had fun watching the drones this morning. You're going to love it. Steve and the boys are heading over to the hobby shop to look at some today. Ginger and I are still over on the West Side. We'll find a good place to have lunch, and then we want to explore. It's a great opportunity to take in Petroglyphs National Monument. See ya in a couple of hours."

The cheeriness in her voice almost convinced him. But DJ knew better. Now he understood her decision to leave the message rather than calling him.

How, by all that's good and true, would he keep her out of this latest adventure?

7

Saturday Afternoon

"Are you sure you want to do this?" Ginger looked over at Harrie while waiting for the red light to turn green.

Harrie knew she'd been too quiet since they'd left the restaurant. While eating lunch, they talked about the drones and their new ham radio friends. But Harrie remained unwilling to discuss the thing most occupying their minds—last night's dream, and today's visit to Petroglyphs National Monument.

What was there to say? She didn't know why the dream came to her, the identity of the deceased person, or how he or she became deceased. As usual, Harrie had only the sketchiest of information, yet a strong sense of urgency.

"I have no choice," she said. "Without more information, or understanding why I dreamed about this event, I don't know where else to start."

Ginger turned the car onto Unser Boulevard. "Have you thought about the reason you receive these dreams?"

"Of course. The first one, when I was a teenager, freaked me out. I didn't know where it came from or why it happened to me."

"But you became accustomed."

Harrie shrugged. "More or less. I'm not sure I'll ever really be accustomed to it."

Ginger persisted. "With your other dreams, once we discovered a connection, you solved the mystery, and the dreams stopped."

"What's your point?"

"It seems obvious. Isn't it reasonable to discuss this one with DJ, or even Swannie, before we embark on our own investigation?"

Harrie shook her head. "I don't view a visit to the Petroglyphs as being an investigation. I meant it when I said I've always wanted to check it out."

"Are you sure the body at the Petroglyphs is the same one you saw in your dreams?"

Harrie thought a moment. "No, and I won't be unless I find

something at the Petroglyphs tying it in with my dream. I had a huge reaction when Nick Ellis told his story, but I can't know if what I'm seeing is what he saw—not until I visit there."

Ginger remained quiet a few minutes. "Maybe you could just explain it that way to DJ. If you made him see your reason for getting involved, maybe he wouldn't be set on keeping you away from the action."

Harrie snorted. "Yeah, right. I have a big picture of that. You've seen how much effort DJ makes to prevent me from getting answers. To him, it's about keeping me safe."

Ginger nodded. "I know, and to you, it's about understanding the dreams and solving the mystery."

"I'm glad you see my point."

"So what's the answer? How do you satisfy your need to know and still keep DJ from having anxiety about your safety?"

Harrie shrugged. "If I knew the answer to that, I could start my own advice column."

Fifteen minutes later, they turned onto Western Trails, the road leading to the Visitor Center at Petroglyphs National Monument. They parked at the bottom of the hill and noticed two pathways. One on the right led to the building that housed the Visitor Center and several other trails leading to the stone art. The longer pathway to the left climbed a slight hill.

Harrie's skin tingled.

"Let's see where this leads us," she said, and walked toward the left path.

"Why?" Ginger hurried to join her.

"I sense it's important," Harrie said.

"Naturally." Ginger shifted her purse to her left shoulder.

They arrived at the amphitheater at the end of the path. It looked ready for use. A graceful roof used canvas sails for shade and sheltering visitors. The structure seemed perfect for small groups or individuals to sit and enjoy the quiet in the peaceful atmosphere. It was a simple, yet elegant semi-circular design. Stone pillars of simulated granite, pockmarked with small stones, stood at intervals wide enough to allow a breath-taking view of the landscape to the east.

In the first milliseconds, it reminded Harrie of photos she'd seen of the ancient Grecian amphitheaters, with their tiered stone seating, and their view of the stage at the bottom. One could almost imagine a performer standing in the pit below the benches, playing to an admiring audience. They would gaze down at him while he strummed a lute.

The overall impression promoted an air of peace and tranquility.

But not for Harrie.

Her imaginary audience would not see the crumpled body that Harrie now pictured in her own head.

Moments after she had stepped into the structure, she knew—this was the source of her latest dream.

The only thing missing was the crumpled, lifeless body.

8

Saturday Afternoon

Harrie and Ginger sat for several minutes inside the amphitheater while Harrie explained all she could about the dream.

Ginger stayed quiet for several seconds after Harrie finished. Then she said, "So if you had to guess, would you say the body was that of a man or a woman?"

Harrie frowned as she gave that some thought. "Hmm. My gut tells me it's a man. It's just a feeling I have."

"Okay," Ginger said, "then the next question seems obvious. Why have we not heard anything at all about this? Forget about television news. The newspapers have the time and the space to report on stuff like this. I read the Albuquerque Journal each morning, and so do you. I can't imagine why one of us wouldn't have seen something about it."

Harrie shook her head. "Beats me, but there must be a reason." She halted and grabbed Ginger's arm. "Something occurred to me."

"Lay it on me," Ginger said.

"I should have paid more attention to Mark when he asked me what DJ had to say about all this."

"I thought you provided a logical answer. There's no way he would discuss an ongoing Bureau case with you. Even I know that."

Harrie stood up and paced. "You're right, but that's not what I meant. I'm thinking if I can get information from someone else—say, for instance, our friend Detective Sergeant Cabrini Paiz, or our other close friend Lieutenant Bob Swanson...."

Ginger shook her head and rose from her seat. "Oh, no you don't." She intercepted Harrie in mid pace and grabbed her by the arm. "You know perfectly well Swannie is a direct conduit to your mother-in-law. He tells her, she tells DJ, then where are you?"

Harrie grinned. "I'm guessing about halfway there. Don't you see? If I go through someone else and DJ finds out, he won't be able to stop himself from asking me about it. Once he brings it up, we'll have a conversation on the subject."

"You know you're nuts, don't you?"

"Probably," Harrie said. She looked at her watch. "Come on, we need to get going."

They walked toward the parking lot. When they reached the adjoining path, Harrie said, "Shouldn't we take a quick peek at the Visitor Center? Maybe we could pick up more information about the Monument. Perhaps it'll give me some ideas."

"Okay," Ginger said, "but let's make it fast. I need to get home and assess the damage to our bank account after Steve's trip to the hobby store."

The Visitor Center was almost as inviting as the amphitheater. A covered area with tables and benches greeted them just outside the entrance. People could sit and enjoy another spectacular view of the city below. Inside, rows of shelving displayed books, maps, and pamphlets about the area. It was inviting and would, Harrie realized, require another, longer visit.

A gray-haired gentleman stood behind the counter. He smiled at them as they entered. "Welcome to the Petroglyphs," he said.

Harrie and Ginger thanked him, then stopped to look at some displays. Harrie selected a map, two books, and a video. She went to the counter to pay for them.

The man behind the counter sported a badge pinned to his shirt. It declared his name to be Ed. Ed smiled at Harrie and Ginger. "Are you ladies tourists?"

Harrie smiled back. "No, just almost-natives who've never taken the time to visit this place until now."

Ginger said, "We were on this side of town today and are remedying that oversight."

Ed grinned and nodded. "Know what ya mean. Lots of folks get so busy with the day-to-day grind, they sometimes don't get around to the interesting things. We're just glad you're here today."

Before long, Harrie and Ginger were having a great conversation with their new friend. He talked about the site, its history, and its being established as a national monument. Harrie could tell he loved this place, and he was a fountain of information.

"Take this building here," he said.

Harrie looked around, then back at Ed. "You mean the Visitor

Center?"

"Yes," Ed said. "I'll be you didn't know a famous lady lived here back in the day."

Harrie said, "She lived here in the Visitor Center?"

He grinned. "Well it wasn't a visitor center then. This was her house. They remodeled it to become the Visitor Center."

"Oh," Harrie said, "you had me going there for a moment. So who was this woman?"

Ed leaned on the counter and said, "Her name was Sophie Aberle, and she lived to be 100. She went to Stanford in 1927 and got her Ph.D. and Yale in 1930 and received her M.D. During those years women rarely achieved that. She spent a lot of time working with the Pueblo Indians too. Came to visit New Mexico for a while right after Stanford. Later she moved back here and continued her work after she graduated from Yale. She was quite the lady, and then being a doctor to boot. Yes sir, Sophie was one of a kind—bright, independent, a real achiever. When she married William A. Brophy, she opted not to take his last name."

Harrie said, "I imagine that choice was unusual, but I can see why she did it. Sounds like she was a real feminist."

Ed shook his head, "Nope, that's not it."

"Really?" Ginger said. "Then why not take Mr. Brophy's name?"

Ed grinned. "Because," he said, "she didn't want to be known as Sophie Brophy."

9

Saturday Afternoon

As soon as they were back in Ginger's car, Harrie pulled out her cell phone and pushed a speed-dial number.

"Who are you calling?" Ginger looked over at her friend before backing out of the parking space.

"Who do you think? Our friend Cabrini."

Ginger groaned and steered the car toward the exit. "Come on, you can't be serious. You shouldn't put her in that position."

Harrie narrowed her eyes. "I need information, and she's a likely source."

Cabrini answered on the first ring, as though already expecting a call. After a couple of minutes of idle chatter, Harrie got to the point. "I have a problem, Cabrini, and I need your help."

On the other end of the line, Harrie heard Cabrini sigh. "Is your problem going to become my problem?"

Harrie put the call on speakerphone. "I hope not," she said. "I'm here with Ginger. I put you on speaker so I don't have to repeat the conversation for her."

"Hi Ginger," Cabrini said. "I gather she's up to something again."

"Just so you know," Ginger said, "I tried to talk her out of this. It won't surprise you to learn she wouldn't listen."

On the other end of the line, they heard Cabrini chuckle. "Okay, what's up?"

"Well," Harrie said, her voice carefully noncommittal, "Ginger and I were having a discussion about police procedures, and since you're my go-to-person for homicides and the like in Albuquerque, I thought of you."

"I'm not sure I like how that sounds, but I understand. What's your question?"

Harrie outlined the events of the morning's drone adventure. Then she explained that one of the drone pilots had found a body.

The other end of the line was quiet for a couple of seconds before Cabrini spoke again. Her voice sounded strained. "What sort of information are you looking for?"

Harrie did a thumbs up for Ginger's benefit. "Have they identified the body found at the Petroglyphs, and can you tell me the cause of death?"

Cabrini didn't speak for such an unusual interval that Harrie feared she'd lost the connection. "Cabrini, are you still there?"

She heard a long sigh, then Cabrini spoke into the phone in a soft voice. "This really isn't a good time. I'm walking into a meeting as we speak. I'll get back to you."

Harrie and Ginger looked at each other. Harrie said, "Umm, okay, can you call me back when the meeting's over?"

Another, shorter pause. "I have to go now. Good talking to you."

The call disconnected. Harrie frowned.

"Okay, Sherlock," Ginger said. "Now what?"

Harrie put her phone back in her pocket. "Good question. I suppose I'll play it by ear. Drop me off at my house." She tapped her fingernails on the arm rest. Then she grinned. "This calls for strategic planning, and it's time I brought in the big guns."

Ginger glanced over at her friend. "And who would that be?"

Harrie raised an eyebrow. "Who else? My wonderful mother-in-law who, as you so nicely reminded me, has great access to the next best source—Lieutenant Bob Swanson."

"Gee," Ginger said, an edge of sarcasm in her voice, "why am I not surprised?"

Harrie grinned. "I love it when a plan comes together."

10

Saturday Afternoon

Detective Sergeant Cabrini Paiz slipped her smartphone into her pocket. She frowned as she stepped back inside the conference room.

"What's up?" Lieutenant Bob Swanson stood beside the whiteboard, dry-erase marker in hand.

Cabrini shook her head. "Wasn't who I expected. Sorry."

Several other APD detectives sat around the table, and Cabrini rejoined them. "What did I miss?"

Swannie shook his head. "Nothing, really. We were trying to brainstorm other ways to determine the identity of our homicide."

Detective Kramer spoke up. "When will we get a report from OMI?"

Cabrini said, "They won't have anything until later this afternoon. I had hoped that call would be them. They said earlier they're swamped and short-staffed."

Kramer blew out a breath. "They should pay those people more. You couldn't get me to do that job for all the tea in China."

Another detective, brand new to the division, grinned and spoke up. "I heard they were using a lot of interns from the medical school, and there's a whole lot of pukin' goin' on."

"Okay," Swannie said. "Let's can the humor. We have a dead guy we can't identify, and we're short on time, so think, people. Think!" His irritation silenced the jokester, who turned pink and studied his tablet with deep concentration.

Cabrini spoke up. "We need to reach out to some of our informants."

They tossed that idea around for a few minutes, and each detective made a list of likely sources of information for follow-up.

"We should reach out to the FBI," Swannie said.

Several groans went up around the table. He held up both hands to silence the complaints.

"Come on," he said. "I didn't say we're turning it over. I'm just saying it's imperative we ID this fellow before the news leaks out."

Cabrini sighed. "I'm afraid we've missed that boat, Sir."

Now it was Swannie's turn to frown. "Do I really want to know what you mean by that?"

Cabrini grinned. "Oh, probably not. But one way or the other, you'll be hearing more."

Swannie sat back in his chair, gazing up at the ceiling. "Okay. Who squealed?"

"Apparently the young ranger who discovered the body," Cabrini said, but didn't meet Swannie's eyes.

She took a breath. "I don't know all the details, but apparently he encountered Harrie and Ginger this morning."

Swannie sprang from his chair and paced the floor, a string of fiery, colorful language erupting from his lips. When he'd finished and regained his composure, he smiled. But to Cabrini, it was a scary smile, and she waited for the words she dreaded.

"I. Don't. Care. HOW you do it," Swannie said, through gritted teeth. "But I want you to make sure our little redheaded dynamo does NOT involve herself in this investigation. And she'd better keep her mouth shut about it. You got that?"

Cabrini nodded, but who was she kidding? This would not end well. "Of course, Lieutenant. Your wish is my command."

Swannie's shoulders slumped, and he sat down, shaking his head. He scrubbed his face, as if to wipe away the consternation he obviously felt.

"Just do the best you can, okay? Maybe we can distract her with something else."

"Oh, sure thing. That always works so well." Cabrini stood and gathered up her folders.

"Keep me posted, will you?" Swannie reverted to downright pleading. "I have to walk a pretty tight rope here."

Cabrini turned back to him and smiled as she prepared to walk out the door. She felt sorry for him.

"I know, Lieutenant. I know."

11

Saturday Afternoon

Lieutenant Swanson closed the door to his office. He gazed at the pile of paperwork waiting on his desk, shook his head, and sighed. Whoever said computers would do away with paper didn't know how the real world operated.

He set a fresh cup of coffee on his favorite coaster, a square tile that read "If I want your opinion, I'll give it to you."

It brought a smile to his face and lightened his heart. His buddy, Bernie Thomas, had given it to him years ago. They'd been partners when Swannie first joined the force. Bernie had seniority, and as a rookie, Swannie found it difficult to know when to speak up and when to defer to his senior officers. One night after a particularly active shift working a DWI roadblock, they were escorting a very tipsy driver to the police van for his trip to the city jail. The fellow was verbose in his objections to being hauled off to the hoosegow for the night. He was a regular they had arrested half a dozen times in as many months.

Swannie told the guy he'd better call his wife so she wouldn't be worried. The inebriated citizen climbed unsteadily into the van, turned to Swannie and said, "If I want your opinion, I'll give it to ya." Then he fell, face down, and passed out.

Bernie and Swannie looked at each other, and Bernie said, "I guess he told you."

They burst into laughter, and Bernie teased Swannie about it for months. Not long after the incident, Bernie got his promotion to detective. He went to a local shop and had the tile specially made. He gave it to Swannie as a reminder of when to speak up and when to hold his tongue.

The current situation looked like a perfect opportunity to hold his tongue. If Harrie McKinsey was on the trail of this murder, he wanted someone else to intervene. He admired Harrie, and he and DJ had become good friends. Swannie's involvement with DJ's mother added another layer of complexity to the situation. Caroline Johnson was a sensible woman, but she often stood firmly with

Harrie when it came to tracking down clues connected to her strange dreams.

The ringing of the phone interrupted his thought process. He eagerly answered when he saw the caller ID. At last. The Office of the Medical Investigator.

He disconnected from the call and heaved a heavy sigh. The report was on its way. All of the medical language—that mess he hated to slog through—would be on his desk in less than an hour. The one immediate question he'd expected resolution for, however, couldn't be answered.

A search through every fingerprint and DNA database available to the OMI, which was extensive, returned no results. They still had no idea who their victim was, what had brought him to the Petroglyphs, or why he'd been killed.

12

Saturday Afternoon

Caroline opened the door and greeted Harrie with a hug.

When they went into the kitchen, Caroline said, "What brings you here on this lovely afternoon? I thought you and Ginger had plans."

Harrie sat in her favorite spot at Caroline's kitchen table and leaned back. "We had a full morning and a great time. But Ginger had to get home and check on things. Steve and the boys bought a drone this afternoon."

Caroline placed a cup of coffee in front of Harrie and sat across from her with a cup of her own. "That sounds like a major purchase."

"Yeah, I suppose it is," Harrie ran her finger around the rim of her coffee cup. She knew Caroline was waiting for a more complete response, and she looked up to see the older woman watching her.

Harrie took a sip of coffee. "I guess I should explain why I dropped by."

Caroline smiled and reached over to pat Harrie's hand. "Hon, you don't need an excuse to be here. You're part of my family, and I love your visits. But I'm guessing something's on your mind."

Harrie grinned. "You know me too well. There is something." She leaned in and propped her elbows on the table. "I had one of my dreams last night."

Caroline set her cup down and nodded. "I thought it might be something like that. You get a particular look when you're struggling with one of your dreams. It's hard to describe, but you turn inward—as though you were consulting an inner resource only you can hear or see."

"Huh," Harrie said, nodding. "I never knew I did that. But it's the most accurate way to describe the experience. I think I dream every night, like everybody else. But these dreams are so different. They're almost like lucid dreams."

Caroline nodded. "I've had quite a few lucid dreams in my day.

It's a strange experience, isn't it? To be dreaming, and aware you're dreaming. It's like standing outside yourself and being both an observer and a participant."

"That's what I mean," Harrie said. "It's so different. And I usually remember them better than my ordinary dreams. I'm glad you don't think I'm nuts."

Caroline frowned. "I would never think that. You're the brightest, most stable young woman I've ever known. But I hate to see you becoming consumed by these dreams. So tell me. What did this one show you?"

Harrie explained the dream and related the events of the morning and afternoon.

After Harrie described their visit to the Petroglyphs, Caroline said, "I'd love to visit there. Maybe if you go again, I can tag along."

"I'd love that. But for now, I need your help."

"If I can, I will," Caroline said. "What do you need?"

Harrie took a deep breath and hoped she wasn't being too outrageous in asking this.

"I'd like you to talk to Swannie. I thought if you would describe my dream to him, maybe he'd volunteer relevant information about the case."

Caroline hesitated. "I'll do what I can. I know that sounds wishy-washy, but I think you understand what I mean. I must be very careful not to take advantage of our relationship. If Swannie doesn't want to talk about it, I'll have to accept that."

Harrie nodded. "That makes sense. I know my request is over the line."

"No, I see why you're asking," Caroline said. "I'm sure I'd try whatever I could to get information if I were in your situation."

Harrie said, "Glad you understand. I know it's a wild shot, and if you feel uncomfortable about doing it . . . ."

"No," Caroline shook her head. "That's not it. It's just that I think I know how he'll react. I want you to be aware it's a slim chance I'll succeed."

Harrie sighed. "Yeah, I figured that. I got nowhere when I talked to Detective Cabrini Paiz."

Caroline frowned. "You already contacted Cabrini?"

"Yes," Harrie said, "and she shut me down when I asked the

question. Said she was going into a meeting. Wouldn't even agree to call me back afterwards."

Caroline chuckled. "Oh, boy. I'm just guessing here, but I'd bet that meeting was with Swannie and the task force."

Harrie perked up. "Task force? What task force?"

Caroline held up a hand to cut Harrie off. "That's as much as I know. Swannie said he had an important task force meeting right after lunch. We had planned to go out to dinner tonight, and he asked if we could postpone it until tomorrow. I could tell whatever's going on is important, and he needs to be available the rest of the day."

"Rats," Harrie said. "I guess I should revamp my plan."

Caroline grinned. "Okay, Miss Amateur Detective. What does that mean?"

Harrie shrugged. "It means this. As of now, your tall, handsome son is my next target in this quest for information."

Caroline leaned back against the chair, closed her eyes, and smiled. "I wish I could be a fly on the wall in your house tonight. The picture I see in my head—as I imagine DJ being pumped for information—is most entertaining."

13

Late Saturday Afternoon

"We need to talk." Swannie's shoulders slumped. He'd been reluctant to make this call. He knew it was the right thing—hell, who was he kidding—it was the only thing left to do. But he hated the necessity.

DJ chuckled before he said, "I realize how much that cost you, my friend. Just so you know, I'd feel the same way if I were in your position."

Swannie relaxed at the sound of DJ's voice. He thanked his lucky stars he had a good relationship with Caroline's son. DJ was a decent young man, and as bright as they came.

Swannie said, "Did you get the OMI report I sent you?"

DJ said, "I have it right here in front of me, but I've been swamped today. Haven't read it yet. Condense it for me?"

So Swannie explained the whole sad story. No record of fingerprints, no ID on the body, and currently no way to identify their victim. They discussed various aspects of the report for several minutes.

Swannie waited.

Finally, DJ said, "Do you want me to try? I know OMI has access to our fingerprint database, but I might have a few tricks I could use."

Swannie grinned and felt better already. "I hoped you'd say something like that."

"I'll do my best. Anything else?"

Swannie took another deep breath before he spoke. "Well, there is one more thing I might need your help with."

"Oh?"

"Um, well, ah . . . ."

"Okay," DJ said, "just get it out. What has Harrie done now?"

Swannie straightened up. "How did you know it had anything to do with Harrie?"

DJ laughed. "Let's say I'm developing my own 'Spidey' sense about my very challenging wife. Has she been after you to discuss this case?"

"Well not me, exactly. But she called Detective Sergeant Cabrini Paiz and pumped her for information." Swannie heard DJ groan.

Then DJ said, "I knew she was up to something. I could feel it, and that voice message she left on our answering machine today was so transparent. Just so you know, she's already taken a trip out to the Petroglyphs."

"What?" Swannie realized it came out more like a croak than a question.

"Relax," DJ said. "I'll handle Harrie. I'm heading home in the next few minutes. I'll nip this thing in the bud."

Now it was Swannie's turn to chuckle. "Oh, my boy. You sound so confident. How I hate to be the voice of experience here."

"Meaning what?" DJ said.

"Meaning, my young friend, you are no match for Harrie. She has the genetic experience, handed down through the ages, from every woman who ever set out to reach a goal."

"What do you suggest?"

Swannie warmed to his subject. "Capitulation my friend, capitulation."

DJ made a noise that sounded as though he might be choking. Then he said, "I can't believe you said that. You want me to hand over everything to her?"

"Of course not," Swannie said. "Get a grip. I'm thinking of something much easier."

"Oh, I can't wait to hear this."

"It's simple," Swannie said. "We make her THINK we're giving her what she wants. But we give her only enough to make her feel part of the investigation."

After a long pause, DJ said, "Swannie, my friend, if this plan of yours works, I will crown you the undisputed master of feminine curiosity."

"And if it doesn't?" Swannie waited for an answer.

"Then I'll say 'told you so.'"

14

Saturday Evening

Harrie finished setting the table as she heard the garage door open. By the time DJ entered the kitchen, she had poured two glasses of wine, set them on the table, and turned to greet her husband.

DJ took her into his arms and kissed her with gusto. Then he said, "Let me go change out of these clothes. After that, I'll join you for a lovely glass of wine."

Harrie smiled at him. "Great idea. The roast needs just a few more minutes."

While DJ changed, Harrie contemplated her best move. She needed a careful approach. DJ was adamant about not discussing Bureau cases. The only reason she'd ever known about any of them was because of her personal involvement. The first time she laid eyes on DJ, he had been there to question her about an FBI matter.

She leaned against the counter, looking out the window toward the east. The mountains were spectacular at this time of day. A New Mexico sunset was a riotous mixture of pinks and yellows in the western sky. The purple reflection of the sun, contributed by the Sandia Mountains in the east, made the view breathtaking.

She jumped in alarm when DJ slipped his arm around her waist and pulled her to him.

"You seem a bit on edge," he said into her ear.

This wouldn't be as easy as she'd thought. "A little. I was drinking in the view, and you startled me."

"Speaking of drinking, let's have that wine you poured for us." DJ smiled as he reached for the glasses and handed her one.

She felt awkward—like she'd been laying a trap for DJ—and here he was, so sweet and trusting. And here she was, trying to figure out the best technique to worm information out of him. How could she?

They went into the den, and Harrie started for her favorite chair. But DJ sat on the sofa and patted the seat beside him.

Harrie changed course and joined him. *Oh Lord. This isn't at all the way I'd pictured this evening.* The smile on her face felt "fixed" in place, as though she was trying to pull a con. *Why do I keep thinking these things? I can't do this right now. Maybe I should wait until tomorrow.*

She didn't hear DJ speak at first.

"Hey, Earth to Harrie. Are you with me?"

"I . . . I'm sorry. Did you say something?" Her heart pounded like a little kid caught slipping her unwanted broccoli to the dog.

"I said, tell me about the drone flight today, and how did you like the Petroglyphs?"

"Oh," Harrie said, and even she could hear the false brightness in her voice. "The drones are amazing. There were so many people out there, and several drones flying. I don't know how they avoid crashing into each other."

"Did anything interesting happen while you were there?"

Harrie frowned. "What do you mean 'interesting?'"

DJ smiled at her, and it dawned on Harrie that he was teasing her. He said, "Oh, I don't know. Did you meet any new people?"

Harrie leaned over and set her wine glass on the coffee table in front of her. "Okay, what's going on? Why so many questions?"

DJ's eyes were wide. "I'm just interested in your adventures today. Sorry I had to miss the drones, and I'm especially sorry I didn't get to go with you and Ginger to the Petroglyphs."

Harrie frowned. She didn't look at DJ. "The Petroglyphs. Who said anything about the Petroglyphs?"

DJ reached over and lifted her chin so she had to look at him. "You did. In the message you left on the answering machine. So . . . how were the Petroglyphs? Did you find anything interesting?"

Things were not working out the way she'd planned. She couldn't think. She had the awful feeling that DJ could see right through her and her elaborate plan to get information. Panic set in and her brain froze.

At that moment, Harrie thought she knew how a deer felt when caught in the headlights of oncoming traffic.

She couldn't have moved if her life depended upon it.

15

Monday Morning

"And what did you say?" Ginger leaned her elbows on Harrie's desk.

Harrie shook her head. "What could I say? I've never been so tongue tied in my life."

"You're kidding," Ginger said, the surprise showing in her eyes. "You always know what to say—even if it happens to be wrong."

"Not this time. He had me, and he knew it. It's almost as though he had prepared for what I was about to do. It seemed like he'd been warned."

"Caroline," Ginger said. "Caroline must have warned him."

"No," Harrie said. "Caroline would never have done that. Besides, when I told her yesterday what happened, she was stunned too."

"Did she get a chance to talk to Swannie about it like she said she would?"

"Nope," Harrie said. "She didn't see Swannie until they went to church together Sunday morning. After church they went to brunch with some friends, and right after that, Swannie said he had to get back to the office for a meeting."

"Hmmm," said Ginger. "That sounds a little fishy if you ask me."

"Well," Harrie said, "according to Caroline, Swannie is very worried about this task force thing they have going. She doesn't think he's had much sleep, and she's worried about him."

Ginger leaned back in the chair in front of Harrie's desk. "Are you sure this murder at the Petroglyphs is the subject of Swannie's task force?"

"It has to be," Harrie said. "Everything makes sense. The secrecy surrounding the murder and the victim. I've listened to the news several times each day and scoured the Journal. I've even looked online for information. There's still not one word about that body. Nothing. If I didn't know better, I'd say the journalists in this town were deliberately hiding information about it."

"So, now what? How do you plan to find out what's going on if you can't even bring yourself to question DJ about it?"

Harrie had been tapping a ballpoint pen against the edge of her desk. She suddenly stopped and looked up at Ginger. "That's it," she said and pushed her chair back. She grabbed her handbag and rummaged inside.

Ginger frowned. "What are you doing?"

Harrie dug around in her purse, removing item after item and piling them on the desk in front of her. "I'm looking for a piece of paper. It's here somewhere." She continued piling things on her desk until nothing remained in the handbag.

Ginger sighed. "If you'll tell me what you are looking for, maybe I can help."

Harrie slumped in the chair. "I had a piece of paper with me on Saturday. I handed it to Nick, the park ranger, and asked him to give me his email address. I told him I'd like to talk to him about what he saw that night at the Petroglyphs. He wrote the email address on the piece of paper, and I put it . . . ." She twisted her mouth, deep in thought.

She grinned and dug among the items from her purse. She grabbed her billfold, opened it and produced a small piece of paper. "That's it," she said. "I found it."

Ginger said, "What's next?"

Harrie waved the piece of paper at Ginger. "How about you and I see if we can arrange a meeting with Park Ranger Nick Ellis?"

16

Later Monday Morning

DJ Scott couldn't remember exactly when he'd formed the idea of becoming an FBI agent. As best he could figure, it had to be when he was about ten years old.

His mother envisioned him becoming a successful lawyer, like the ones she worked with every day. But he had a different dream.

From the time he started first grade as a six-year old, his mother's best friend took care of him before and after school. Because his father had died prior to his birth, his mother had always needed to work. DJ didn't mind the arrangement for his care. He loved Joan Werner, and her house was like a second home to him. There were always freshly baked cookies after school, with a big glass of milk. Many nights DJ and his mother ate dinner with Joan in her large comfortable kitchen. She made the most amazing Eggplant Parmesan he'd ever tasted, and to this day it was his favorite Italian food.

But the thing he loved most about her house was the extensive collection of FBI memorabilia.

Joan's father had been a career FBI agent who retired from a high position in the Bureau. After his death, Joan had taken possession of all his papers, photographs, awards, and books. As DJ grew up, he was allowed to inspect this treasure trove any time he wished. He read most of the books, and his admiration for the man who'd owned them increased each year. Then one day he'd discovered reruns of the television show *The FBI,* starring Efrem Zimbalist, Jr. From then on, young DJ's fate was sealed.

After graduation from UNM, he enrolled as a law student at Georgetown University. His mother was delighted, of course, but she still didn't know his secret dream.

At Georgetown he became close friends with another student who was also interested in a future with the FBI. Tim Burns was taking various science courses to qualify for FBI employment. He had lived in the DC area all his life, had often toured the FBI as a kid, and enthusiastically fueled DJ's mind further about the venerable institution. After graduation they had maintained their friendship—especially after both became employed at the FBI.

Today, DJ hoped his friend could help.

Tim had become a specialist in the Fingerprint Division at the FBI's lab at Quantico, Virginia. He was a miracle worker when it came to difficult IDs. He had many resources not normally available to the average investigation.

"All right. What have I done to deserve this call?" Tim's friendly, jovial voice made DJ smile.

DJ returned the barb. "I'm scraping the barrel for an ID, so naturally I thought of the guy who lives at the bottom of one."

"You know, I've been pulling your sorry ass out of the fire for years, Scott. When are you gonna learn some of this stuff on your own?"

"Why bother?" DJ felt his own big grin shining through the typical male bantering. "If I can get you to do the work, it leaves me time for better things."

"Typical," Tim said, then he became serious. "Okay, what's the situation?"

DJ outlined the case thus far, including the apparent failure of a DNA match, and no fingerprint identification.

"Can you send me the pertinent data? I'd also like to see the OMI report on the autopsy. Oh, and photos if you've got 'em."

"Not a problem," DJ said. "They made lots of photos. You should have a great time going through those."

"Okay, then. Shoot it to me. I assume you still have my email address."

DJ grinned. "I keep it tattooed on my wrist just for these occasions."

"You owe me, Bro," Tim said.

"I'll ship you an entire case of Hatch's Green Chile today, will that do?"

"Now you're talking. You got me hooked on that stuff, Dude, so you're obligated to feed my habit."

"Keep dreaming, my friend." Then DJ paused. "Seriously, Tim. When can you have an answer for me?"

"If I don't get back to you in the next two days, you'll know we have a problem."

DJ felt his jaw tighten. "I'm really counting on you, buddy.

This one is major."

On the other end of the line, Tim's voice sounded equally serious. "I know, man. I've heard. I'll do what I can."

As DJ disconnected the call, he looked at the file in front of him.

If Tim Burns couldn't ID this guy, no one could.

17

Monday Lunchtime

Earlier in the day, Harrie contacted Nick Ellis and discovered the young park ranger had Mondays free. He seemed reluctant, but agreed to meet her and Ginger at a small sandwich shop close to his apartment in the Northeast Heights.

Harrie drove, and Ginger kept a lookout for the sandwich shop.

"Why do you suppose he hesitated about meeting us?" Ginger asked.

Harrie shrugged. "Based upon the roadblocks we've run into, I'm not surprised."

Ginger said, "I think that's it." She pointed to a small strip mall and a large sign proclaiming the best sandwiches in town.

When they entered the restaurant, Harrie spotted Nick Ellis. She waved to him, and he stood. They headed for his booth on the far side of the room.

"Thanks for agreeing to meet us, Nick." Harrie flashed her best smile as she and Ginger seated themselves opposite him.

"Yeah, sure," Nick said, revealing his lack of enthusiasm for the encounter.

Immediately, a perky young server presented Harrie and Ginger with menus and flashed her big blue eyes at Nick. He ignored her and continued studying his own menu with—Harrie thought—inordinate interest.

Harrie turned to the girl. "Could you give us a few minutes to decide?"

The server nodded and left them in peace.

Harrie made small talk, hoping to break through Nick's reluctance to look her in the eye. But it didn't work. She said, "Is there a problem, Nick?"

He put his menu down, and leaned in. "I'm almost sure meeting you like this will get me in trouble."

Harrie glanced at Ginger. She leaned back. "Why do you think that?"

"Well, it could be because ever since Sunday morning,

someone's been following me."

Harrie started to turn. Nick reached across the table and grabbed her hand. "Don't look now, for God's sake." His voice sounded low and urgent. "Trust me when I tell you something is off. I think the cops believe I killed that guy."

Ginger said, "Maybe you're overreacting. Finding a body would make anyone jumpy."

Harrie removed her hand from his grip. "Are you sure about being followed?"

Nick frowned, and his shoulders slumped. "I thought so, but I'm not sure. I know I don't like being involved with the police.'"

"Have they invited you down to the police station yet?" Harrie studied his face. He seemed frightened.

"Only that first night when I . . . you know . . . when I found it. The body, I mean. They wanted me to come down and make a statement. But that's the only time."

Ginger said, "Nick, maybe you should call your lawyer."

Nick's surprised look seemed genuine. "You think I need a lawyer?" His voice broke on the last word.

"Maybe not," Ginger said. "But my husband is an attorney, and he always says people should consult an attorney before they agree to questioning by the authorities."

Nick glanced around the room, as though making sure no one could hear what he said next.

"Have you heard of the Ancient Ones who inhabit Petroglyphs National Monument?"

Harrie nodded. "As it happens, I bought a video last Saturday when Ginger and I went to the Visitor Center at the Petroglyphs. It mentions them and how they roam the area."

Nick looked down at his hands. He'd been twisting is paper napkin and stopped abruptly. "I've even thought maybe the Ancient Ones are following me—or maybe it's the spirit of that dead guy."

A cold chill ran up Harrie's arms. "I didn't get the impression the Ancient Ones would do that sort of thing. I don't know about the dead guy, but if I had to guess, I'd bet your stalker is just a human with an agenda."

The young man seemed relieved. He managed a weak smile. "I suppose that's good news. I really don't want to believe the

Ancient Ones or any other spirits are out to get me."

Harrie put her hand on Nick's. "Let's talk about something else."

He nodded and took a sip of water.

Harrie said, "What else can you tell us about this body you found?"

Nick set his glass on the table and looked at her with an expression hard to interpret. "What makes you think I know anything about the victim?"

Harrie looked at Ginger, who shrugged.

Harrie tried another tactic. "I think it's odd nothing about this homicide has appeared on the news. Any ideas why?"

Nick said, "Well, I heard the detectives talking at the scene. One of them said they needed to keep a lid on it."

"But you were telling everybody about it Saturday morning at the drone field," Harrie said.

"I know," Nick said. He looked down at his hands. "That morning I was still in shock at what happened. I didn't remember hearing their conversation until later."

"What made you think about it now?"

"Yesterday I went to work and stopped for coffee on my way to the Petroglyphs. I saw a guy at the donut shop who looked . . . well . . . he looked out of place."

"And," Ginger said.

"So afterwards, I went to fill up my car. It was early, and there were only a few people in line. I saw this same guy in the second car behind me."

"Are you sure?"

"I wasn't then, but when I got here today, the same guy came in and sat down right after I did."

Harrie almost turned her head to look. She stopped. "Is he still here?"

"I didn't see him leave, but that table is empty now."

Ginger frowned. "You should tell the police."

Harrie said, "Do you know the names of the detectives you heard talking?"

Nick's brow knitted in thought. "Not that I recall." Then he brightened. "But one of them—the lady detective—was giving the orders. In fact," he smiled at Harrie, "she had red hair like yours, and looked at lot like you."

Harrie and Ginger grinned at each other. In unison they said, "Detective Sergeant Cabrini Paiz."

18

Monday Afternoon

"But what good did this do?" Ginger watched Harrie backing out of the parking spot at the sandwich shop.

Harrie didn't respond until she had the car back on the street and in the flow of traffic. "Because now we know for sure Cabrini is working the case. You heard him say the detective resembled me. And we know she and Swannie are working together on something."

"How did you leap to that conclusion?"

"When I told Caroline about my short conversation with Cabrini, she let it slip that Swannie was conducting a task force meeting on Saturday afternoon. In fact, he expected it to run into the dinner hour. She believed Cabrini was in that meeting too."

"Okay, I'll give you that. But it doesn't change things. They're not gonna talk to you."

"Maybe not," Harrie said, "but if I tell Cabrini about this guy following Nick Ellis, she might be more willing to share."

Ginger sighed. "You are the eternal optimist about your schemes. Why is that?"

Harrie grinned. "Have you noticed my success rate? That's why I'm an optimist."

"So, tell me this," Ginger said. "Have you formulated a plan using this knowledge you imagine you have?"

Harrie frowned. "Well, not yet."

Ginger laughed. "That's what I thought. Let's get back to the office. I have work to do, even if you don't"

"Killjoy," Harrie said. "On another subject, I think I'm becoming paranoid."

"Why?"

"Well, when we first walked in I noticed a guy sitting at a table a few feet away from where we sat. He watched us as we settled in with Nick."

"Sweetie, you always draw male attention. I'm used to it by now, and frankly I don't even notice anymore."

"It wasn't that kind of attention." Harrie stopped at a red light. She turned to look at Ginger. "This was different. He looked like he knew us, or was surprised. It was more like . . . I don't know how to explain it. It seemed significant."

"Was he still there when we left?"

"Yes, and I felt his gaze on us all the way out."

Ginger sighed and shook her head. "You're going into suspicious mode. You do that every time you involve us in murder."

Ten minutes later they pulled into the parking lot at Southwest Editing Services, the business they'd been running for the past six years. The first thing Harrie noticed was a black SUV.

"Uh, oh. I didn't count on this."

Ginger frowned. "Isn't that DJ's Bureau car?"

"Yep," Harrie said. "Follow my lead. He doesn't need to know everything yet."

"All right," Ginger said. "But you'd better come up with something pronto."

When they entered the office, the receptionist pointed to Caroline's office. "They're in there."

Harrie tapped on the doorframe. Caroline smiled and motioned them in.

"We were just talking about you two."

"Something good, I hope," Ginger said with a grin.

"Always," Caroline said. "DJ says he wants to see the new drone Steve and the boys bought last weekend."

DJ put his arm around Harrie and bent down to plant a husbandly kiss on her forehead. "Maybe we could all get together this weekend. Would that fit into your schedule?"

Harrie hesitated only a second. "Sure. Sounds good."

"Great," He said and turned to Ginger. "I'll give Steve a call this afternoon and make arrangements."

He turned back to Harrie. "Will you be home early tonight?"

A tiny alarm went off somewhere in Harrie's head, but she decided to ignore it. "Sure, will you be?"

He grinned. "Well, not early, but basically on time. See you around 6, okay?" He bent to kiss her again.

"Okay," she said. When DJ turned to go, she flashed a look at Ginger. Ginger responded with a tiny lift of her left shoulder, as if to say, "So, you dodged a bullet—this time."

Harrie turned to go back to her own office, and Caroline said, "Okay, what was that all about?"

Ginger had already left the room, and Harrie sighed. "What do you mean?"

Caroline sat behind her desk and reached for a manuscript. "You still haven't said a word about your conversation with DJ Saturday night. How did it go?"

Harrie plopped herself down in the chair facing Caroline's desk and tilted her head back. "Not well. I'm embarrassed to tell you I failed miserably. Not only did I not even get a chance to bring it up, I think he suspected my intentions. He cut me off at the pass. I couldn't believe how lousy my great plan turned out. The man intimidated me, can you believe it?"

Caroline chuckled. "Yes, in fact, I can. You know, by the time he was eleven-years old, he could wrap me around his little finger without my even realizing what happened. He would set his mind on something, but he didn't nag me or make a big deal. Instead he'd be so sweet and charming, before I knew it, he'd convinced me to agree to some adventure he'd planned, or some other darn thing. It all seemed so innocent at the time, then I'd think about it later and realize I'd been had."

"Huh," Harrie said. "You failed to warn me about that aspect of my husband. How come?"

Caroline shook her head. "Didn't think of it. It wasn't like he did it often, and I can't even remember the last time I fell victim to his charming ways." She grinned. "I suppose I should have at least warned you on Saturday."

"Yeah, well," Harrie said and stood to leave. "Now that I know what he's capable of, I'll be ready next time."

"Don't be too hard on him," Caroline said. "You're pretty darned good yourself at getting what you want. It's really difficult for him to say no to you."

Harrie said, "That's exactly what I'm counting on."

19

Late Monday Afternoon

For several hours Harrie had racked her brain, trying to come up with the perfect gambit to entice information from her super-secretive husband. Her concentration on editing manuscripts suffered. Then half an hour ago, DJ had called to say he wouldn't be home until late. Now her mind really went into overdrive. Could this possibly mean DJ was now part of the Petroglyph Murder task force with Cabrini and Swannie?

The original idea of trying to pump information from Sgt. Cabrini Paiz seemed less doable the more she thought about it. In the first place, she didn't want to strain her relationship with the detective. They hadn't known each other very long. Besides, she already owed Cabrini, big time, for pretending to be Harrie in some dangerous situations.

Her fallback scheme—trying to elicit information from Lt. Bob Swanson— seemed even less palatable. She now realized she shouldn't do anything to damage Caroline's relationship with the man. Caroline had every right to guard him from Harrie's insatiable curiosity.

That left her back where she started—her wonderful husband. But he was sworn to secrecy, and she'd never known a more tight-lipped individual. He was her only hope, but how did she get past all that and become part of the investigation? And what if he really was now part of the task force? She shook her head in tired resignation. She'd pondered this question, from one end to the other, all afternoon.

She faced a bitter truth. Getting DJ to help her was a lost cause. It was clearly impossible. She put down her pen and looked at the clock: 3:30 PM.

She stood, stretched, and headed for the break room for a fresh cup of coffee. Only an empty carafe and an unplugged coffee maker greeted her. *Dang! Too late for brewing another pot.* She reached in the refrigerator and selected a bottle of water instead.

When she turned to leave, she caught a glimpse of the familiar plaque on the wall by the door. She hadn't noticed it for a long time. Funny how things like that worked out. She'd loved that piece of wisdom so much when she saw it at the store, she was inspired to buy it. She'd settled on putting it in the break room so everyone would benefit from its positive message.

Now, as she looked at the words again and let them sink in, they jumped out at her and spoke to her current dilemma. The quote came from Audrey Hepburn.

"Nothing is impossible. The word itself says, 'I'm possible'!"

Harrie breathed in new energy. Exactly what she'd needed.

20

Tuesday Morning

"Ladies, I have a problem."

Harrie and Ginger sat at the conference table in Harrie's office, going over an almost completed manuscript from a budding writer. The problems they'd found in the young man's work were troubling. They happily turned their attention to Caroline, who stood in the doorway.

Harrie said, "Come in. Might as well add your problem to ours."

Caroline joined them. "I'm probably overstating the situation. At least my problem is easily solvable."

Ginger grinned and removed her reading glasses. "That's refreshing. We haven't had one of those today."

Caroline said. "All I need is a decision from the two of you. It's time to order letterhead."

Harrie groaned. "Oh, crud. We were supposed to decide about the company name, weren't we?"

Caroline nodded and spread out the pages. "It's a simple design. It shouldn't be difficult to make the change. The real issue is settling on the name you're most comfortable using."

Ginger said, "Why do we have letterhead with two different company names?"

"Oh, how quickly we forget," Harrie said. She went to her desk, returned with some business cards, and put them in front of Ginger.

Ginger looked at one, then the other. "Oh, yeah, now I remember. You messed up an order, and we changed the name of the company."

Harrie frowned at her friend. "That's not the entire story, and you know it. We've had several long discussions over the last six years. I say the company name should better reflect what we really do. You, on the other hand, love to be clever."

Caroline shook her head. "Hold on. I don't think I've heard this story. Fill me in."

Harrie sat again, leaned back in her chair and picked up one of the cards. "This is the name we originally planned to use. I felt strongly that Southwest Editing Services let everyone know immediately what our business offered."

Caroline nodded. "Makes sense to me. So how did it switch to being Southwest Office Systems?"

Harrie looked at Ginger. "Why don't you tell Caroline your clever idea?"

Ginger sighed. "Okay, I'll admit it didn't turn out as clever as I thought." She turned to Caroline. "But honestly, don't you think people would be intrigued with an ad in the phone book that said, 'S.O.S for all your editing needs'? Using the initials of the name would get attention, don't you agree?"

Caroline's face took on a comic look of dismay. "Not really. How did you come up with that?"

Ginger's right shoulder lifted in a half-hearted shrug. "I think it came to me one night after a couple of glasses of chardonnay. That's usually when I get my best ideas."

"I think the larger question," Caroline said, "is why you keep going back and forth? We have letterheads and business cards with each of these names. Can we please standardize?"

"I'm ready," Harrie said.

"Me, too," said Ginger.

Harrie looked at Ginger. "You mean you're ready to throw in the towel?"

Ginger's faced scrunched up to produce a look that sent both Harrie and Caroline into fits of laughter. Caroline recovered first.

"I'll take that as reluctant consent. The new letterhead will show the name Southwest Editing Services. I pray it sticks."

Ginger stood to leave. "It probably will—unless I come up with another great idea."

A hail of rubber bands and paper clips flew in Ginger's direction as she beat a hasty retreat from Harrie's office.

21

Tuesday Noon

"I need to meet with you."

It took DJ a couple of seconds to recognize the voice on the other end of the line.

"Crider?"

"Let's stick with Mr. Smith today, okay?"

DJ frowned. This did not sound good. It had been close two years since he'd met Colin Crider. "Whatever you say. What'd you have in mind?"

"Are you familiar with Old Town?"

"It depends on how far off the beaten path you're thinking."

"Meet me at the bandstand in the Plaza in one hour."

"Is there anything I should bring?"

A soft chuckle preceded the next words. "Only your usual equipment."

The line went dead. DJ looked at the receiver as though it might provide answers to unspoken questions. Why was CIA Operative Colin Crider, or his alias—John Smith—asking to meet with the FBI?

Within half an hour, DJ had located a parking spot in Old Town Albuquerque. He sat quietly in his vehicle while he scoped out the area. His mind went back to the first memory he had of exploring Old Town when he was a young boy. His mother liked to visit the area during the Christmas season and soak up all the Christmas lights, luminarias, and holiday music. They would have dinner at La Placita restaurant afterwards—just the two of them DJ remembered being served hot chocolate with a cinnamon stick on his first visit there. He had always looked forward to this elegantly served treat each Christmas. It made him feel grown up.

He smiled as he remembered the sense of joy he felt each time they walked through the plaza, with the colorful lights and the pungent smell of piñón logs burning in fireplaces in the area.

He sighed and forced his mind back to the present.

Today happened to be a lovely, spring day. Although it was a weekday, a fair number of tourists strolled around the plaza, meandering in and out of the shops. He'd been lucky to find a parking place so easily. He checked his watch: twenty minutes before his appointment with Crider. He decided to spend the time strolling around like a tourist while he watched for his subject. He couldn't help wondering if this would turn into a case file. He sincerely hoped not. He had his hands full at the moment and didn't need the distraction.

A few minutes later, he found himself on the south side of the Plaza in front of Treasure House Books & Gifts. Harrie had brought him here several times and introduced him to the shop owner. DJ decided to stop in and say, "Hello." He could keep an eye out for Colin Crider from the large picture window fronting the building.

Treasure House was a tiny store, but held a huge selection of books about New Mexico, many of them by local authors. DJ waived to the owner as he walked in. John Hoffsis waved back but was busy with several customers. DJ browsed the shelves at the front of the store, occasionally stealing a glance out the front window. One minute the bandstand was empty. Moments later, DJ looked again and saw Crider. The CIA agent seemed to be looking directly at him.

DJ noticed John was still ringing up sales. Maybe he'd come by later.

By the time DJ crossed the street, Crider had seated himself on one of the old iron benches in front of the bandstand.

DJ joined him on the bench and waited for Crider to speak. A young couple had apparently decided the bandstand would make a lovely backdrop for photographs. They took turns with a camera, playfully posing for pictures. They laughed and teased each other, oblivious to their audience. After a few more photos, they moved on to other landmarks.

For the moment, the only humans now in the plaza were DJ and Colin Crider.

"I need your help." Crider had leaned forward, forearms resting on his thighs. His gaze seemed focused on the area in front of him, but DJ knew he was aware of everything in all directions.

"I don't suppose you could be a bit more specific?"

Crider chuckled and looked down at the ground between his

feet. "Always a wise ass, aren't you Scott?"

"Isn't that why you called me?"

Crider leaned back against the bench. "I'm missing an operative."

DJ took a breath. "Okay. How can I help?"

"Do you know anything about a body found at The Petroglyphs last Thursday night?"

DJ groaned softly. "Oh, brother. Now you're opening a can of worms."

"I think it might be my guy."

"Does your guy have a name?"

Crider looked at DJ and lifted an eyebrow. "We could always call him James Bond, I suppose."

DJ sighed. "Okay, that'll work for now. Tell me more."

Crider looked directly at DJ for the first time since they'd sat on the bench. "We've been following someone who snuck into the United States about six months ago. He's a mean S.O.B. He's left a string of bodies in more than a dozen countries. Mr. Bond was able to get close to him. They were supposed to meet at the Petroglyphs Thursday night."

"For what purpose?"

"You know I can't tell you that."

DJ shook his head. "And yet, you want my help."

Crider looked down at the ground again. "This scumbag is a terrorist. He's planning something or knows something about a plan. Bond offered to be a messenger. The terrorist was supposed to give him a package to deliver."

"But instead, your guy Bond—at least you think it's your guy—got himself killed."

"In a nutshell, yes."

"Have you been in touch with OMI? You could identify the body if it's your operative."

Crider shook his head and sighed. "You know I can't do that. We are not supposed to be operating covertly within the U.S. I can't expose this thing by making an official request."

DJ lifted an eyebrow. "Hmmm. So it would seem your choices are limited. But I still don't know what you want with me. Why doesn't your boss just call my boss. They should be able to come up with something without making it official."

"It might come to that, but I don't think you'll want things working out that way."

DJ shook his head. "You lost me again. Why would I care how it works out?"

"Because," Crider said, "apparently your lovely wife is now involved."

22

Tuesday Afternoon

An hour later, DJ Scott tapped on the door to Lt. Bob Swanson's office.

Swannie looked up from his take-out lunch and grinned. "I'd ask you to join me, but I ate all the fries."

DJ shook his head and took a seat in the chair facing Swannie's overflowing desk. "I had lunch before I came. Needed a bit of time to think."

Swannie frowned, wiped his fingers on the paper napkin in front of him, and leaned back in his chair. "What's up?"

"The situation has become dicey." DJ described his visit with Colin Crider and briefly explained the covert nature of the CIA operative's involvement.

Swannie said, "I'm puzzled. How can Crider be so sure our deceased is his operative? Even we don't know who the fellow is."

DJ shrugged. "Don't know. I was about to ask him that very thing when he took the discussion in an unexpected direction."

"Dare I ask?"

"He claims Harrie's involved."

The look of surprise on Swannie's face was almost comical, but DJ wasn't in a laughing mood.

Swannie seemed to regain some composure and said, "I wasn't expecting that. I knew from you and Caroline that Harrie is trying to inject herself into the investigation, but how could she possibly be part of it?"

"She and Ginger apparently met with someone yesterday—someone Crider has in his sights. He wouldn't tell me any specifics."

"It has to be a coincidence." Swannie gathered up the remains of his lunch, crumpled up the bag it came in, and tossed it in the trash. He studied DJ for a moment. "How will you handle this?"

DJ sighed. "I hoped you might have some suggestions along those lines. I obviously can't tell her about meeting with Crider."

Swannie grinned. "I think I have an idea." He placed a phone call and said into the receiver, "DJ Scott is here with me. Could you join us?"

Within two minutes there was a tap on the door, and Detective Sergeant Cabrini Paiz entered the room.

"Hello, Agent Scott. What brings you here today?"

DJ said, "I think your boss is hatching a plan to help me out. It appears to includes you."

Swannie quickly explained the situation, with DJ filling in the details. When they finished, Cabrini sat quietly for a few seconds. Then she said, "Any ideas how I'm supposed to approach her?"

"It should be relatively simple," Swannie said. "After all, she did call you first—you said so yourself."

"Wow," she said, the look on her face hard to read. "You guys are something, you know that?"

The squinted look she gave the men sent a chill through DJ. He looked down at his hands, not willing to meet her gaze. "Umm, I'm guessing you don't think this will be such an easy task?"

She took a breath, tilted her head back, and gave a good impression of mentally counting to ten. "For a couple of smart, accomplished guys, you can be pretty thick."

DJ shot a look at Swannie. They both shrugged.

She sighed and waved her hand in a dismissive gesture. "Never mind. Here's what I'll need from the two of you. First, let's get our stories straight. We need to be sure we're on the same page, and that I won't be saying something that's classified. Next, where are we on ID-ing the victim?"

DJ said, "I've put in a call to a friend in DC who might be able to help us with that. He should get back to me by tomorrow."

Cabrini nodded. "That's good. Now let's discuss exactly how much I can reveal, and what she must not hear."

23

Later Tuesday Afternoon

Harrie was pleased with her accomplishments today. She and Ginger had met with the budding writer and relayed their concerns about his manuscript. They also finished preliminary reviews on two other manuscripts. Harrie's desk was now cleared of several pending projects she'd been putting off. She'd made a list of current projects in the pipeline. Her desk had a clear work space. She'd need it for her "information gathering" project.

Before she could switch gears from her work routine to her snooping one, her cell phone rang. She couldn't believe her good luck when she saw the caller ID.

"Hi Cabrini."

"Sorry I'm so late getting back to you. We're really swamped."

"I understand. I know all you law enforcement types are overworked these days."

"Anyway," Cabrini said, "I'd like to make it up to you. Could you meet me for coffee?"

Harrie hesitated for a couple of seconds. She sensed something a little off about the invitation. Still, it was the perfect opportunity to learn more, and she should take it.

"Sure, where and when?"

Half an hour later the two women were seated in a booth at The Flying Star on Montgomery and Juan Tabo in the Northeast Heights. They had exhausted the usual greetings and chitchat. Harrie still hadn't figured out how to start her inquisition.

Cabrini leaned back and took a sip of coffee. "So, are you still interested in our homicide at The Petroglyphs?"

Harrie almost choked on her own coffee. She covered with a little cough and set the mug on the table. "Ah, sure. Absolutely."

Cabrini grinned. "Don't you want to get out your pad and pen?"

Harrie hoped she didn't look as guilty as she felt. "No, of course not. I'm just curious about what happened. My friend Nick was really shaken about finding that body, and when there wasn't anything in the news about it . . . Well, you know . . . I mean, it had me wondering and . . . ." She shrugged and took another swig of coffee. She focused on keeping her hand steady.

Cabrini said, "I didn't realize you and Nick Ellis were friends. How long have you known him?"

Harrie blinked. *Damn, this is NOT going well.* She automatically smiled. "Actually, Ginger and I just met him Saturday at George Maloof Airfield. We went out to see the ham radio guys fly their drones. Nick was there, too, and he told us about discovering a body at The Petroglyphs. He seemed pretty rattled."

"So, have you talked to him since then?"

Harrie opened her mouth to speak, then quickly shut it. Something was definitely going on here. "Why do you ask?"

Cabrini shrugged. "Just curious. We asked him not to talk about the case to anyone. Next thing I know, you're calling me, asking for information about it. Want to tell me why you're so interested?"

Harrie briefly considered making a quick getaway. Then it occurred to her she now had the opening she needed. She set her cup down.

"I had one of my dreams. It matches what I heard from Nick Ellis, and what I saw with my own eyes at the Petroglyphs."

Now it was Cabrini's turn to be startled. "You were at the Petroglyphs? When?"

"Ginger and I decided to check it out on Saturday after lunch."

Cabrini frowned. "Why would you do that?"

Harrie shrugged. "When I have one of my dreams, it leaves me . . . Well . . . It's sort of hard to explain. Let's just say having one causes me to push for the reason. I always know there's some point to my receiving the dream, and I always feel responsible for learning why."

"Okay, I get that." Cabrini nodded. "So, what did you learn?"

"Very little," Harrie said. "When I walked into the center of the amphitheater at the Petroglyphs, I knew it was where I saw the body in my dream. What I still don't know is why that dream was given to me, and what I'm supposed to do about it."

Cabrini was quiet for a moment and absently stirred her coffee. She seemed to be pondering a difficult decision.

At last, she put the spoon on the table and looked at Harrie intently. "Are you willing to do whatever I tell you?"

Harrie was startled to the point of speechlessness—a rare occurrence. She sensed this would be her only invitation into the inner circle. "That's a hard question to answer. You might ask me to do something I'm not comfortable doing. Could you give me a hint so I can make a better decision?"

Cabrini grinned. "Do I sense hesitation in the normally adventurous Harrie McKinsey?"

Harrie stiffened. She suddenly felt defensive but also wary of ruining her only chance at getting the information she needed. She forced herself to relax her tense muscles and take a few breaths.

Cabrini gave her a quizzical look. "I assure you I'm not planning anything unpleasant. The only thing you risk is being shut out of the loop if you don't hold up your end of our bargain."

Harrie felt a tiny smile forming around her lips. "You really know how to turn the screws, don't you? Okay. I'm in. But this better be worth it."

"That," Cabrini said, "is totally up to you."

24

Late Tuesday Afternoon

Swannie took off his glasses and massaged the bridge of his nose. Tiredness washed over him like a warm, gray cloud. He picked up his phone and dialed the extension for his administrative assistant.

"Abigail, could you come in, please?"

A tap on the door, and Officer First Class Abigail Baker stepped into Swannie's office. She had notebook and pen in hand, and took a seat in the chair in front of the Lieutenant's desk.

She flashed a smile at her boss and said, "What's up, Sir?"

"It's talk-through time, Abby. You up for it?"

"Of course, Lieutenant. You want to start?"

Swannie leaned back in his chair, the tired feeling slipping away. When he got stuck in an endless loop while investigating a new case, the talk-through technique always helped. Abby introduced it when she started working for Swannie six months ago. He didn't like to think of himself as a dinosaur—or worse—an old codger unable to accept new ideas. At first he considered it just another new-age, psycho-babble gimmick. So he surprised himself when he agreed to it the first time.

Thing is, it seemed to work. Hell of a thing to have to admit, even to himself, but there it was. So he cleared his throat and opened the file folder.

He said, "This case seems like no other I've ever investigated. The fact that not a word has leaked to the media is something I would never have imagined possible. I'm equally amazed at the lack of clues to follow, evidence to assemble, and ideas of how to proceed. And we won't even talk about the fact the victim's identity remains a mystery."

Abby nodded. "We have a cause of death, don't we?"

"Blunt force trauma, weapon currently undetermined, but possibly a baseball bat or a piece of heavy material."

Abby said, "What, exactly, did the victim have on his person when he arrived at OMI?"

Swannie flipped through the file. "Not much. It says here there was a wallet, but no ID or credit cards. There was quite a bit of money in it—over $2,000, so robbery seems off the table. He wore an inexpensive Timex that could be had at any discount store."

"What about his clothing?" Abby asked.

Swannie turned to another page in the file. "Says he had on underwear consisting of shorts and T-shirt, jeans, a faded denim shirt, brown leather belt, white socks, white sneakers. Fairly typical for a guy in his thirties. That's the age range OMI estimated him to be."

"Anything in his pockets?"

"A couple of receipts from fast-food joints, a pack of gum, a book of paper matches, and a small notepad."

"Hmm," Abby said. "Does it say if there's any writing on the notepad?"

Swannie shook his head. "Nope, and that's odd." He frowned. "Why didn't I notice that before?"

Abby grinned. "I'm sure you did, and I'll bet you jotted a note to yourself."

Swannie felt a flood of relief. "Of course I did," he said. He grabbed his calendar and flipped the page over to the previous day. And there it was. The note he'd written to remind himself to check back with OMI to get the clothes and actual contents of the victim's pockets sent to him.

He sighed and smiled. "How did you know that?"

"Because, Boss, I've seen you do it nearly every day. No reason to think you wouldn't have done it yesterday."

"Abby," he said, "I don't know how or why your new-fangled technique works, but I'm a true believer."

"Happy to hear that, Sir. Would you like me to place the call to OMI?"

"If you would be so kind," he said. "And it's getting late. After you make the call, why don't you take off."

"On my way." She stood and hurried back to her own desk.

Swannie's relief was mixed with just a small dose of annoyance. Why, with all his vast training and experience on the job, did it take a whip-smart young officer to point out the obvious? He sighed. Maybe he was getting old and slow. Not exactly what he wanted at this moment.

Only one cure for this journey into the doldrums. He picked up his phone again and dialed an outside number. It rang twice before Caroline Johnson answered.

"Hey, Lovely Lady," Swannie said, and felt a smile creasing his face. "Would you take pity on an old guy and have dinner with him tonight?"

"Sure," she said. "Just one question, though. Who's the old guy?"

Was it any wonder he loved this woman?

25

Early Tuesday Evening

As soon as Harrie arrived home, she headed for her cozy little office. She'd made notes on Sunday about Saturday's events at George Maloof Airpark and the subsequent trip to The Petroglyphs. Then Monday night while DJ was working late, she summarized the meeting she and Ginger had with Nick Ellis at lunch that day.

She figured she had about an hour to make notes on today's events before DJ would be home. Cabrini's invitation to coffee had been a surprise, and Harrie still wondered if she was being "handled." In fact, that seemed to be the most logical explanation for the sudden outreach. It made her determined to use that to her advantage.

She finished her notes and had just put them away when the phone rang. Ginger's phone number popped up on Caller ID.

Ginger wasted no time with preliminaries. "So, what happened? Is Cabrini ready to cooperate and let you in on stuff?"

"I didn't exactly get that impression. In fact, she made it clear that if I didn't cooperate with them, I'd be out."

"What do they want from you?"

"I'm supposed to write up a report. It should include the details of my dream—as far as I can remember them—everything about our escapades on Saturday, and one other thing."

"What else is there?" Ginger's voice always sounded higher when she became annoyed.

"Our lunch date with Nick Ellis."

After a long pause, Ginger said, "How does she know about that?"

"It would seem," Harrie said, "that the fellow who Nick said followed him, reports to APD."

The sound of Ginger's voice went up another half step on the scale. "For crying out loud, are you that well known to APD?"

"I honestly don't know," Harrie said, "but apparently you are."

"Me?" Ginger all but screeched out the question.

"I know," Harrie said. "I had the same reaction. But it made sense. Do you remember any of your students from your teaching days?"

"My teaching days?" Puzzlement replaced annoyance.

Harrie chuckled. "Yes, you remember those days, don't you? Up at dawn, work all day with a bunch of kids who don't want to be there?"

"Ah, but don't forget I had summers off."

"Now you remember," Harrie said. "Well, one of those students of yours, who is now a young man, serves as a police aide. He happened to be at the restaurant having lunch while we were there meeting with Nick Ellis."

When she spoke next, Ginger's voice sounded more confused than annoyed. "So how does something like that get back to Cabrini? Don't they have more important things on their plate than tracking where I have lunch?"

"You'd think," Harrie said. "I asked the same question. Turns out this young police aide was riding with one of the responding officers who got called out to the Petroglyphs Thursday night. They let him hang around while CSI was there, and he got permission to stay and watch the detectives at work. That's when he first met Cabrini."

"Oh," said Ginger. "Now I get it. Another impressionable young male falls under the spell of the gorgeous and glamorous Detective Sergeant Cabrini Paiz."

"Something like that," Harrie agreed. "Anyway, he was aware of the orders given that night—speak to no one about this case. When he saw you and I talking to Nick, he happened to overhear the words "murder victim" and his young ears perked up to see what else he could hear."

"Geeze, Louise, where was this guy? In the next booth?"

"You got it," Harrie said.

"Oh, man." Ginger didn't say anything else. Harrie heard running water.

"What are you doing?"

"I'm taking some ibuprofen. I've got a nasty headache, thanks to you."

Harrie laughed so hard she started hiccuping. That was apparently more than the annoyed Ginger could take.

"That's right. Laugh it up, Moose Face. You're always getting me into trouble."

Harrie got her giggling under control before she responded. "I apologize for my reckless behavior. Please forgive me. I've seen the error of my ways and will make amends."

Whatever Ginger said next was only speculation on Harrie's part. It sounded something like "harrumph," then lip noises, followed by an unladylike guttural sound.

"I'm sorry your head hurts. Anything I can do?"

Ginger sighed. "No, I'll be fine. I just hope this whole thing is over soon. By the way, did you find out the name of my former student/turned aide/turned Benedict Arnold?"

"I think she said his name is Randy Rigby. Does that ring a bell for you?"

Ginger's voice rose at least an octave. "That little weasel. After all I did for that kid. You wouldn't believe the trouble that young man was in, and I stood up for him."

Harrie decided to let her friend vent her anger. Eventually, she'd run out of steam. Anyway, now was probably not the best time to tell her about the rest of the promise Cabrini had extracted from Harrie.

Or how it might impact them both.

26

Wednesday Morning

Lt. Bob Swanson felt infinitely better than he had the previous afternoon. It amazed him how spending the evening with Caroline washed away all his frustrations and left him feeling serene. Today he had renewed purpose and fresh energy in his walk.

He took the steps in front of APD headquarters two at a time, and when he reached the top, he stopped to get his breath. He bent over, hands braced against his knees, taking in great gulps of air.

Slow down, old man. Remember you're a sedentary sixty plus—not a teenager.

He straightened up and opened one of the big doors, almost colliding with the energetic DJ Scott.

"Whoa, Swannie." DJ stopped just short of bumping into his friend. "I dropped by your office and they told me you weren't in yet. Playing hooky today?"

Swannie felt his face reddening. "Umm, got a bit of a late start this morning. What's up?"

They chatted about nothing in particular as they headed for the second floor and Swannie's office. Abby wasn't at her desk, so Swannie gathered up the messages she'd left him.

DJ dropped down in a chair. Swannie removed his suit jacket and sat in his own chair.

"Any news from your friend in DC?" Swannie thumbed through his phone messages.

"Not yet, but I do have a little something."

Swannie looked up, all interest in the messages gone. "And?"

"Don't get your hopes up too much. It's not what I'd hoped to hear."

Swannie sighed. "Enough with the talking. Tell me what we have."

DJ handed Swannie a document. "I'm telling you. It's almost worse than nothing."

But Swannie was busy reading the document and didn't respond. When he finished, he looked up at DJ. The frown on his face spoke volumes.

"Am I to understand that the FBI has verified that there are fingerprints on file somewhere but that they cannot access them? How is that possible?"

DJ sighed. "Not all fingerprints taken in this country end up at the FBI. There are plenty of situations and circumstances under which this sort of thing is possible."

Swannie's mouth gaped open, and his eyes looked unnaturally large. "Seriously? In this day and age? Are you kidding?"

DJ ran his index finger across his forehead while he seemed to search for a way to explain. He said, "There are, for want of a better word, 'groups' within the federal government who sometimes maintain their own files. I have a hunch that's what's happening here."

As Swannie spoke, his head shook in slow motion. "I thought by now I'd heard everything. Not even close, I guess." He stopped shaking his head. "So what happens now?"

DJ blew out a breath. "We wait to see if my friend Tim comes through. I have confidence in him. The guy's amazing."

Swannie shrugged and tossed the document on his desk. "And to think I felt so good just a few minutes ago. Thought I had the world by the tail."

"I know, and I'm sorry to burst your bubble. Look, why don't I go with you to the task force meeting this morning. I'll be the bad guy and you can all beat up on me."

Swannie's sour look almost slipped into a tiny grin. "Now that's something I can almost get on board with. But judging by your slightly haggard look, I'm guessing you have your own problems today. Care to share?"

DJ sighed. "There is one little thing that has me worried. I've been trying to find a way to get to the bottom of it, but all I have at the moment is a tiny piece of information."

"Any way I can help?"

"You're the only person I can think of who could help. But it's touchy."

"Why's that?"

DJ stopped pacing and looked directly at Swannie. "Remember I mentioned yesterday that Crider said Harrie was involved in all this?"

Swannie nodded. "Yeah, you said he saw her having lunch with Nick Ellis, the park ranger."

"Well, it's more than that."

Swannie's face displayed concern. "What's got you so worried?"

DJ let out a breath he'd been holding. "According to Crider, Harrie has some sort of connection to our victim."

Swannie looked toward the ceiling—apparently seeking guidance from above. "Oh, dear Lord. What has she gotten herself into now?"

"I don't know," DJ said, "but you have to help me find out. I'm depending on you."

27

Wednesday Afternoon

Caroline Johnson frowned as she returned the receiver to the phone. Swannie had been in such a good mood this morning before they both left for work. They'd had a wonderful evening the night before at a quiet, restaurant, with amazing food and wine, and soft violin music. She'd seen the lines on his brow melt away.

But this afternoon, it was all wiped away, and he was tense and irritable. She knew he tried really hard to not let his work interfere with their time together. Usually he pulled it off quite skillfully. This current case, though, had him twisted in knots.

Time to bring in reinforcements.

She knocked on the doorframe of Harrie's office. Harrie looked up and smiled at her mother-in-law.

"What's up, lovely lady?"

"Are you up for an impromptu dinner party tonight?"

She smiled. "Who are we cheering up today?"

"Swannie—and you, if you need it."

Harrie broke eye contact with Caroline. "What makes you think I need cheering up?"

Caroline said, "Oh, let's call it intuition. I'm sensing tension in you, and quite a bit in my son." She held up her hand to stop Harrie's attempt at a comment. "It's just a mother's instinct. Besides, I noticed Ginger isn't her usual tranquil self, and I just got off the phone with Swannie. I thought I'd been able to get him out of his funk with our lovely dinner out last night. But he's back in the dumps. So, it occurs to me that our little informal dinner get togethers often produce wonderful results. How about it?"

Harrie tilted her head. "Have you ever heard of the phenomena of what happens when Mercury is in retrograde?"

Now it was Caroline's turn to look surprised. "As a matter of fact, I have. Why do you ask?"

"Every time things get like this—people being out of sorts, things going wrong, stuff like that—every time that happens I look up Mercury's position in the solar system. And you know what

I've discovered?"

Caroline grinned. "I'm betting you'll tell me."

"Almost every time these situations present themselves, I find out Mercury is in retrograde. It's uncanny, really. I looked it up today, and bingo! We are slap dab in the middle of one."

"Well, I suppose that could explain a lot. But have you given consideration to the idea that people often go through rough patches with work, relationships, illnesses, and a hundred other things? I'm betting somewhere in this world, on any given day, people all around us are experiencing difficulty with life. It can't all be laid at poor little Mercury's doorstep."

Harrie started laughing so hard she wiped tears from her eyes. "You are so classy. Thanks for not calling me a whining wimp."

Ginger appeared in the doorway, a frown on her face. "What's going on in here?"

Harrie took one look at her friend and started laughing again. "See what I mean?"

Ginger walked into the room and stood looking at Harrie. "What is wrong with you, woman?"

Caroline smiled and shook her head. "I think my point has been made. What do you say, ladies? Are you up for dinner at my house this evening?"

Ginger looked confused. "Is somebody going to tell me why Harrie is laughing like a hyena, and her mother-in-law is putting on a dinner party for us tonight?"

Harrie caught her breath at last. "It would take too much effort to explain. Besides, it's one of those things where you needed to be there to see the humor. Trust me. Dinner tonight at Caroline's is the best idea I've heard all day. You need to let Steve know the plan."

Ginger nodded, still looking confused. "Okay, whatever you say. I'm nothing if not cooperative."

Harrie shook her head. "You are so pathetic."

Ginger grinned. "I know. I get it from you." She hurried out the door before Harrie could come up with a clever retort.

28

Later Wednesday Afternoon

After Caroline's call, Swannie's spirits felt recharged. Moments ago he'd been frowning and even a little annoyed. Then Caroline called and announced they were having a dinner party for the gang tonight. She had asked if he could stop by Rising Star and pick up the takeout dinner she'd ordered.

The warm, happy feeling still surrounded him when Abby walked into his office.

"Here ya go, Lieutenant." She set an evidence envelope and a very large brown paper bag on his desk. Both items were stapled shut.

"What's this?" He looked blankly at the items.

"It's the contents of the victim's pockets and his clothing from OMI. Did you forget you asked me to call them yesterday?"

Swannie opened the clasp. "Oh, of course. Sorry. My mind was elsewhere. Good job, Abby. You must have really put the screws to them over there."

His assistant smiled sweetly. "Oh, Lieutenant. You know I never coerce. I usually get what I need by gentle persuasion."

Swannie grinned. "And you do it well, Abby. Thanks for coming through for me."

She smiled and left, quietly closing the door.

For the next half hour, Swannie went carefully through the various items in the envelope. The wallet, minus any sign of a driver's license, had seen very little wear. The $2,000 was intact inside the bill compartment. He found a small, shirt-pocket sized, flip-top notebook. Some pages were used, but the majority were empty. Swannie spent extra time to figure out what the names, numbers, and other scribblings meant, if anything. But nothing made any sense. Maybe DJ would be able to decipher it.

Next he tackled the large brown bag. The victim's clothing seemed exactly as described in the OMI report. Swannie went through everything carefully, examining the seams and pockets. It yielded nothing, but again, he wanted DJ to have a look.

At the bottom of the bag were the victim's shoes and socks. Swannie's first impulse was to ignore those items, but some instinct told him to give them the same scrutiny.

The socks were nondescript, plain, white athletic socks. Nothing remarkable and certainly no hiding places—unless the very threads in them were somehow important. He shook his head. Perhaps someone with an infrared device, could check out the socks for hidden clues.

The shoes, at first glance, seemed dirty and old. But something caught his eye, and he looked closer. He picked up the right shoe, wet his finger, and rubbed it against the toe cap. Underneath was a white leather athletic shoe that seemed almost new. He peeled back the tongue of the shoe and saw it had no visible signs of wear. Odd, he thought.

When he looked at the inside, it confirmed his suspicions. The lining was clean and undamaged. These sneakers had been deliberately coated with dirt on the outside to make them look used and unattractive.

He felt around the inside of the shoe, running his finger along the edge of the insole piece. He felt something sticking out, ever so slightly, from underneath the insole. He pulled it loose to observe the footbed. Nothing unusual or damaged about it.

Before reinserting the insole, he thought to turn it over. He saw a white business card stuck to the underside. It had a foil sticker on its face and looked a bit faded. He thought he might be able to read it if he used a strong enough light.

Swannie pushed his chair back and went to his filing cabinet. He reached for his trusty "super inspector." He smiled as he remembered rescuing this particular treasure from a trash heap. It was probably originally a jeweler's or watchmaker's tool. The thin, metal, adjustable band fit over the artist's head and a small, high-intensity lamp perched in the middle. An adjustable magnifying glass finished off the rig.

Swannie affixed the device to his head, turned on the little light and focused on the dirty business card. He flipped it over and noticed some writing on the back. He couldn't make any sense of it, but his detective juices flowed like he hadn't felt them in a long time. Somehow he knew this card had importance to their case.

Temporarily stymied, he turned it back to the side with the

large gold foil sticker. The sticker had been placed right in the middle of the card. It was big enough to largely cover the printed face. *Crap! Is somebody deliberately messing with me?*

He pulled out his trusty pocket knife and released a tiny nail file from its slotted home. He eased it under the edge of the foil sticker and gently pried it up from the card. To his surprise, it came away cleanly.

Swannie reached into his top drawer and grabbed one of the dozens of 3x5 cards he kept there. He carefully placed the foil sticker on it and set it aside.

He repositioned the metal headband into a comfortable position, picked up the business card, and used the magnifying glass to closely study its front. His first thought had been to look for a microchip of some sort. But something nagged at him and he removed the headband. He put on his reading glasses, and took another look at the business card.

When he stopped focusing on the magnified letters the entire the name of the company clicked into place. His mind reeled.

Southwest Office Services.

Then he saw the name of the individual: *Harrie McKinsey, Owner/Editor.*

29

Wednesday Evening

In Harrie's mind, an evening together with her best friends and relatives seemed like the perfect end to the mid-week weirdness. As she turned into her own driveway and pressed the garage door opener, it occurred to her that in the past few years, much of her life had taken on a weird quality. She supposed the prophetic dreams were mostly responsible. But realistically, even she must admit her own curiosity, and the need to obtain as much information as possible, played a big role in complicating her life.

She gathered up the pile of mail from her mailbox, shaking her head at the usual number of advertisements, specialty catalogs, and enticements from Publishers Clearinghouse Sweepstakes. No time to go through it all now. It would be added to the larger pile on her home office desk to sort through later. No wonder she so often felt stressed and overwhelmed with the everyday clutter finding its way into her retreat.

She hurried to change into a casual, comfortable outfit, and ditch her high-heeled shoes. Why she still bothered with high heels puzzled her. She supposed she needed the added height. She envied her best friend at times like these. Ginger's extra five inches gave her a natural look of being in charge, while Harrie fought to seem like someone other than a school girl.

She checked her appearance in the full-length mirror beside her closet—good to go. A look at her watch surprised her. Far from running late, if she left now, she'd arrive a good hour before the rest of the crowd. DJ planned to meet her there since he'd been a bit uncertain about when he'd leave his office. With this unexpected chunk of time, she'd see what order she could bring to her desk.

Half an hour later, Harrie felt a sense of accomplishment. She had sorted everything into categories. The stack of mail still needing her attention was much smaller. Ditching most of the catalogs and all the ads went a long way toward taming the beast. She looked through the stack of other envelopes and found what looked like a letter.

A letter? Nobody writes letters anymore, do they?

Then she noticed the return address. It was from their previous home on Sagebrush Lane. They'd only met the new owners once—when they closed on the sale. She'd even forgotten their name.

She slit the top edge of the envelope with her letter opener. From inside she removed a single page, folded into thirds, and another, smaller envelope. She sensed something out of the ordinary and felt a familiar electrical charge of energy flood her body. She swallowed the lump developing in her throat.

"Dear Ms McKinsey:

I hope you don't mind, but I contacted our realtor for your new address. I thought this piece of mail could be important. If you wish, I'll forward anything else I receive addressed to you."

It bore the signature of the new owner, Ellen Coleman. Enclosed was the woman's business card with phone number and email. Harrie set that aside and picked up the smaller envelope. She saw her name and the address of the old house. The postmark was faint, so she concentrated instead on a printed logo in the area reserved for a return address. It looked vaguely familiar.

She thought she caught a faint whiff of something like aftershave lotion. She held the smaller envelope up to her nose, but couldn't recapture the smell. A shiver went through her, as though a cold, icy draft had entered her cozy office. Goosebumps rose up on her arms and the image of a man flashed through her mind. Who?

She slid her finger under the flap of the sealed envelope and opened it. A small rectangular card fell out and landed on her desk. It featured the same logo appearing on the envelope. She stared at the cryptic, hand-written message, willing her brain to make sense of it.

"Ms. McKinsey - Please destroy the manuscript. My life may depend on it."

30

Wednesday at Dinner

The guests for Caroline's impromptu dinner party arrived within minutes of each other. Harrie had hoped to be the first one there. She wanted to speak to Caroline alone, but it was not to be. Before she could exit her car, Ginger and Steve arrived. She had barely locked her car before Swannie, laden with the food order from Rising Star, drove up. They all joined her as she approached the front door.

Caroline had not even had a chance to open the door before DJ arrived in his personal car and joined the rest. Harrie smiled and returned his greeting kiss. Then she took a deep breath and resolved to find a way to talk to Caroline alone later.

Even though they displayed their usual light-hearted banter, Harrie sensed tension from the group. DJ seemed lost in thought, his mouth in a grim line. Swannie showered most of his attention on Caroline, but even he seemed distracted. She knew Ginger was still stewing about being seen by her former student at lunch on Monday. Perhaps Harrie's own confusion about the strange mail she'd received caused her to be more cognizant of the moods around her. She decided dinner could go one of two ways. People would talk too much, dancing around whatever was on their minds. Or they might retreat into themselves, thinking over the subject troubling them. Harrie vowed to act normally—at least normal for her.

Caroline, alone, seemed serene. As usual, she was an amazing, gracious hostess—taking the food Swannie delivered and transferring it into the waiting serving dishes. Within minutes, the hungry group seated themselves at the table, ready to dig in.

Conversation was light and sparse. As dinner ended, Harrie decided she might as well break the ice and get into the subject that probably occupied most of their minds.

"So," Harrie started, with the bright, calculated cheeriness she'd chosen to adopt. "What's new with the Petroglyph murder?" She paid extravagant attention to her delicate little cup of jasmine tea and waited for the axe to drop.

She heard Ginger gasp and clear her throat. When Harrie looked up, Ginger's look clearly said, *"What are you? Nuts?"*

She steeled herself and looked around the table at the rest of her companions. "I had an interesting thing happen to me today. I thought it might be useful to those of you looking for clues to your homicide."

Harrie noticed DJ's jaw was tightly set, but Swannie's mouth hung open in obvious surprise. Steve looked puzzled, and Caroline had the faintest of smiles.

"What's going on, Harrie?" Swannie said.

Harrie sighed. "I think, it's time we compare notes."

Swannie opened his mouth to protest, but DJ held up his hand. "Hold on, Swannie. Perhaps she has a point. There are a couple of things we should ask her. By rights, we should let her in on whatever we can, agreed?"

Swannie displayed a range emotions. After a few seconds, he took a breath and slowly nodded. "Okay, perhaps this is the time."

Harrie hadn't expected such quick reversal in attitude. She decided extreme caution should be her guide.

"Good—that's good—okay, then. Where do we start?"

DJ's smile seemed authentic, but sometimes he tried to "handle" her by using almost that same smile. "Why don't you tell us what happened to you today. Then maybe we can connect some of the dots in this case."

Harrie glanced at Ginger.

Ginger gave her a fierce look and slowly nodded her head. The message was *Take what you can get and cooperate*. Her actual words were more blunt. "I, for one, would love to hear what happened to you."

Harrie nodded. "Okay. I received a piece of forwarded mail today from our old house on Sagebrush Lane. It had a cryptic note in it that I don't understand."

She excused herself from the table and went to get her purse. When she returned, she had the envelope in her hand. She handed it first to DJ.

He looked at it. "This is from the people who bought the house?"

"Look inside. Mrs. Coleman forwarded me a smaller

envelope."

DJ retrieved the smaller envelope and held it gingerly by the edges. Swannie left his seat and came to stand beside DJ. He leaned in while they both studied the envelope.

"It's handwritten. That might be useful," Swannie said. "But what's inside?"

DJ reached inside the small envelope, being careful, once again, to handle it only by the edges. The two men silently studied the sparse message.

DJ looked at Harrie. "I'm assuming you know who sent this?"

A sinking feeling coursed through her. "Actually I don't. I hoped Ginger or Caroline could help with that."

Ginger popped up from her chair and joined DJ and Swannie to view the message. When she reached out to take it, Swannie said, "No. Do not touch. There are too many people's fingerprints on it already."

"Oh," Ginger said. "Sorry. I didn't think about that." She bent over closer to read the message. "How does this person expect any of us to know what manuscript he's talking about? Caroline, come take a look."

Caroline obediently joined the others to peer at the note. She shook her head. "Beats me. There's not much to go on."

Meanwhile, DJ had gone back to the small envelope. He placed it on the tablecloth, address side up. "Here's something we might use." He turned to Harrie. "How many clients do you have out of the country?"

Harrie frowned. "Off the top of my head, I'm not aware of any who are out of the country. Where did you get that idea?"

"Didn't you notice the postmark?"

Harrie shrugged. "It's so faint. Besides, I was too anxious to examine its contents. What's the big deal anyway?"

"Because," DJ said, "if you look very closely, you'll see that this very faint postmark on your mystery envelope indicates it was sent from Greece."

31

Wednesday After Dinner

"I don't understand." Harrie looked at each of the people around the table. "I don't know anybody in Greece."

Ginger frowned. "I thought your father's parents came to this country from Greece."

Harrie shrugged. "They did, but as far as I know, they didn't leave any family behind. It was right after World War I, and there was so much destruction in so many places in Europe. My grandparents had just married. My father wasn't born until about ten years after they arrived in the United States. I never heard him say anything about there still being family in Greece."

"It wouldn't have to be family," DJ said. "Your grandparents probably had friends there. Maybe they stayed in touch."

Swannie had been quiet up until now. "I'm trying to make the connection to a manuscript. Do you have large numbers of manuscripts hanging around your office?"

Ginger said, "We hold on to copies of manuscripts for our clients. We do have that walk-in vault, and from the beginning we offered to maintain the original and a paper copy for them. Many are not that comfortable with their own digital storage, and they jump at the idea."

"How many manuscripts would you guess are stored in the vault?" DJ addressed the question to Harrie, who had been unnaturally quiet for the last couple of minutes.

"Two or three hundred, maybe more. But I still don't think we ever received any work from Greece."

Caroline cleared her throat. "I think we're missing a point here."

They all focused their attention on her. Harrie said, "What point is that?"

"Well," she said, "just because this note is postmarked as having been mailed in Greece, doesn't mean that the writer lives in Greece or has anything to do with Greece. Lots of people travel overseas and mail home letters and postcards. Why couldn't that be the case with our mysterious correspondent?"

Swannie smiled. "That's my girl. Always thinking and using that amazing brain of hers."

Caroline blushed a bright pink. "Nonsense. It's just a thought that occurred to me."

"It was a good one," Harrie said. "It gives us a lot more clients to choose from."

"So," Ginger said, "I take it the first order of business tomorrow will be a search of the manuscripts in the vault."

Harrie nodded. "It seems the logical place to start. Now, how about you guys share something." She pointed to Swannie and then DJ.

Swannie looked at DJ. DJ nodded.

"We have reason to believe that you are somehow connected to the victim at the Petroglyphs."

Harrie felt a surge of that familiar electric energy race through her body. Her heart beat wildly, and the memory of last week's dream hit her without warning.

DJ reached for her hand, a look of concern on his face. "Are you okay?"

She nodded mutely and reached for the glass of water she'd been sipping with dinner. She took several large gulps and willed her heart to return to a normal rhythm.

Ginger said, "Sweetie, I know this is upsetting news, but why the huge reaction. Those dreams of yours always end up associating you with the victim, don't they?"

Harrie shook her head. "I know, but this is different. I have this awful feeling that this time, the victim could actually be somebody I know."

32

Still Wednesday Evening

In the silence that followed Harrie's statement, Swannie frowned. Something was wrong—she could feel it—and she dreaded whatever was coming.

Swannie sighed. "I shouldn't be telling any of you this. I vowed I wouldn't. There are things I need to verify . . . I . . . I haven't even shared this with the Task Force . . . . " he turned to DJ.

DJ said, "Should we talk first?"

A look of pure relief swept across Swannie's face. "Yes, we should." He stood and gestured toward Caroline's den.

Ginger had returned to her chair beside Steve. She picked up her wine glass, and Caroline reached for the bottle of chardonnay. She refilled Ginger's glass, as well as her own.

DJ stood to join Swannie. He put his hand on Harrie's shoulder. "Stay here. Don't worry about anything right now. We need to compare notes."

Harrie had half risen from her chair when she saw both Caroline and Ginger's faces. By their expressions, each clearly encouraged her to leave it alone. She sank down, torn between her sense of danger and her intense need to know.

Caroline reached for Harrie's empty wine glass. "I think tomorrow we should divide up the alphabet and the three of us can eliminate many of the manuscripts we have in the vault."

She handed the glass back to Harrie, who took a sip, then shook her head. "Why do we so often discuss crime while sitting around this table?"

The four of them reminisced about other occasions when they'd had similar dinner discussions. By unspoken agreement they kept the conversation light, even chiding Harrie for some of her more outrageous escapades in recent times. They avoided references to the current situation.

Harrie took another sip of wine. At that precise moment, the grandfather clock in Caroline's entry hall chimed the hour. Harrie jerked reflexively, and sloshed wine down the front of her blouse.

"Oh, no!" She put her glass down, grabbed her napkin, and blotted at the wine.

Caroline sprang into action. In less than a minute she appeared at Harrie's side with a damp cloth and sponged away the offending spill.

"Thanks," Harrie said. "I think I'm wound tighter than your clock." She turned and looked toward the den. "What's taking them so long in there?"

Caroline gathered up the used dishes. "Who's ready for coffee?"

Both Ginger and Steve responded, "Me."

Harrie leaned her head back to look at the ceiling. "I might as well have some too. I'll be up all night anyway."

As Caroline returned with a tray of cups and saucers, DJ and Swannie entered the dining room.

DJ rubbed his hands together. "Thanks, Mom. How did you know I needed one of your great cups of coffee?"

Caroline smiled. "Mother's instinct, my boy."

Harrie contained herself until everyone had been served, and Caroline rejoined them. Then her patience came to an end.

"So, what's going on?" She looked from DJ to Swannie and back again. She noticed Swannie's clenched jaw.

He blew out a long breath before he spoke. "I discovered something just before I left the station this afternoon. I've been struggling ever since to figure out how it came to be. I wanted to talk it over with DJ before I said anything to you." He reached inside his jacket and extracted his smart phone. He scrolled through it until he arrive at a photo.

"Do you recognize this?" He handed the phone to Harrie.

She peered at it. "It looks like one of my old business cards. How did you get this photo?"

Swannie sighed. He spent the next few minutes explaining his examination of the articles of clothing from the Petroglyph victim. When he got to the part about finding Harrie's business card hidden under the inner sole of the victim's shoe, Harrie could contain herself no longer.

"Why would anybody go to that much trouble to conceal one of my business cards? It makes no sense."

"I agree," Swannie said. "But people do crazy things for a variety of reasons. And the question remains. How did our victim end up with your business card?"

Harrie opened her mouth but nothing came out. She turned up the palms of both hands and shrugged.

Ginger spoke up. "May I see that photo?"

Swannie handed the phone to Ginger who studied it briefly. "Huh," she said, and gave it back to Swannie. "Whoever had this must have found it, or they got their hands on it at least five years ago."

"Why do you say that?"

"Because," Ginger said. The look on her face left no question of her certainty. "These were the very first business cards we made. I know because I designed them on the computer and took them to the copy store in our complex to have them printed on card stock."

Steve frowned. "Sweetheart, you seem so sure. How can you possibly tell from just looking at a photo?"

But Harrie said, "Of course. I should have seen that myself. She's absolutely right."

DJ addressed his comment to Ginger. "What's so unique about this card, other than the fact that you designed it?"

Ginger grinned. "Because I only had ten printed up for Harrie to okay, but she hated them. I hadn't used the company name she wanted. Besides, we decided then and there not to put our individual names on our cards."

Caroline started laughing and everyone turned to look at her. She was shaking her head and consumed with such gales of laughter it completely broke the tension in the room. She finally got her control back, and wiped tears from her eyes.

"That certainly explains the whole name confusion thing we talked about yesterday. One question though. Why did you girls decide not to have your individual names on your business cards? That's pretty unusual."

This time Ginger's face had a sheepish look. She held up her hand. "My fault. I convinced Harrie it would be more efficient and less expensive if all the business cards were the same. Without our names, we could order in bulk."

DJ had been quiet for the past several minutes. He frowned.

"So, back to the original question. How did the victim at the Petroglyphs end up with one of ten cards that had the alternate name of the company and included Harrie's name printed on it?"

Harrie drew in a breath as realization came to her. She must have made a tiny noise of some sort because everyone turned at once to look at her.

"I think I did it myself. I kept those ten cards in my desk drawer for a long time. One day, I couldn't find any business cards, and I was in a hurry. I reached into my desk and grabbed one of those first ones Ginger made. I didn't even remember that until now."

"Who did you give it to?" DJ's voice sounded strained.

Harrie shook her head. "Sorry. I have no idea."

33

Thursday Morning

After an early staff meeting Thursday morning, DJ Scott had barely started on a stack of paperwork when his phone rang.

"DJ Scott," he said into the receiver.

"What do you have for me?"

DJ shook his head and settled back in his chair. "What do *you* have against identifying yourself on the phone, Crider?"

"You're a smart guy, Scott. You have an instinct for these things. No need to repeat the obvious."

"As it happens, I do have a little something for you."

"Meet me inside the mall at Coronado Center."

"That covers a pretty large area. Where specifically?"

"How about in front of Victoria's Secret at 10:00 AM?"

DJ sighed. "You have a wicked sense of humor, but I'd feel more comfortable loitering around the entrance to the old Sears store."

Crider chuckled. "No sense of adventure, Scott. I'm disappointed. Have it your way. Sears it is." With no further sign off, the line went dead.

DJ checked his watch—9:45 Eastern Time. Did he dare place a call to his buddy Tim Burns? Tim said he'd get back to him in two days, and it was now three since they talked. DJ had an uneasy feeling about all this. He picked up his phone again and punched in the number.

Tim answered with. "What are you, a mind reader?"

"You have something for me, don't you?"

"Well, I do and I don't. I found something, but you won't like it."

"How so?"

"I'll spare you the annoying details 'cause I'm pretty sure you don't really care what I had to go through to get it."

"That bad, huh?"

"Well, let's start with the fact that your victim isn't a US citizen."

DJ sucked in a breath. "And how did you determine that?"

"You don't want to know. Besides, if I told you I'd have to kill you. So just listen, okay?"

"Okay, but get to the point because you're scaring me."

"All right, but don't say I didn't warn you. Your victim is a foreign national. He's from one of those small countries that used to belong to our friends, the Soviets."

"Go on."

"At one time he became an asset, or at least that's how he was listed by the agency to whom he reported in those days. Turned out he was a double agent and they cut him loose."

"Did all this take place overseas?"

Tim paused a few beats, then said, "What you don't know about that is probably to your advantage so just shut up and listen."

"Aye, aye, Captain." DJ scribbled notes as he talked.

"Anyway, he dropped off the radar for a couple of years, during which time he apparently found another sponsor for his information. Then last year, the CIA sent in an undercover to deal with him."

DJ frowned. "How in the hell did you find out something like that?"

"Tsk, tsk, Buddy. Need to know, comprende?"

DJ groaned. "You know, Tim, you really should get out of the lab more often. You display an unhealthy obsession with spy movies."

"I'm as serious as a crutch, DJ. This stuff is too cheesy to make up. I'm giving you the straight scoop here."

"Okay, okay," DJ soothed him. "Can you just get to the point before I'm eligible for retirement?"

"Here's the part you're waiting for. The name of the victim, at least his latest alias, is Viktor Ivanovitch, and he showed up in this country about two months ago. The Intelligence Division has been watching him since he slipped in through Mexico. They had him under surveillance in south Texas until about three weeks ago. Somebody's ass is going to be grass because they lost him. When I ran his prints from here, I got called in to have a private chat with one of the deputy assistant directors."

DJ moaned. "Oh, great. Did you tell them I was the one who asked to have his prints run?"

On the other end of the line, Tim Burns let out a long breath. "That's the part you're not going to like. They already knew."

DJ felt his heart rate shoot up. "Do they want me to back off?"

"No, I've been told to offer you whatever's needed."

"Really? Why would they do that?"

On the other end of the line, DJ heard Tim's familiar chuckle.

"Dude, let's put it this way. *You* don't have the clearance to know what clearances *I* have. So believe me when I tell you this. Even *I* don't have the clearances to know the answer to that question."

34

Later Thursday Morning

Dozens of files from the Southwest Editing Services vault covered the large conference room table. Since 7:30 AM, Harrie, Ginger, and Caroline had worked in virtual silence as they pored through them. Two hours later, they seemed no closer to discovering who wrote Harrie's mysterious note.

"You know," Ginger said, "many of these manuscripts have absolutely no handwritten material on them. How are we expected to compare Harrie's note to any of them?"

Harrie shrugged. "We'll have to hope the right one contains handwriting."

"Let's take a break," Caroline said. She laid aside the manuscript she'd been reviewing.

Ginger sighed. "Fabulous idea. I'll get us a cup of coffee."

Harrie straightened up and massaged her neck. "Sounds heavenly. I feel like a human pretzel."

When Ginger returned with the coffee, Caroline had cleared a space. They sipped gratefully and chatted about things having nothing to do with their current pursuit.

After a few minutes Harrie said, "It occurs to me we may be on a wild goose chase."

"Why?" Caroline set her cup on the tray, as did Ginger. Both women waited for Harrie's response.

Harrie added her cup to the other two. "I believe it's possible we're on the wrong track. Because I'm so anxious to get answers, I may have jumped to conclusions."

Ginger and Caroline looked at each other, and both laughed.

Ginger recovered first. "Now there's an admission I never expected to hear from you."

Harrie grinned. "I know. Don't get used to it."

She picked up a copy of the note DJ had made for each of them last night. He had insisted on taking the original.

"Why did we assume this note has anything at all to do with the Petroglyph murder? Other than an annoying gut feeling, I have no other reason to make that association."

"But Sweetie," Ginger said, "that's the point. Your 'gut feelings' have been creepily accurate up to now. If you feel there's a connection, I say we're obligated to make sure."

"She's right," Caroline said. "In view of the business card Swannie discovered yesterday, and the fact that you received that note on the same day . . . ." She stopped and shook her head. "I don't know," she continued, "but I'm with Ginger on this one. I think we have to keep going and see what turns up."

Harrie shook her head. "You two never cease to amaze me. Half the time you both think I'm off my nut when I get one of these obsessions about my weird dreams. I'm always pushing you to see connections when they aren't obvious. Now, I'm unsure about this, and you're suddenly convinced I'm on to something. How's that for turning the tables?"

Ginger smiled and hugged her friend. "We're keeping you on your toes, that's all. Don't we always come around to your viewpoint in the end? We simply arrived earlier this time."

"Well okay then," Harrie said, and returned to the files on the conference table. "Let's get back to work."

They spent another forty-five minutes looking through manuscripts. There was little conversation as they studied the files.

Harrie interrupted the relative quiet. "Well I'll be dipped. Look at this." She held up a manuscript.

Ginger said, "You found it?"

Harrie nodded. "Yep."

Caroline and Ginger looked over Harrie's shoulder. The manuscript had a small logo on the title page consisting of a triangle inside a circle.

"Is that what I think it is?" Ginger's grin stretched wide.

"Jackpot," Harrie said. She held up the copy of the card and envelope she'd received in the mail yesterday.

Both items bore the same triangle set inside a circle.

35

Late Thursday Morning

By 9:45 AM, Special Agent DJ Scott had found a chair and a small table near the south entrance to the old Sears store inside Coronado Mall. He seemed like any other business man having a quick cup of coffee and scanning the morning paper.

He assumed somewhere close by, Colin Crider had already arrived and, even now, had DJ in his sights. This cat and mouse game seemed essential to the CIA operative, and DJ certainly didn't want to disappoint the man. But he found it tiresome on a day as busy as this one.

DJ felt Crider's presence seconds before Crider's low, resonant voice reached him from the other side of the table. "Anything worth my attention in there?"

DJ folded the newspaper and put it beside his almost empty coffee container. "Just the usual. An inordinate number of automobiles are being stolen. Seems to have something to do with people leaving their cars warming up in the driveway, keys inside, just begging to be taken."

Crider chuckled. "They never learn, do they?"

DJ drained the rest of his now lukewarm coffee. "So what's up?"

"You said you had something for me."

DJ lifted an eyebrow. "Ah, but you called me requesting a meeting. That would imply you had something too."

The first time he met Colin Crider, DJ thought the man's icy blue eyes were his most outstanding feature. At the time, they seemed cold, ruthless, and frankly, a bit creepy. Before long, it became apparent they were a weapon Crider used to intimidate people. Now the cold stare had lost its effect.

DJ stared back at Crider, who shrugged and shifted his gaze. "Good point. I have nothing new from my efforts. I counted on you coming through for me. You said you might have something soon. I hoped by now you had it."

DJ decided to let him off the hook. "I do. I just talked to my contact, and it's good news."

Crider's face gave away nothing of the emotion he might be feeling. DJ had to admire the man's stoic persona. When he spoke, even his voice didn't betray him.

"What do you consider 'good news'?"

"Well," DJ said, "I'm assuming James Bond's real name isn't anything close to Viktor Ivanovitch."

Crider's face paled. "I haven't heard that name in a very long time. And you're correct. James Bond isn't Viktor Ivanovitch."

DJ frowned. "But that's good news, isn't it?"

Crider nodded. "I'm glad it wasn't James Bond. But that begs the question. If the victim at Petroglyphs National Monument isn't my operative, then where is he, and why haven't I heard from him?"

36

Still Thursday

When DJ left Colin Crider, they had reached an agreement. If Crider's operative reappeared, DJ would be notified. If DJ learned anything else about Viktor Ivanovitch, he would get back to Crider.

DJ had decided not to mention anything to Crider about the business card hidden in the victim's shoe. Since the victim wasn't Crider's operative, he didn't need to know—yet.

So why did none of this make DJ feel any better about Harrie's possible involvement?

Once back in his Bureau car, he took time to place a call to Lt. Bob Swanson.

"What's up, DJ?"

DJ frowned. "How did you know it was me calling? There's no Caller ID associated with this number."

On the other end, Swannie chuckled. "Precisely, my boy. The designation, 'Unpublished Number' that pops up is a dead giveaway it's a Fed."

"Point taken," DJ said. "On another topic, I've just concluded a meeting with Crider. We should talk in person."

"Are you coming here?"

"Not this time. I have a better idea. Let's meet at Harrie's office. I discovered a text from her a couple of minutes ago. They found the manuscript in question. I think you and I should check it out."

"Interesting," Swannie said. "Okay, I can be there in about twenty minutes."

DJ's thoughts bounced from one thing to another as he wove his way through the mid-morning Uptown Albuquerque traffic. Why would Viktor Ivanovitch have one of Harrie's old business cards hidden in his shoe? It was one thing when they still hadn't known the man's identity, but the information this morning from Tim Burns ignited more worry in DJ's mind. Then there was the question of the cryptic note Harrie received in yesterday's mail.

Could that be a connection with Ivanovitch? How could it be? For that matter, was the manuscript now stored in Southwest Editing Service's vault a completely separate issue? If so, it was an amazing coincidence, and DJ, like many other law enforcement individuals, didn't generally believe in coincidences.

He pulled into the parking lot at Southwest Editing Services so automatically it took him a second to realize he'd arrived at his destination. He turned off the ignition and considered waiting for Swannie to arrive. But his curiosity outweighed his patience.

DJ entered the reception area and found it unattended. There seemed to be an unusual amount of activity emanating from the conference room. He headed there.

Tapping gently on the doorframe, he peered in to see the source of the noise. Harrie, Ginger, and his mother were gathered around the table, oblivious to his arrival.

"Hey, Ladies," he said. "What's going on here?"

Harrie let out a tiny squeal and spun around to face him. Caroline and Ginger laughed at Harrie's outburst.

Caroline said, "Good grief, DJ. Are you trying to give us heart failure? When did you sneak in?"

DJ frowned. "I didn't sneak. There wasn't even a receptionist out front. Then I heard all the hilarity and thought I missed the party."

Harrie slipped her arms around him. "The girls out front took an early lunch. It's DeeDee's going away party."

DJ told himself he overreacted, but he still wanted to get his point across. He tilted her chin up so he could see her face. "I remember a time, very recently, when an old man with a tentative grip on reality snuck in here toting a pistol. Do you happen to remember that incident?"

Now Harrie frowned. "I'm not likely to forget, but it's hardly the same situation today." She grinned and reached up to pat his check. "You worry about me too much. It'll give you wrinkles."

Caroline spoke up. "Don't rain on our parade Sweetheart. We're celebrating. Finding this manuscript was tedious. We deserve a break."

Before DJ could respond, he heard a voice behind him.

"Hey, young fella," Swannie said, "are you giving my lady a hard time?"

"I wouldn't think of it," DJ said.

Swannie went to Caroline and gave her a hug. "What's this I'm hearing about your finding the manuscript? You ladies are amazing."

"Thank you," Caroline said. "But we haven't even had a chance to check it out."

Both Swannie and DJ approached the conference table. DJ reached out to take the manuscript, but apparently Harrie had other ideas.

"Not so fast." She clutched it against her chest.

"What are you doing?" DJ hoped he didn't look as exasperated as he felt.

Harrie raised her chin, and her eyes blazed. "Our clients expect anonymity. We sign non-disclosure agreements when we take possession of their work. I can't just let you look through this manuscript. We could be sued."

DJ tamped down his immediate response. He smiled tightly, took a breath, and said, "So, what would you have us do? Get a warrant?"

Harrie blinked, opened her mouth, then shut it abruptly. She turned to Caroline, who stepped forward and put her hand gently on DJ's arm. "Sweetheart, you need to take it down a notch. Harrie has a point. Let's think of a way around this, okay?"

DJ tilted his head toward the ceiling and took another, longer breath. "You're right, Mother. As usual, my concern for Harrie's safety has made me a tad . . . Shall we say, 'impatient?'"

Swannie grinned. "I think my young friend is simply saying we are all concerned, not only about your safety, but also the pressing need to solve this case." He gestured toward the tightly held package Harrie still clutched. "We can go about this a couple of ways. Can you at least give us the name of the owner?"

Harrie relaxed her grip on the document and frowned. "I suppose that would be all right. But I can't let you see it until I get permission."

DJ realized he had relaxed enough that he his hands were no longer balled into fists. His brain buzzed, and he suppressed a grin. "That reminds me of another question I have for you."

The eyebrow over Harrie's left eye arched. "I'm almost afraid to ask what that would be?"

DJ rubbed his hands together. "Well, considering the cryptic note you received yesterday, it would seem our currently unknown writer has already let you off the hook."

Now Harrie frowned. "How did you reach that conclusion?"

"He asked you to destroy the manuscript. Doesn't that imply he's no longer planning to use it?"

Harrie turned to Ginger, who simply shrugged her shoulders. She turned back to DJ, loosened her grip on the manuscript, and held it out to him.

"I have a bad feeling about this. If Southwest Editing Services gets sued, you're paying for my lawyer."

DJ took the manuscript. "Worse things could happen."

"Meaning what?"

DJ rested his hand on Harrie's shoulder. "It's possible the author is already dead."

37

Thursday Still

Harrie frowned. "Why would you say that?"

Swannie spoke up. "Good question." He turned to DJ. "Did you learn something about my victim's identity?"

DJ said, "You and I need to talk."

Swannie nodded. "It would seem so."

"Ladies," DJ said, "please excuse us. We need to borrow your conference room for a few minutes."

"But," Harrie squeaked out before DJ pressed his fingers to her lips.

"You know how this works," he said. "Once again, you've managed to get yourself mixed up in one of our cases, but the rule still holds. I cannot discuss this with you." He turned to include Ginger and his mother in that statement. "Not any of you."

Harrie gently pushed his fingers away from her lips. "You must get tired of saying that to me. It's okay, but will you promise me one thing?"

DJ sighed. "You know I can't promise—"

This time Harrie interrupted. "I'm only suggesting that if the manuscript has nothing to do with your case, will you promise to return it to us?"

He frowned. "Don't hold your breath."

Caroline spoke up. "Come on, ladies. Let's give these guys a chance to do their jobs. How about we go to my office?"

Both Harrie and Ginger nodded and the threesome left the conference room, closing the door behind them.

"Okay," Swannie said, "what's the story?"

DJ described his conversation with Tim Burns about the identity of the victim.

"Well there's a twist I never expected," Swannie said. "Does that mean the FBI will take the case?"

DJ shook his head. "It's possible, but until I talk with the bosses, I can't be sure. I need to determine what, if anything, this manuscript has to do with the case. I may be imagining things that aren't connected."

Swannie rubbed his chin. "What about Crider? How did the meeting go?"

DJ filled Swannie in on Crider's reaction to the fact that Viktor Ivanovitch was the victim rather than his operative.

Swannie said, "But he still doesn't know what happened to his operative?"

"No, and I think that has him even more worried."

"Hmmm," Swannie said, and the faintest of smiles creased his face, "you don't really think that manuscript is related to the investigation, do you?"

"Well this much I do know. There's something hinky about it, even if it's not involved with this case. My gut tells me it's still something I need to pursue."

"You planning to read it, or just turn it over?"

"I have to read it," DJ said. "If it was written by Ivanovitch it could be relevant. If it was written by Crider's operative, even that could be important."

"And what if you can tell right away it has nothing to do with the Petroglyph murder, Ivanovitch, or Crider's operative?"

"I'll still be in a better position to make sure Harrie doesn't get involved in another mystery with an unknown author who, by the way, is using a phony name."

Swannie frowned. "How do you know that?"

"Take a look for yourself." DJ held out the manuscript so Swannie could read the cover page.

Swannie looked blank. "I still don't get it."

"Seriously?" DJ said. "This guy is using the name Keyser Söze. That's the tip off."

Swannie shrugged. "So?"

"Come on," DJ said, "you must have seen that movie from the Nineties. You know, the one everybody talked about? *The Usual Suspects*?"

Swannie groaned. "Oh, of course. But who's dumb enough to pawn off his manuscript using the name of a movie character?"

"A guy who thinks he's pretty smart, or someone who wants others to figure it out."

Swannie grinned and patted DJ on the back. "Well, I wish you luck. Enjoy your reading assignment. I'd offer to help you out, but crime hasn't come to a standstill in Albuquerque. It's back to the office for me."

DJ managed an exaggerated sigh. "Thanks a bunch, friend. I'll be sure to return the favor sometime."

Swannie started to open the conference room door, stopped, and turned back to DJ.

"You know, I love how you're always trying to protect that little gal of yours. But be forewarned. You know as well as I do Harrie won't let this rest. One way or the other, you'll have to let her in on how the manuscript fits into this case."

DJ nodded. "I agree."

Swannie smiled wickedly and opened the conference room door. "Brother, I don't envy your life for the next few days."

38

Thursday Afternoon

DJ Scott hunched over the manuscript from Southwest Editing Services for almost four hours. He checked his watch and realized he'd forgotten to eat lunch.

The day had been quiet for a change. He'd found an empty conference room and stayed out of sight.

A flood of contradictory thoughts competed for his attention. First, who needed to see this? How much was pure fiction, and how much reflected the actual work of an enemy agent? It seemed like a cheesy rip-off of a James Bond thriller.

Or it could be a clever way to hide a secret file in plain sight. It seemed unlikely, even to DJ, that it would ever be published.

It occurred to him that Harrie must have cross references in her records. He hoped it included both the writer's legal name and his pen name. How else could she contact the author?

Harrie answered her cell phone on the first ring.

"So, what's the verdict?" Her voice sounded tense.

"If I give you this guy's pen name, can you tell me his legal one?"

There was a pause before she answered. "If I can, will you tell me what you found?"

Before he had the chance to deliver his pre-planned speech, an inspiration struck. "Do you want in on this case?" No response. "Harrie? Are you still there?"

"Sorry," she said. "I'm having a surreal experience. I could swear you asked if I want to become involved in the case? That can't be what you said."

"It's precisely what I said, my love. I plan to name you as a confidential informant. You'll help us analyze this manuscript. We'll ask you to research your files to help us fill in missing information. Is that something you would like?"

The musical sound of Harrie's laughter filled DJ with a warm glow. *God, I love this woman!*

He felt the warmth of her voice through the phone "I'll give you whatever info you need. You don't have to tell me any more than necessary. I want to sort out this mess, find out who committed a murder, and end these dreams. If that sounds good, we have a deal."

"Just when I think I have you figured out, you surprise me." He heard her soft chuckle and imagined the smile on her face.

"In the event you hadn't noticed, I'm a woman. You should realize it's a waste of time trying to understand what goes on in my head."

"Thanks for the tip. I think I knew that." He waited a beat and returned to the reason for his call. "So, back to my original question. Can you match up the pen name with the real name?"

Harrie chuckled. "Of course. How else could we communicate with our clients?"

"Ok," said DJ. "Keyser Söze is the name on the manuscript."

"What an unusual name."

"Doesn't that mean anything to you?"

"No, should it?"

DJ snorted. "Am I the only one who saw a lot of movies in the Nineties?"

"I can only answer for myself," Harrie said. "I spent my time in the Nineties reading. But I assume one of your movies during that period featured this Söze guy?"

"Yes, *The Usual Suspects*—and Söze was the most important character."

"Sounds strange."

"It was."

"Ah hah." Harrie's voice had a note of triumph.

"You found it?"

"I did, but you won't like it."

"I don't need to like it. Lay it on me."

"Don't say I didn't warn you. The name in our file is Richard Tracy."

DJ hesitated. "Okay, so, why would that upset me?"

Harrie laughed. "Now who's out of the loop. When you were a kid, didn't you read the daily comic strips in the newspaper?"

DJ's patience snapped. "No. I already explained I spent all my time at the movies."

"For your information Mister FBI, I grew up being a big fan of a comic strip about a handsome homicide detective. His name was Dick Tracy. Warren Beatty even starred as him in a movie around 1990. You must have seen that one."

DJ groaned. "Right. Of course. Now I remember. But that means we still don't know this guy's real name."

"Don't give up," said Harrie. "Maybe that's actually his real name. His mom could have been a fan. Anything's possible."

He considered making a comment about misplaced optimism when a lightbulb went off in his head. He reversed course. "Sweetheart, that's the best advice you've given me today. Gotta go. Thanks for your help."

New energy had replaced his earlier discouragement. He grinned as he dialed the number for Colin Crider.

39

Early Thursday Evening

DJ looked at his watch for the third time. It wasn't like Colin Crider to be late for a meet. In fact, he could usually be found lurking somewhere nearby, checking for whatever or whoever could pose a threat. And while DJ supported situational awareness, Crider seemed overboard on the subject.

DJ noticed that the small coffee shop, which had been almost empty when he walked in, had filled to a capacity crowd. On the heels of that discovery, he noticed Crider sitting at a table against the far wall. As soon as DJ saw him, Crider stood and ambled over to where DJ sat nursing his coffee. Crider pulled over a chair from the next table and sat at a right angle from DJ.

DJ said, "I thought you'd stood me up."

Crider looked at the coffee cup he'd brought with him from the other table. "Just waiting for an invitation. You looked deep in thought."

"You know, I don't think I'd make it in the CIA. Too much drama."

That seemed to amuse Crider. "No surprise there. You guys are so uptight and proper you'd get yourself killed the first time you had to go deep cover."

DJ resisted the urge to respond to that statement. No point in giving away tactical information Crider needn't to know. Instead, DJ smiled and took a long swig of coffee.

Crider seemed to study the other occupants of the coffee shop with casual interest. "So, what's this information you've brought me?"

"Has your operative ever used the name Richard Tracy?"

The cup halted on its way to Crider's lips. He returned it to the table, and his eyes narrowed. "Where did you get that name?"

"I'm guessing from your response I hit a nerve."

Crider's jaw clinched, and his icy blue eyes narrowed. "Don't mess with me Scott. I'm out of patience. Tell me what you know."

DJ put his cup on the table and leaned toward Crider. "Calm

yourself, Buddy. Let's not give those people over there anything else to talk about." He nodded to a table two rows away.

Crider took a deep breath and twisted his head from side to side, causing a soft 'crack.' And with that sound, his entire body seemed to relax. "Sorry. I've been tense. Losing an operative has that effect on me."

"As it happens, I have information about that. I don't know what it means. Maybe you do."

Crider listened without comment as DJ filled him in. He explained about the cryptic note Harrie received. That led to a discussion about the manuscript referred to in the note. He described how Harrie, Ginger, and his mother located that manuscript in their files earlier today.

When DJ mentioned the odd logo on not only the card and envelope but on the title page of the manuscript, Crider smiled. It was so out of character for the man that DJ stopped talking and stared at him.

Crider shook his head. "It's okay. This is good news. My co-worker is safe."

DJ frowned. "How did you jump to that conclusion? I've been all but sure he was dead."

"Tell me," Crider said, "this note your wife received. Was the envelope postmarked from Greece?"

DJ's pulse raced. "Yes, but how could you know?"

Crider stood and tossed two, one-dollar bills onto the table. He returned his wallet to his pocket. "Let's just say we always have contingency plans. This was one. Now, if you'll bring me that manuscript tomorrow, I'll explain how it all works."

And with that, Colin Crider left the coffee shop, leaving behind a very annoyed and worried DJ Scott

.

40

Thursday Evening

Harrie sighed in relief when she opened her garage door. She hadn't realized until that moment how much she'd counted on arriving home before DJ.

The glowing red button on their kitchen landline phone blinked the presence of an unheard message. Maybe it would be from DJ, indicating he would be a little late this evening. She pressed it, listened, and smiled. It was, and he would.

Since he hadn't indicated how late, she hurried to her home office with her briefcase. She removed the laptop and plugged it into the power strip.

As she waited for the computer to boot up—which always seemed annoyingly slow to the impatient Harrie—she marveled at her second bit of luck in the past half hour. She smiled at how her mind worked. She had just entered the gates of Canyon Estates this evening, thinking about what she would prepare for dinner. Then, without warning, a stray thought popped into her head.

I'm pretty sure I have a digital copy of that manuscript.

Naturally, from that point on, she'd been eager to reach the relative privacy of her home office to verify this belief. So now, her only obstacle was the glacially slow boot-up process.

She sighed and went to her file cabinet, unlocked it, and reached in the middle drawer. A small box about 8 x 10 inches sat at the bottom. She took it out and twirled the dial on the combination lock. It contained a collection of labeled thumb drives. If her good luck held, she would find the manuscript on one of them.

Caroline had come up with the idea of off-site backups for client manuscripts. They instituted the plan three years ago and settled on assigning a new thumb drive to each client. Although the original and duplicate copies were in the vault at Southwest Editing, Harrie and Ginger had both agreed it was important to maintain copies off-site.

Harrie found the one marked "Keyser Söze" and inserted it in her computer.

She waited for the Word document of the manuscript to load. It didn't take long. The title page bore the proposed name of the book. In Harrie's humble opinion, *The Karaoke Kaper* was a lousy name for a serious effort at writing a Suspense/Thriller novel. She vaguely remembered when the manuscript arrived at Southwest Editing but hadn't worked on it personally.

The editor who had done so mentioned it in a staff meeting one day. She said it was one of the most disjointed pieces of writing she'd encountered since coming to work at Southwest Editing. According to her, it didn't make much sense.

Harrie checked her watch. Probably not much time left before DJ came through the door. Still, she might get some idea of why this manuscript had caused so much trouble. She settled down to read.

An hour later she had skimmed through about half of the novel and felt more confused than when she started. It appeared that at least two people were involved in writing this mess. It also seemed disjointed and amateurish.

The drive contained another file with the client's information. She clicked on that file to see what she could determine about the author. It was no surprise to see the name listed for the client was Richard Tracy—she'd already shared that with DJ.

But when she looked through the rest of the client information form, the name of the person to contact in an emergency took away Harrie's breath.

"In case of emergency," it said, "please contact John Smith," and it showed a local Albuquerque number. Harrie shuddered, suddenly feeling a cold breeze in the room.

She already knew that John Smith was the pseudonym for Colin Crider.

41

Late Thursday Evening

When Harrie heard DJ's car in the garage, she removed the roasted chicken breasts from her Instant Pot. She'd been going over and over in her mind how to get into the discussion she knew she must have with her husband.

He walked through the door, and before he noticed her, Harrie caught a glimpse of the tiredness he carried. As soon as he saw her, his expression underwent a dramatic change. He grinned broadly, put down his briefcase, and took her in his arms.

"Wow, something smells good," he said. He seemed reluctant to let her go.

"It's roasted chicken breasts with extra touches. I used a variety of herbs this time, and I poured a light coating of brandy over them the last five minutes to add a subtle flavor."

She reluctantly pulled away from his embrace and grinned at him. "Dinner's ready."

He grinned back. "I'll go wash up, and be back in less than five minutes."

She set the table with candles—one of her favorite rituals on nights he worked late. He needed relaxation, and soft candlelight gave that. She sensed he tried to keep her from seeing just how tired or worried he might be. He wouldn't understand her sensitivity to his mood, his energy level, and any number of other things about him. She supposed it could be related to her tendency for prophetic dreams.

They finished dinner and were sipping the last of their wine when Harrie decided to make her move.

"I have news for you," she said brightly.

"Oh?" He seemed guarded.

"Not to worry," she said. "It's should be helpful."

"I'm all ears. Enlighten me."

First she explained about the off-site storage situation for Southwest Editing. Next she plunged ahead and told him about her decision to locate the manuscript file in question and read it for herself.

He remained surprisingly quiet during this entire recitation, so she continued.

"I also checked through the rest of the customer information we collect on all our documents. You'll be happy to know it contains the name and phone number of an emergency contact."

That statement didn't elicit the reaction she'd anticipated. "But you already have that information, don't you?"

DJ took his last sip of wine. "Yes, as you've surmised, I do."

42

Still Thursday Evening

Harrie leaned back in her chair. She closed her eyes while she put together a reasonable response. "When did you learn Colin Crider might be involved in the Petroglyph murder?"

"This past Tuesday, but for accuracy, he's not *involved* in the way that word implies. That's also when I found out your involvement was more than your adventures on Saturday."

Harrie sat up straight and sighed. "And you're just now telling me?"

He shrugged. "I think you know I've been walking a very tight line. Besides, I still don't know to what extent Crider thinks you're 'involved' in this thing. At first he only revealed he knew you and Ginger had met with the Park Ranger. But he said more this evening."

Harrie felt a chill. "Meaning . . . ?"

She looked at her husband and could see the tiredness. She felt a guilty twinge because of her intense questioning. A sudden, fierce need to protect him overwhelmed her.

"Sweetheart, you're tired. We don't have to get into this tonight."

DJ shook his head. "No, let's get it done. Each day brings its own set of problems. If we spend a few more minutes now, it'll be out of the way."

Harrie stood. "Then I suggest we do it over a cup of herbal tea. It will relax us both and help us sleep."

DJ nodded and followed her into the kitchen. He got out cups while Harrie prepared the tea. She smiled at him when she set the cups on the table.

"You look better already." She leaned down and kissed him before she took her seat and sipped her tea.

"Okay," DJ said. "Since you've already read much of the book, and since I told you earlier I would designate you as a source of information, I'll fill you in on what I can."

Harrie smiled. "That's wonderful, Honey. I really . . . ."

DJ interrupted her. "Don't get all excited yet. I meant it when I said I could use your help, but you must understand I can only give you limited information. We'll see how things go, and maybe down the line I'll be able to share more with you. Deal?"

For the first time in days, Harrie had hope this would soon be over. She felt like hugging herself.

"Deal," she said. "I promise I'll behave."

"Ok, then." DJ outlined Crider's problem with losing track of his operative, and how DJ had intervened to discover the true identity of the victim. At that point, Harrie took a breath, and DJ cut her off.

"I know how your brain works. So for now, save your questions."

Harrie made a 'zipping' motion across her lips, and resumed sipping her tea.

DJ told her about the significance of the note she received from the author of the manuscript. He explained Crider's confidence in his operative's safety, thanks to that note. Then he mentioned Crider had revealed on Tuesday he had someone following Nick Ellis, and that person reported back to Crider that Harrie and Ginger were talking with Ellis.

"Hold on a minute," Harrie said. "I know I'm not supposed to be asking questions, but this is more of a comment."

"Okay, go ahead."

Harrie set her cup on the table. "You said Crider had someone following Nick Ellis, and that a 'person' reported Ginger and I were having lunch with Nick."

DJ nodded.

"Did you know that Cabrini and I went for coffee on Tuesday? Did you have anything to do with that?"

DJ looked a bit sheepish. "Well, Swannie and I did ask her help finding out what you were up to."

Harrie chewed her lip briefly. "Did Crider tell you the identity of this person following Nick?"

DJ frowned. "No way. There's no reason he'd ever tell me something like that."

"Well," Harrie said, "just so you know, Cabrini gave us the name of the person who outed us."

DJ looked completely surprised. "That's not possible. I had no name to give her, and I never said you were being followed. I just told her and Swannie that Crider said you were involved in some way."

Harrie grinned. "She not only had a name, but she told me who it was. She said a former student of Ginger's got a job as a police service aide, and he happened to be having lunch at the restaurant where Nick Ellis met us. He also accompanied the detectives to the murder scene last Thursday night. At that time Cabrini personally told Nick not to discuss the murder with anyone. This kid supposedly overheard our conversation and reported back to Cabrini that Nick had been talking."

DJ finished his tea and took his cup to the sink, rinsed it out, and dried it. She joined him with her own cup. They looked at each other.

"Something strange is going on," he said. He took Harrie's cup and treated it to the same cleaning process.

"There's something else," Harrie said. "I just now thought of it. When we got to the restaurant on Monday, Nick told us he thought he was being followed."

"That sounds reasonable," DJ said.

"But wait, that's not the interesting part. When I started to turn around to look, he said not to bother because the guy had left before we came in."

DJ stared at Harrie. "That means there's somebody other than the police aide who knows you and Ginger were at that restaurant on Monday."

"No, that can't be. The only reason the service aide reported back to Cabrini about us was because he recognized Ginger. He sat in the booth behind us and overheard our conversation."

"Interesting," DJ said.

The nerves in Harrie's arms and legs tingled.

"Wait," she said, "if Crider's guy left just before we arrived, how could he know who we were, or that we met Nick Ellis?"

43

Friday Morning

A repeat showing of Harrie's dream during the night—and the dark, angry-looking rain clouds hanging in the sky this morning—combined to dampen her normally cheery mood.

She and DJ had talked until well after midnight, discussing her being followed. Harrie felt inclined to discard that idea—especially since discovering Crider's operative was the author of the mysterious manuscript. But DJ still believed she could be in danger, and all their talking failed to convince him otherwise.

This morning he had gone for his usual early run, but Harrie took one look out the window at the sky and declined to join him. Instead, she burrowed back under the covers and tried to make up for lost sleep. She didn't wake again until after he'd returned from his run, showered, and left for the office.

In Harrie's opinion, a hot shower constituted the ideal wake-up remedy—almost as effective as a cup of steaming coffee. It also served as the ideal place to let ideas flow over you. Today the ideas flowed almost immediately, and her plan formed.

It was still early, but she felt fidgety and anxious to get going. She dressed quickly and within ten minutes declared herself ready to face the day—needing only that perfect cup of coffee.

She'd just taken her first sip when the landline phone rang. Harrie checked her watch. At this hour, it was probably either DJ or Ginger. She grinned when she saw the caller ID.

"To what do I owe this early morning check in?" Harrie sipped her coffee and waited.

"And a happy good day to you too," Ginger said. Harrie noted the slightest edge of irritation.

"What's up?" Harrie adjusted her voice to better fit her friend's mood.

"I need to talk to you."

"Sure," Harrie said. "You sound like you have a particular topic to discuss."

There was a slight pause before Ginger responded. "I have

some concerns, I'll admit."

"You wanna give me a hint?"

"Not really. Will you be at the office at the usual time?"

Harrie looked at the clock on the stove. "I may be a little late. I have a small errand to do first."

Ginger let out a long sigh, which Harrie recognized from many years of friendship. She knew her friend was struggling with something and would tell her only when she was ready.

Harrie said, "You know what I think? This has been a hellacious week and we should spend an hour or two talking. Let's take a long lunch today."

"How do you do it?" Ginger's voice had softened slightly.

"Do what?"

"No matter what's going on, no matter how many other things you have on your plate, you can always sense my moods better than anyone I know, with the possible exception of Steve."

Harrie laughed. "Tell you what. Let's have an early lunch at Jinja's in that booth on the east wall where we always sit. We'll have Lemon Soufflé iced tea and some pot stickers. It's a great place to talk. Would you mind calling and making a reservation for us?"

Harrie heard a small laugh before Ginger spoke. "I'd be happy to. And, thanks."

"No need to thank me. I'm the one bending your ear."

"About what?"

"What else? My husband is trying to cramp my style again"

Ginger sighed. "I don't wish to disappoint you, but I'm thinking I'll probably side with DJ. If this is a situation like so many others we've had in the past few years, you're up to something, and DJ's trying to stop you."

"Oh ye of little faith. You make it sound like I have a habit of doing dangerous things."

"Gee, I wonder what ever made me think that? You don't suppose it could be because of your reckless history, do you?"

"You cut me to the quick, woman. But I forgive you because you're making the lunch reservations, and I'm in a hurry."

"What are you up to now?"

"It's the most innocuous thing you can imagine. I'm taking a few moments this morning to scope out my old neighborhood on

Sagebrush Lane."

"Why, for the love of toothpicks, are you doing that?"

"I'm trying to prove a point to DJ—and probably you, too, by the sound of it. Trust me. There's no danger, and it will satisfy my curiosity about something."

Ginger laughed. "If I had a dollar for each time you've said that and been wrong, I'd buy your lunch today."

"Tell you what, if I'm wrong about it, I'll gladly pay you that dollar."

Ginger's voice sounded strained. "Just don't take any stupid chances, promise?"

"You have my word," Harrie said. She disconnected the call, uncrossed her fingers, and picked up her car keys and sunglasses.

44

Still Friday Morning

Harrie opted to leave her car radio off. She could never resist the urge to sing along with the artist, and that wouldn't work today. For reasons she didn't fully understand, she left her mobile amateur radio on, tuned to frequency 145.33 Megahertz. Knowing she could pick up the microphone and summon help if she needed it, always gave her a sense of security.

In the shower this morning it had occurred to her she had some experience being followed—and shaking the offending car. Back when they still lived on Sagebrush Lane, she'd been followed more than once. While it had been a bit unnerving, she felt rather proud of herself for being able to ditch the tail.

The dark clouds scuttling across the sky might present a problem. She really needed the sunglasses to pull this off. Not only did they give her a degree of anonymity, but her expressions would also remain a mystery to anyone watching her.

"Harrie," she said to herself, "I think you're enjoying this too much." She removed the glasses and dropped them into her lap. The whole point of this exercise was to prove no one was following her, right? To achieve that goal, she had to see clearly.

As she crossed Eubank Boulevard, going east on Academy, she systematically scanned the cars in her rearview and side mirrors. She made a mental note of the color and make of cars behind her, and realized they had been with her since she pulled away from the gate at Canyon Estates. A little blue sports car was immediately behind her. Further back was a brown SUV, a black Prius sedan, and a red VW.

The next traffic light up ahead was green, so she slowed a bit to see who would go around. As expected, the driver of the little blue sports car whipped around her and sped past. She kept her eyes on the road, imagining the irritated look he probably bestowed as he swooped passed. He moved to her lane again—this time two cars ahead. She smiled and relaxed.

Approaching the red light at Tramway and Academy, she

checked which cars were still behind her. As far as she could tell, only three had stuck with her this far.

She sped up, quickly signaled a right turn, and edged into the far right-turn lane. At the same time the light turned green, giving her the opportunity to ease into the merging lane on Tramway. Behind her, the brown SUV, and the black Prius, copied her maneuver. Significant? Too soon to tell.

She got up to the 50 mph speed limit on Tramway and quickly maneuvered into the far left lane. The traffic light cycled to green as she approached Spain and Tramway. She moved into the left-turn lane without signaling, and the brown SUV, which had been with her since somewhere around Eubank, sped on through the green. Harrie searched her rear view mirror for the Prius and saw it move into the left-turn lane. She hadn't noticed the red VW sitting right behind her, now hiding her view of the Prius. The heavy morning traffic gave little opportunity to turn onto eastbound Spain. The light cycled to red, and, as if on cue, the sun popped through the clouds.

Harrie tried her sunglasses again. They made her more comfortable checking out the cars. She noticed a man drove the VW. Much as she tried, she couldn't get a look at the Prius driver.

When the green arrow came on, she wasn't paying attention, and the VW tapped on his horn. She recovered and made her turn. But now what? This wasn't the best way to her old neighborhood.

She drove through the winding streets of the High Desert subdivision, all the while keeping track of the two cars behind her. She noticed the VW had what looked like a rabbit's foot dangling from the rearview mirror. It swung back and forth as they traveled the winding road. She kept going east until she reached a cross street. She knew it would take her, eventually, to her old neighborhood. She turned left again, and headed back north.

The VW continued east on Spain, and Harrie let out the breath she'd been holding. Looking through her rearview mirror allowed her a glimpse of the driver's side door on the black Prius still sitting at the stop sign. It sported a big dent, like something ran into it. She went around a curve and lost sight of it. She turned onto a side street and waited. After a few minutes, it seemed obvious the Prius had either continued east or turned south at the stop sign. She got back on the northbound street and congratulated herself for her resourcefulness.

Now she had to pay close attention to her driving. You could take a wrong turn and end up in one of the dozen or so cul de sacs in that area. She chided herself for taking such a circuitous route when it would have been easier going the old, familiar way.

It took at least ten minutes longer than it should have, but she finally turned the corner onto Sagebrush Lane. She crossed another short street and arrived at the cul de sac of her former home. A "For Sale" sign was planted in the lawn of the corner house. To her amazement, the home of her former next-door-neighbor also displayed a "For Sale" sign. Then she noticed something else.

The same black Prius with the dented door was now parked in the driveway, next door to her old house. A chill went down Harrie's spine. The driver sat in the car. She saw his eyes peering into his rearview mirror.

She completed the half circle she'd started around the cul de sac and tamped down her panic. At the corner she turned right and proceeded slowly. Once out of sight, she took off at several miles over the speed limit.

Harrie gripped the steering wheel.

"Damn!" Now she owed Ginger a dollar.

45

Late Friday Morning

Sgt. Cabrini Paiz tapped lightly on the doorframe to Lieutenant Swanson's office. He seemed concentrated on the file folder in front of him. At her knock, he looked up and closed the folder.

"Am I interrupting you, Lieutenant?"

He smiled. "It's okay. I needed a break." He leaned back and ran a hand through his thick gray hair. "What can I do for you?"

Cabrini sat in a chair facing his desk. "Where are we on the Petroglyphs murder? Have you heard anything new?"

Swannie blushed. "Um, well, about that . . . ."

He cleared his throat, but seemed unwilling to continue.

Cabrini almost laughed at the picture he presented. At that moment he looked like a small boy caught with his hand in a candy jar. She bit her lip and forced the smile from her face.

"I take it you have, but you can't tell me."

Swannie shook his head. "No, no, it's not that." He paused and frowned. "Yeah, I guess it really is that. I'm sorry Sergeant. I hate being in this spot. I hope I can fill you in by the end of the day—or tomorrow at the latest."

Cabrini felt sorry for the guy. "It's okay, Lieutenant. I assume the FBI is more involved in this than we originally thought."

The weak, embarrassed smile on Swannie's face conveyed more than words. "Let's say circumstances have arisen which put things in a slightly different context."

Cabrini nodded. "Well stated, Lieutenant. Don't misunderstand me, I know the constraints you're under, but I must tell you I have a strong feeling this new development, whatever it is, involves our friend Harrie McKinsey."

Swannie's eyes widened. "How did you . . . I mean why would you . . . Um have you talked to Harrie?"

This time Cabrini didn't even try to suppress her laughter. "I had coffee with her on Tuesday. Don't you remember? You and DJ asked me to see what I could find out."

Swannie relaxed. "Oh, right. I forgot." He shuffled a stack of papers on his desk. "Anything else?"

Cabrini stood to leave and dropped a file on his desk. "I only came in to brief you on this new case. It's a bit weird, but we can talk about it later."

Swannie picked up the folder and opened it. He scanned the top page. When he looked up, he frowned. "When did this happen?"

"They're not positive, but apparently it was sometime between midnight and 6 AM last Thursday morning—a little over a week ago."

"You've got to be kidding me."

Cabrini shook her head. "Nope. I'm as serious as a heart attack. I called over there and verified the situation."

"And they're just now reporting it?"

She nodded.

Swannie looked at his watch and grinned. He stood, took his suit jacket off the back of his chair, and put it on. "Thanks, Sergeant. You've brightened my day. I'm headed for a luncheon meeting, and I can't wait to tell DJ Scott about this."

Now it was Cabrini's turn to frown. "I don't understand, Sir."

Swannie walked toward the door and gestured for Cabrini to go in front of him.

As they walked down the hall together, Swannie's grin grew even bigger. "Sergeant, lately I'm always the one at the table who listens to the interesting activities of our young FBI friend. Now, thanks to what you just brought me, I have something to add to the conversation for a change."

"You think this new case is interesting? I thought it was only about somebody over at OMI dropping the ball."

Swannie shook his head. "Maybe, maybe not. Either way, how often do I get to tell DJ that the Office of Medical Investigation misplaced a body?"

46

Later Friday Morning Still

Harrie arrived at Southwest Editing Services shortly before 9 AM. She had assumed, based on her earlier phone call from Ginger, that her friend would already be there. Caroline and two of their editors were in the conference room, but Harrie saw no sign of Ginger.

Once in her own office with the door closed, she felt calmer. Running a few errands, in between her morning adventure and her arrival at work, had given her time to ponder the situation. It occurred to her that what happened earlier today might have nothing to do with her.

She almost convinced herself she had overreacted. After all, the black Prius in the driveway next to her former residence could have a perfectly legitimate reason for his presence. It was probably the guy who lived there. He looked vaguely familiar, and she'd never really gotten to know those neighbors, so it was possible.

At first, she'd been absolutely positive the car in the driveway was the same one following her—or at least going on the same zigzagging route she'd chosen. But she had to confess there might be a different, logical explanation. After all, a For Sale sign adorned that yard. The man might have been a realtor or a prospective buyer.

Still . . . .

A knock on the door startled her. "Come in."

Ginger opened it and leaned in. "Are you deep in thought, working hard, or just want to be alone?"

Harrie grinned. "Mostly just goofing off, I'm afraid. How about you?"

Ginger sat in one of the guest chairs. "I had to drop off some papers for Steve this morning. What were you doing earlier?"

"Working on a theory."

"And . . . " Ginger prompted.

Harrie shrugged. "I have no idea. I neither proved nor disproved my theory. I probably have more questions now than I did before I started."

"Uh-oh," Ginger said. "Tell me what you did."

So Harrie described the conversation she and DJ had the night before and her decision to engage in the experiment this morning. During this recitation, Ginger's expression took on a range of emotions. When Harrie finished, she waited for Ginger to actually say something, but her friend sat there, shaking her head.

"All right, say whatever it is you're thinking. I know you have an opinion."

Ginger sat back and crossed her arms. "How long have we known each other?"

"Since seventh grade, but I know you're not that forgetful. Your point?"

Ginger shook her head and looked briefly toward the ceiling. "Well, here's the thing. When you were twelve, you were a shy, mousey sort of kid."

Harrie started to make a wisecrack. But Ginger stopped her.

"Hold it. Hear me out."

Harrie nodded.

"My point is," Ginger said, "the older you get, the more reckless you've become. You never seem to consider the danger you might be courting. You go off on one of your hair-brained adventures and never give it a thought. You leave the people around you in a panic. We never know what you'll do next or what kind of trouble you'll get yourself into."

Harrie sat in silence. Then she said, "Okay, I agree with almost everything you said. I'm an inconsiderate jerk who gets into dangerous situations without much thought. But I'm sensing something else going on here. What's up?"

Ginger's shoulders drooped, and when she looked at Harrie, there were tears in her eyes. Harrie immediately got up and hurried to her friend.

"What's wrong?"

Ginger shook her head and reached for a tissue from the box on the edge of Harrie's desk. She blew her nose loudly, and they both laughed.

"I think I'm just being hormonal. I hate it when I get this way."

"Well, something must have triggered it. You're one of the most emotionally stable people I know—with the possible exception of Caroline."

Ginger took a long breath. "It's Christopher. I just found out last night that he's applied to attend the Air Force Academy."

Harrie shook her head. "Is that what all this angst is about? I thought you were going to tell me something terrible happened—like you broke your grandmother's Victorian tea set."

Ginger frowned. "It's not funny, Shorty. I'm really upset about this."

Harrie returned to her desk. "Well, I can see that. But you knew the boys were checking out a bunch of colleges. Why does this upset you so much?"

"Colleges, yes. Even a university far away, maybe. But a military academy? And why did he not tell me before he applied? Why am I just now finding out?"

"Did Steve know?"

Ginger's eyes narrowed. "Yes, and that's the other thing. Why would he keep something like this from me?"

Harrie grinned. "I'm guessing the man has a highly developed sense of self preservation. He must have known how you'd react. Have you ever talked about this possibility before?"

Ginger opened her mouth to speak. Her expression clearly showed her anger, but it melted almost immediately. She said, "About a year ago. The boys participated in a special testing program designed to help them find their career path. One of the suggestions for Christopher was the military. At the time, I assumed he would stick with his first choice—computer science."

"Did you and Steve discuss it then?"

"Of course. I told both Steve and Christopher how I felt. Don't get me wrong. I really admire people who choose to be career military. We need them, and I'm grateful they are there for us. I just don't want either of my sons to go down that path."

"Why not?"

The look Ginger bestowed on Harrie clearly questioned her sanity. "People in the military die or get maimed."

"Well, maybe you should insist he become a priest and take a vow of isolation for the rest of his natural life. Of course, if he travels in a car, he might be killed. And then there's all that unhealthy food they eat. He could have a heart attack."

Ginger looked down at her hands. "Now you're making fun of

me."

"No," Harrie said, "I'm trying to make you look at what you're doing here. You can't protect those boys from life. They'll be eighteen soon—the threshold of adulthood. You have to let them lead their lives, Mama."

Ginger sighed. "I know that, I really do. It's just that . . . ." She held up her hands.

"Are we still on for an early lunch?" Harrie opened a file folder and put on her reading glasses.

"Of course," Ginger said. "I'm not finished raking you over the coals about your dangerous behavior." Ginger stood and headed for the door.

Harrie said, "It's because I'm short, isn't it?"

Ginger stopped at the door and turned around. "What are you talking about?"

"I'm just now getting it. All the flak I get about taking chances and doing dangerous things. You're trying to mother me just like you do the twins."

Ginger laughed out loud. "Why do you think I constantly tried to get you married to somebody. I didn't want the responsibility of being your mother and the worry that goes with it."

Now it was Harrie's turn to laugh. "Didn't work, did it?"

"Give me time, Short Stuff. Give me time."

47

Friday Lunchtime

Since both Swannie and DJ were hooked on Mexican food, they almost always ended up at one of the many fine restaurants that specialized in their favorite dishes. Today was no exception. They chose Monroe's downtown.

When Swannie walked into the restaurant, he waved at DJ, and headed for the table. DJ noticed the lieutenant had a big grin on his face.

"You seem unusually cheery." DJ liked to see the older man having a good day.

Swannie sat and took a menu from the efficient waitress. "Well," Swannie said, "when a good day comes along, I celebrate."

"Care to share?"

Swannie explained the mix-up at OMI last week. "I'm aware it's petty of me, but the police often get such bad press. It's about time people focused on some other division of the criminal justice system."

DJ nodded. "I can't say I disagree, but did the report explain how it happened?"

Swannie waved a hand in dismissal. "No, but I think it was just a matter of missing ID tags. Some new employee probably got flustered, someone else moved the body, and now there's a problem. They'll iron it all out in the next day or two."

Their waitress reappeared with a big smile and her pen poised to take their orders. "You guys ready?"

Swannie chose the chile rellenos while DJ went for the red chile enchilada platter. When their meals arrived, they dug in. In between bites, their talk swirled around the Petroglyphs murder. While they waited for their hot sopapillas, Swannie broached the subject on his mind.

"Sgt. Paiz caught me by surprise just before I met you today."

"Let me guess. She's curious about our progress."

Swannie nodded. "And I want to share with her."

"And you should. But go easy."

"How easy?"

DJ paused. "For starters, don't mention any names. With the CIA involved in this thing, we can't risk it."

"Oh, I agree. But how do we give her information without giving her information?"

"I have an idea about that. In fact, I talked to my SAC, and he thought it was a good way to handle things."

"And . . ."

DJ grinned. "Well, as I recall, Sgt. Paiz already knows Colin Crider. She met him at the dinner party we had for everyone involved in the Sagebrush Lane Murder two years ago. I'd like to be the one who explains what's going on, and how he's involved."

Swannie frowned. "But you said we can't give her any names."

DJ said, "Crider is the only name she'll get for now. We still can't tell her the identity of the body, and that will be difficult."

Swannie snorted. "That's putting it mildly. She's a seasoned detective. She'll feel insulted that we don't trust her with more information—especially since she caught the case."

"That's why I want to be the one to tell her. The FBI will have to take over on this one. It's too touchy with the CIA involvement. It wouldn't be fair to expect APD to deal with the fallout."

"I suppose you have a point," Swannie said. But he didn't seem happy about it.

"I'll meet with Sgt. Paiz this afternoon. Is that okay with you?"

"Sure, but do you mind if I tag along?"

DJ grabbed one of the hot sopapillas and bit off a corner. He poured honey into the steaming pastry before he responded. "I'm counting on it. But could we finish lunch first?"

"Only if you pass the sopapillas," Swannie said.

He reached for one, and with a look of bliss on his face, bit into it.

48

Friday Lunchtime Número Dos

"At least Rob is predictable. He's interested in athletic scholarships for soccer. He hasn't decided yet where he wants to go."

Harrie grinned. "Good for Rob. I hope you're proud of that boy." She took another sip of her Lemon Soufflé iced tea.

"Of course. Why wouldn't I be? He works hard to receive scholarship offers. He wants to become a coach. He's always been the more athletic twin."

"And yet?"

Ginger ran her index finger around the rim of her iced tea glass. She didn't seem inclined to answer.

"Sweetie." Harrie reached over and touched Ginger's hand. "You should discuss this Air Force thing with Chris. Get things settled. Tell him how you feel. Listen to how he feels."

"I know. Steve says that—over and over. He's like a broken record."

The waiter approached their secluded booth. "You ladies need anything?"

Harrie tapped the top of her iced tea glass. "A refill, if you don't mind."

He departed with the empty glass. Harrie tried again.

"How does Rob feel about Chris's plans?"

Ginger frowned. "That's an odd question."

Harrie sighed. "Not really. Those boys are close. Besides having shared a womb for nine months, they've always been great friends and supportive of each other. They seem to read each other's thoughts."

"What's your point?"

The waiter returned with Harrie's refill. He turned to Ginger. "And how about you, young lady. Would you like more tea?"

Ginger shrugged. "Sure, why not?"

He retreated with her glass.

Harrie sighed. "My point is, once you talk to Rob, you might feel better about Chris's decision."

Ginger opened her mouth to speak, and the waiter placed the freshly filled glass in front of her. "Would you ladies like to see the dessert menu? We have a wonderful selection today. The double chocolate pecan tart is to die for."

Harrie said, "Thanks, we're doing fine. We won't be much longer."

His eye opened wide. "Oh, please. Take your time. No rush. No rush at all." He hurried away.

Ginger shook her head. "You love doing that, don't you?"

Harrie said, "It annoys me. They always choose exactly the wrong moment to be solicitous. It's a mood breaker."

Ginger laughed. "You're right. Where were we before he interrupted?"

Harrie frowned, trying to remember the conversation. "I think I was making a point that Rob might help you understand. Maybe even change your mind."

Ginger lifted the iced tea glass to her lips but stopped short of the target. She put it on the table and stared at Harrie a few seconds.

"That's an interesting idea. Why didn't I think of it?"

"I'm guessing because you're too close to the situation."

Harrie signaled for the check. Ginger insisted on paying, and for once, Harrie let her.

On the drive back to the office Ginger seemed more relaxed. They discussed plans to get together the next day and fly drones.

Ginger said, "Speaking of drones, did you know DJ and Steve talked about them the other day? DJ asked where to look for one."

"Oh, good grief," Harrie said. "He didn't mention that."

Ginger signaled a right turn and pulled into the parking lot at the office. "That's what I figured. Thought you should know."

They were still discussing drones as they walked into Southwest Editing Services. The receptionist and a man were engaged in conversation.

Once they reached Harrie's office, Ginger said, "Do you recognize the guy talking to Azalea?"

Harrie shook her head. "Maybe it's a new customer." They decided to let their newest employee handle the situation. They settled in around Harrie's conference table, and Harrie handed

Ginger a manuscript.

 Almost immediately, Azalea opened Harrie's office door. "Excuse me Mrs. McKinsey, may I speak to you?"

Harrie looked up. "You can call me Harrie, Azalea. We're on a first name basis around here. What's up?"

Azalea closed the door behind her. She fidgeted with her silver necklace. "There's a man outside who wants to pick up a manuscript. He said we were expecting him, and he's in a hurry."

The two friends looked at each other. Ginger shrugged. "So, go get him the manuscript. What's the problem?"

"I went to look for it, but I couldn't find it. I asked Mrs. Johnson—I mean Caroline—and she talked to the man. But then her next appointment came in. She said you were the only ones who could handle this."

Harrie picked up a pen and notebook. "Hold on a minute. What's the man's name?"

Azalea handed Harrie a piece of paper, printed with the name *Ted Gunderson*.

A small shiver coursed down the middle of Harrie's back. She glanced at the note and passed it to Ginger. "I'm not familiar with this name, are you?"

Ginger shook her head. "Nope."

Harrie's nerves danced now, and she turned back to Azalea. "Let's try this. What's the name of the manuscript?"

Azalea frowned. "It's kind of odd. I swear I looked everywhere and—"

"Just tell me the name of the manuscript."

Azalea said, "*The Karaoke Kaper*."

49

Friday Afternoon

Harrie and Ginger exchanged glances. Harrie said, "Tell the gentleman I'll be with him in a minute." Azalea retreated and closed the door.

As soon as they were alone, Ginger said, "What the hell?"

Harrie shook her head. "I know. With everything that's happened, I suppose we should have expected something."

"Do you plan to call DJ?"

"Damn. I didn't even think of that."

Ginger quickly put away the manuscript they'd been editing. "Don't you think you should?"

"What? And make this guy sit out in reception for the next half hour? That's not gonna fly."

Ginger said, "I know, but do you doubt what DJ's reaction will be when he finds out?"

"No, and I refuse to think about it right now. We are here. That guy is waiting. There's nothing else to do but talk to him."

Ginger bit her lip. "You worry me, friend. Even when you see it coming, you walk right into danger."

Harrie adjusted the neckline on her blouse and smoothed her skirt. She forced herself to smile. "That's me. Harrie's my name—danger's my game."

Ginger groaned. "Oh, please. You're enjoying this, and I'm about to faint."

Harrie reached for the doorknob. "Pull yourself together, Stretch. I need you."

Harrie left her office door open and approached the visitor. He wasn't much taller than her own five feet, five inches. He paced back and forth in front of the receptionist's desk, resembling a caged tiger more than an irate customer. When he turned to face her, she saw a weak chin, bushy, unkempt eyebrows, and a thatch of greasy brown hair.

Harrie extended her hand to greet him. "Mr. Gunderson, I'm

Harrie McKinsey."

The man glared at her, and didn't return the handshake.

Harrie shrugged. "Let's talk in here."

She gestured toward her office and stepped in front of the man to lead the way. She noticed Ginger had arranged the chairs around the circular conference table so the guest's back would be toward the door. Ginger sat across the table, and Harrie grinned at her.

"Mr. Gunderson, meet my business partner, Ginger Vaughn. Please have a seat." Harrie pulled out the chair Ginger had prepared for the man, and Mr. Gunderson settled himself. She took her seat next to Ginger.

"I understand you're a client of ours? I'm embarrassed to say I don't recall having met you."

Gunderson cleared his throat and leaned forward. "I'm not actually your client. You have a manuscript in your possession. I'm here to pick it up."

Harrie lifted one eyebrow. "Oh?"

The man shifted in his chair and lowered his gaze to the tabletop. "Yes. My late brother engaged your company to edit his manuscript."

Harrie shot a quick look at Ginger, who squinted at the man.

Harrie said, "I'm sorry to hear your brother is no longer with us. What's his name?"

"Richard Tracy."

Harrie felt the tiny hairs on her arms stiffen.

"Okay." She and Mr. Gunderson locked eyes. He dropped his gaze first.

Ginger said, "Do you have legal authority to speak for your brother?"

Gunderson seemed surprised at the question. "Legal authority? What do you mean? He was my brother. I'm his only living relative."

Ginger gave him her "don't mess with me" look. "Do you have paperwork giving you power of attorney, or a will naming you executor of your brother's estate?"

Gunderson's eyes opened wide. "I . . . Well, I never . . ."

He pushed back his chair and stood. Both Harrie and Ginger watched him without speaking.

Gunderson pulled himself up as far as his height allowed. His jaw clenched, and Harrie could see the anger welling in him. "My attorney will be in touch with you. This is outrageous. I've never been treated so disrespectfully."

Harrie and Ginger both stood. Harrie said, "I'm sorry to hear that, Sir. But it's not our policy to speak with people representing themselves as a relative of one of our editing clients. I'm sure you understand we're obligated to protect your brother's privacy. Without the proper documents, we can't allow you access to this manuscript."

Gunderson's hands shook, and Harrie feared he might hyperventilate. He walked to the door, turned, and gave his parting shot.

"Don't expect me to recommend this company to any of my friends." And with that, he stormed out.

Harrie and Ginger stood rooted to the spot. They looked at each other, and when they heard the front door close, they burst into laughter.

"Gee what a shame—we won't get to meet any of his friends," Harrie said.

Ginger shook her head. "Yes, and we dodged a bullet. Now what?"

"What else?" Harrie said, "I call DJ and relate this latest development. It will become his problem—not ours."

Ginger rubbed the back of her neck. "From your lips, to God's ears."

50

Later Friday Afternoon

Sgt. Cabrini Paiz looked from one man to the other. She shook her head and sighed. "So you're saying I'm not allowed to discuss this."

They had gathered in Lt. Swanson's office, seated at his conference table. Swannie studied his hands and remained silent.

DJ looked her straight in the eye. "You and Lt. Swanson are the only ones who know anything about the real situation. There's so much information missing. The three of us may never hear the full story."

Cabrini frowned. "I didn't think the CIA had authority to conduct operations within the United States. I thought laws restricted them to undercover stuff in foreign countries."

DJ gestured palms up. "Let's say this is an unusual departure."

"So why am I here?" Cabrini didn't want to sound confrontational. But the situation frustrated her.

"Because," Swannie said. "DJ and I believe you have a right to know at least this much."

DJ said, "We'll need your help. If nothing else we may need you to keep the task force out of our hair. Plus, I'm worried about Harrie. There might be someone following her."

She frowned. "Why would anybody be following her?" She stopped. "I take that back. Dumb question. Harrie has a knack for drawing attention from bad people."

Swannie grinned. "As my southern-born Mamma used to say, 'Bless her little heart. She can't help it.'"

DJ nodded. "It's true. The day I met her, I realized she attracts trouble like ants to a picnic."

"Which brings up another question I expect you won't answer." Cabrini leaned in closer to the two men. "Why would Crider conclude Harrie had anything to do with his operation?"

"Maybe he made a wild guess," DJ said. "Or it could be because someone is following Ellis."

Cabrini wondered if she had understood him. "Who's following Nick Ellis?"

DJ said, "For a while I suspected you were."

Cabrini found herself momentarily speechless. "That never crossed my mind. What would be the point?"

Swannie said, "Have you forgotten about your observant police aide? Harrie told us he reported back to you about the luncheon meeting she and Ginger had with Nick Ellis on Monday."

"Oh, that." Cabrini massaged her forehead. She felt a headache coming on and wanted to get back to her desk.

"Have you spoken to Ellis this week?" Swannie asked.

Cabrini shook her head. "We took his statement and questioned him for more than an hour that night. I saw no point in another interview. And now . . ." She broke off and looked at them.

DJ said, "According to Harrie, Ellis was nervous when they met him for lunch. He told them someone had followed him on Sunday and again on Monday to the sandwich shop."

"And you're saying perhaps one of Crider's associates took the assignment?" Cabrini reached in her pocket for two ibuprofen. She popped them in her mouth and took a swig from her water bottle.

"It's the only thing that makes sense," DJ said. "*We're* not following him, and if APD isn't, that leaves Crider as the obvious culprit."

Cabrini massaged her temples. "Well, Ellis did discover the body. Maybe the murderer thinks he saw more. Or, perhaps our park ranger has enemies we don't know about. Did that occur to you?"

DJ and Swannie looked at each other. Swannie said, "I suppose it's possible. Hell, anything is possible. Maybe we need another talk with him."

Despite her headache, Cabrini grinned. "Is that the 'royal' we Lieutenant? Are you suggesting I talk to the young man again?"

A big grin Swannie's face. "Why, Sergeant Paiz, what a great idea."

51

Still Friday Afternoon

"I told you to call him before we talked to Gunderson. Didn't I say that?" Ginger crossed her arms and leaned back in the chair.

Harrie sat forward, elbows on the desk, and chin propped in her hands. "Yes, you certainly did. I admit my decisions are not always right."

"Gee, I didn't expect that. Are you okay?"

"You mean other than being a complete airhead?"

"Hey, if you're one, I'm one too. It never crossed my mind to get his information."

"True, but you did suggest I call DJ before we talked to him."

Ginger grinned at her friend. "So now what?"

Harrie said, "Now I face the music. After dinner tonight we'll talk. Or to be more accurate, DJ will talk, and I'll listen. Then I'll take the drubbing I'm due for not getting the man's contact information before I told him to take a hike."

"It can't be as easy as that."

"You think that's easy? When's the last time you had to admit a huge mistake to Steve?"

Ginger grinned. "It will be right after I talk with Chris about the Air Force Academy."

"Really?" Harrie couldn't believe her ears. "When did you decide that?"

"When we were at lunch. Then just now, I watched you take responsibility for not getting creepy Mr. Gunderson's contact information, and I realized something."

Harrie tilted her head to one side. "And what was that?"

Ginger turned both hands up. "What do I have to lose? Chris is set on attending the Air Force Academy, and Steve's all for it. Plus, I really should talk to Rob and get his take on it. I can't expect the entire family to change their opinions just because I'm not happy."

Harrie nodded. "True. I just didn't think you'd come around so soon. I'm impressed."

"You should be. I can't believe I'm using you as a role model, but then I'm willing to admit when you're right."

"So tell me," Harrie said, "how do you intend to handle it? Do you let him bring up the subject or will you?"

"Considering my attitude last night, I doubt he's willing to approach it again. Tomorrow night I'll prepare their favorite meal—that always makes conversation easier. Then I'll ask Rob what he thinks of Chris's plans. After he agrees with Chris, as I predict he will, I'll tell them I've changed my mind."

"Well thought out. Would you like to advise me now?"

Ginger frowned. "I thought you already had a plan."

Harrie realized she didn't have a sassy comeback to the question. She looked down at her hands resting on the desktop. The normal hum of the office and its inhabitants filled her ears. Odd. She hadn't heard it until seconds ago. If she focused her attention, she could make out individual voices. She heard Caroline's gentle laugh, Becky's giggle, the sound of the copy machine churning out paper. All these normal, everyday things going on around her. Yet she hadn't heard anything but her own voice and Ginger's until she focused on the world outside herself.

It dawned on her she'd drifted away from being a planner. She saw herself now as a reactor to events. No wonder she so often found herself in trouble. No wonder her family and friends worried about her.

The sound of Ginger's voice brought her attention back. "I'm sorry. Did you say something?"

Ginger frowned and leaned forward. "Are you feeling okay? You were a million miles away."

Harrie shook her head. "I think I checked out for a few minutes. What were you saying?"

"Never mind. Tell me what's going on in that head of yours."

Harrie knew her smile must be weak. "I had an epiphany. I realized I don't plan. I get a wild hair and run with it. Probably why things get dicey for me."

"Who are you, and when did you switch bodies with Harrie?"

Before Harrie could respond, Azalea burst in to the room. "Excuse me Mrs. McKinsey. Mrs. Johnson just concluded her meeting. She said it was urgent you have this information." Azalea shoved a folded piece of paper into Harrie's hand and rushed out the door.

Ginger said, "What is wrong with that girl? Did we made a mistake hiring her?"

"Caroline's the office manager. I suggest we let her handle it."

Ginger pointed to the note. "Whatever that is, I hope it's important."

Harrie unfolded the piece of paper. It revealed a buff-colored card clipped to a note. She felt a big grin spreading across her face. "Well I'll be damned."

Ginger said, "What's wrong now?"

Harrie shook her head. "It's a note from Caroline. I sometimes forget she's always on top of things."

Ginger perked up. "What does it say?"

Harrie unclipped the card and read the note. "Girls. This fellow is a strange one. Don't know what to think. He handed me this card when I asked for his contact information. It's sparse but better than nothing."

Ginger said, "You dodged a bullet—again."

Harrie glanced at the buff-colored card. Giddy relief spread throughout her body. Her mother-in-law and office manager—famous for her attention to detail—had given Harrie what she needed.

52

Early Friday Evening

Cabrini Paiz looked through her notes one more time. In her opinion, Lt. Swanson's suggestion for another interview with Nick Ellis seemed overkill. But he was the boss, and it was not her job to question his orders.

She dialed the cell phone number Ellis had given her the night she interviewed him. He answered within three rings.

"Hello?" The cheery voice sounded like Ellis.

"Mr. Ellis, this is Detective Sergeant Cabrini Paiz. Do you have a moment?"

There was a short pause before Ellis said, "Why? What's going on?"

Cabrini sensed hesitation on his part. "I need to clear up a couple of things, and I hoped we could meet somewhere convenient for you. Is that possible?"

Over the phone connection, Cabrini heard a releasing of breath. Was is fear? Or annoyance?

Ellis's voice sounded tired. "I'll clock out in the next twenty minutes. Then I plan to get a bite to eat before I go out with some friends tonight. Could you meet me at the Flying Star on Rio Grande Boulevard about 6:00 PM?"

"The one next to Bookworks, right?" Cabrini took a quick peek at her watch.

"That's the one." Nick Ellis seemed a bit more relaxed now.

Cabrini's mind zipped through her plans for the evening. Little Jay would be having dinner at his best friend's house, and Jason was on duty tonight at Station 16. Perfect.

"Sure," she said. "It won't take long."

This time, his voice sounded almost cheerful. "Good. I'll grab a table and watch for you."

The call disconnected, and Cabrini pondered their conversation. The kid had seemed frightened. He certainly came across as cautious. Maybe there *was* something to the idea he was being followed.

Or . . . perhaps he had something to hide?

53

Friday Evening

The proprietors at Flying Star Café didn't seem to mind when a person came in, ordered coffee or tea, and sat at a table with their laptop for several hours. People still came and went all day and evening. The food was good, and all locations had a particular energy, drawing in the young and studious.

Bookworks, the large bookstore next door to the Flying Star on Rio Grande Boulevard NW, also drew a good crowd. Patrons of the popular store often stopped in at the restaurant to read their latest purchase or get something to eat or drink while awaiting a talk by an interesting author.

Over the years, Cabrini had spent many hours at this location. She appreciated its generous attitude toward people's leisurely occupation of space. When she opened the door, it felt familiar and welcoming.

She spotted her subject as soon as she entered. Nick Ellis had selected a small table up against the brick western wall. Cabrini approved its relatively secluded location.

"Thanks for meeting me here," Nick said. He pulled out a chair for Cabrini, and she mentally gave him points for good manners.

"That goes both ways," she said. "After all, I'm the one who requested this meeting."

Nick absently dunked his tea bag and looked around the room. Cabrini thought he seemed a bit haggard since the last time she'd seen him. But when he fixed his attention on her, it seemed he'd lost some of the tenseness she noticed earlier.

"I'll get right to the point, Mr. Ellis—"

"Please," he said, "call me Nick. I'm too young to be called 'mister.'"

Cabrini grinned. "Okay, Nick. I remember feeling the same way at your age."

Nick leaned back in the chair and sipped his tea. "So, tell me what I left out."

"It's not that," Cabrini said. "I'm concerned about something that came up since we talked last." She watched him before she spoke again. "I've been told you believe you're being followed."

Nick's eyes widened. He leaned forward and put the tea cup back on the table. "Who told you that?"

Cabrini shook her head. "Trust me when I tell you that's not important. My concern is that if you *are* being followed, it could be significant to our case."

"How do you figure?"

Cabrini exhaled a deep breath. "Look at it this way. You discovered a body at your workplace a bit over a week ago. You notified the authorities. We've interviewed you. We asked you not to discuss the case or mention it to anyone."

At this point, Nick Ellis dropped his chin in a "hangdog" look. "How did you find out about that?"

"Nick, even though Albuquerque has a decent sized population, it's still a small town in many ways. Let's just say I know a variety of people, and fate brought you into contact with one of them."

Nick's shoulders slumped. "And that 'someone' ratted me out."

"I wouldn't put it that way. You have to realize some people devour information like other people scarf donuts. They're information junkies. One little piece, dropped casually, can put them on a search for more details. That's sort of what happened in this case."

"Is that the person following me?" Nick seemed alarmed again.

"No. I can guarantee you of that. At this point we can't tell if anyone's actually following you. That's why we need your help."

Nick frowned. "I hadn't thought of it in those terms. What can I do?"

Cabrini took out a notebook and pen. "Write down your statement and a description of this individual. Give me as much detail as you can."

Nick reached for the notebook. He opened his mouth, as though about to say something. But nothing came out, and Cabrini saw his eyes grow larger. His face lost all its color.

"Nick?"

The young man bowed his head as if in prayer, keeping his eyes fixed on the table top. He whispered. "Don't look around."

It took all of Cabrini's willpower not to turn and look. "What's going on?"

Nick leaned in closer across the small table. "It's him. It's the guy who's been following me."

Cabrini said, "Is he looking at you right now?"

Nick raised his head just enough to see. "No. He has his back to us. It looks like he's placing his order at the counter."

"What's he wearing?"

"A dark brown suit."

"Okay," Cabrini said. "I want you to slip out the patio door."

Nick started to move, but she grabbed his arm.

"No, wait. I have a better idea. Leave by the front door. From that angle he'll be less likely to spot you. Once you're safely gone, I'll speak to him."

"Then what happens?" Nick said.

"Look for me tomorrow at the drone field. I'm taking my son to watch them fly." She stole a look over her shoulder. "But for now, just get the hell out of here."

Nick surveyed the path he needed to take, but he didn't move.

Cabrini pushed on his arm. "Go."

He looked at her one more time. She sensed he wanted to leave. His eyes were saying go, but his body thought it should stay.

His eyes won the battle.

As soon he left the building, she rose and turned toward the order counter.

The man in the brown suit was having a quiet conversation with the cashier. He seemed completely oblivious to anyone else in the room. Cabrini inhaled a deep breath, walked over to the counter, and stood a couple of feet behind him. She touched the badge on her belt with her left hand, making sure it could be seen.

Then she rested her right hand lightly on the butt of her pistol.

54

Dinner Friday Evening

When Harrie called DJ late in the afternoon, he made a good suggestion. She readily agreed. The "gang of six" would have dinner tonight at Harrie and DJ's house.

A few hours later, she picked up two large takeout boxes of food from Rising Star Chinese Eatery. Thanks to restaurant owners Ike and Judy, her dinner guests would eat well again tonight.

The wonderful smells emanating from the takeout boxes awakened Harrie's appetite. For the moment, her attention centered on the food, rather than creepy dreams and dead bodies. Her buzzing cell phone interrupted her thoughts. She pressed the answer button on the car's steering wheel.

"What can I do for you, my sweet friend?" She waited for Ginger's response.

"May I bring the wine? I have two bottles of a killer Pistachio Rosé from Heart of the Desert Winery in Alamogordo."

"When were you in Alamogordo?"

"Don't you remember? We took Chris and Rob to see White Sands week before last. I told you all about it."

"Ah. Yes you did. Sorry, I forgot. My latest dream is messing with me."

"So should I bring the wine?"

"Of course. It sounds delightful. Can't wait to try it."

"Okay, then. See you in fifteen minutes." Ginger clicked off, and Harrie let her mind drift back to the evening's plans.

Though the details Caroline squeezed out of Ted Gunderson were pitiful in their brevity, Harrie had immediately called DJ and passed it along. She hoped he had good things to tell them tonight.

She arrived home in time to meet Caroline and Swannie. They went inside together. Caroline and Harrie took the food to the kitchen. Ginger and Steve walked in as the dishes were set on the dining room table. DJ came through the door from the garage shortly thereafter.

When all were seated, Harrie said. "We're in for a treat. Ginger and Steve brought us a special wine."

Steve uncorked a bottle and filled their glasses. He lifted his glass and said, "Here's to all of us. And here's hoping we get the answers needed to uncover the facts."

Everyone returned the toast with, "To us."

When they finished eating, Harrie brought out the coffee pot and cups.

DJ said, "Let's talk drones."

A groan came from the three women.

Harrie said, "Steve, you're responsible for this."

Steve grinned. "Yes, I am. And I'm glad. It's essential DJ become involved. With the boys preparing for college, I'll need a drone buddy."

They discussed plans for another Saturday morning get-together at George Maloof Air Park.

Steve said, "I talked to Mark Goodrum this morning on the SCAT Net and he's bringing a couple of friends with him."

Even Swannie got involved in the drone discussion. He asked Caroline if she'd like to tag along the next morning.

"I will if you promise to take me to the Petroglyphs afterwards."

Harrie said, "Ginger and I will be there too, Caroline. We can be the cheering section."

Ginger clapped her hands. "Thanks for the support, Ladies. There's so much testosterone in my family. I'm glad I'll have help tamping it down."

They finished their coffee, and Steve brought out his drone. Harrie, Ginger, and Caroline opted to clean up the dinner debris.

When they returned from the kitchen, they discovered the drone had been put away. Harrie took advantage of the opportunity.

"Did you find any information about our strange new visitor this afternoon?"

Swannie frowned. "What visitor?"

Caroline smiled and patted Swannie's hand. "You know. That guy I mentioned earlier when we talked. Remember? He wanted us to hand over the manuscript."

Swannie sighed. "Sorry. I forgot. Yes, let's hear about him."

DJ shrugged. "There's not much to tell yet. Turns out, Ted Gunderson is a desk clerk at the Hyatt."

"Whoa!" Harrie said. "Why would a desk clerk come to

Southwest Editing looking for Richard Tracy's manuscript?"

"You asked me for information about your visitor. He's a desk clerk. He wasn't working today. That's probably why he visited your office. It was his day off."

Harrie frowned. "But you must have more than that. You're the FBI."

"I also called the phone number he gave you and left a message. He hasn't returned my call."

"Did you email him? Your mom got his email address."

"No. But I requested a search on his email address. We should get his home address with that."

Steve said, "Wait a minute. You said you only had his email address and his phone number?"

"That's right," DJ said.

"Then how did you find out he worked at the Hyatt as a desk clerk?"

"Ah, Grasshopper," DJ said with a phony accent. "The ways and means of the FBI are mysterious and many."

Caroline laughed. "My son is quite the kidder. Mr. Gunderson handed me the card on which he had written his name, phone number, and email. After he left, I turned the card over. It was from the Hyatt downtown."

Ginger said, "But how did you know he was a desk clerk?"

This time it was DJ who laughed. "I called and asked the manager if he knew Ted Gunderson. He said your buddy Ted was employed as a desk clerk."

Swannie sighed. "You live a charmed life, my boy."

DJ put his arm around Harrie. "You bet I do, Swannie."

Harrie frowned. "Not so fast, chum. I expected something juicy to be revealed about Gunderson. He acted deranged when we refused to hand over the manuscript."

DJ tilted her chin up and kissed the tip of her nose. "You must have learned by now nothing comes as fast as you'd like. We have to be patient about these things."

"And I would have thought you understood that patience was not one of my many virtues."

DJ grinned. "Luckily, my sweet, I have enough patience for us both."

55

Saturday Morning

When he awoke early Saturday morning, Lt. Swanson assumed his day would be relaxing and fun. In fact, that only applied to the first half hour.

Before he walked out the door to meet Caroline, he received an urgent text message from Sergeant Paiz, asking him to meet her for coffee. Since this was a pretty unusual request, he agreed. Next, he phoned Caroline and asked to meet her at the Air Park. Fortunately, Caroline was a self-sufficient woman—one of the many things he admired about her.

She'd been a single mother after her young husband was killed in Vietnam. She was alone, seventeen, and expecting DJ. In the ensuing years she accomplished a great deal. She'd worked for a huge prestigious law firm, while raising her son and putting him through UNM. Fortunately the young man earned a scholarship to Georgetown University to receive his law degree. But Caroline was always there for him, helping with expenses whenever needed.

Swannie pulled into the parking lot of The Village Inn on Wyoming. He recognized Cabrini's car and pulled into the spot beside it.

She had established herself at the end booth on the southwest wall of the restaurant and nodded at him when he walked in the door.

His favorite server spied him and waved. Swannie grinned and waved back.

Edee was a friendly young woman and always remembered what her repeat customers liked to order. As Swannie took his seat across from Cabrini, Edee set an empty coffee cup on the table in front of him. She picked up the large coffee carafe and poured him a cup.

"Your usual scrambled eggs, Lieutenant?" She set the carafe back on the table and waited for his response.

"Not today, Edee. I won't be here that long. Got a hot date."

The slender, attractive young woman grinned and punched him

on the shoulder. "Good for you, Lieutenant. That lady is lucky to have you." Then she hurried over to her next group of hungry customers.

Swannie blushed furiously, and Cabrini almost giggled. She'd never seen her boss so embarrassed.

"You must come here often, Lieutenant. I didn't realize you knew Edee."

Swannie shook his head. "Anybody who comes in here with any regularity at all knows our Edee. She's amazing. Has a memory like nothing I've ever seen."

Cabrini took another sip of her coffee and got down to business.

"Thanks for meeting me. I'm sorry to make you late."

Swannie sipped his own coffee. "No worries. I told Caroline I'd meet her at the air park a little later."

He set his cup on the table. "So what's going on? Your text sounded pretty urgent."

Cabrini quickly outlined her interview with Nick Ellis the previous evening. Then she got to the point—the individual following Ellis.

Swannie said, "Why didn't you call me then?"

Cabrini slowly shook her head. "For one thing, there wasn't time. I got Nick out of there as soon as I could and focused on the man in the brown suit. I was all ready to arrest him for stalking."

Swannie now frowned. "Are you saying you didn't?"

Cabrini grinned. "I think you'll agree it could have been a tad awkward."

"Uh oh. What happened?"

"Well," Cabrini said, the grin on her face a bit wider now, "when I tapped him on the shoulder, he reacted with a strange sort of calm. I guess I expected him to jump or act surprised. He didn't."

Swannie looked at his watch. "Sergeant, I can tell this is fun for you, and I don't want to ruin what little joy you find in your day-to-day work, but could you get to the point a little faster?"

Cabrini sighed. "Shoot. There you go. Spoiling my whole reveal."

The glare she received lit a fire under her.

"Okay, sorry. The guy isn't a stalker. He's employed by the government."

Swannie frowned. "In what capacity?"

Cabrini shrugged. "I'm guessing maybe CIA but he wouldn't get into specifics. And his ID only indicated 'US Government Security' when I asked to see it."

Swannie's face brightened. "This is wonderful."

Cabrini frowned. "I thought you'd be upset. Why so happy? "

"Because," Swannie said. "This means it'll be the Feds problem, not mine."

Cabrini nodded and grinned. "Ah. I see what you mean. So you don't mind DJ taking over the case?"

"Mind? Are you nuts? I'm thrilled out of my freakin' gourd!"

56

Saturday Morning

Last night, the dream had returned.

Harrie sipped her steaming coffee. She hoped its warmth would loosen the cold knot in her chest. Her neck muscles ached, and her shoulders felt stiff. But the soreness wasn't her worst problem. Each time she had the dream, it left her more and more apprehensive. She hoped the coffee could melt those feelings away.

Yesterday DJ had expressed his eagerness to get to the Airpark early. Today would be the first opportunity for Steve and the twins to launch their new drone on the big field. His excitement would normally generate a similar feeling in Harrie. Not today.

"Did you hear what I said?"

Harrie looked at him blankly. He grinned at her.

"Hey, wake up. What were you thinking just then?"

She shook her head. "Sorry. I'm still half asleep. Who in their right mind goes out at the crack of dawn on Saturday morning?"

DJ shrugged. "Well—drone enthusiasts for one. And don't forget hot-air balloon pilots."

"Crazy people. I'm surrounded by crazy people."

"You're just now figuring that out?"

"Tell me something, my wide-awake husband. Have you always been an early riser?"

DJ grinned. "Of course. It was just me and my Mom when I was a little kid. She had to be at work pretty early at the law firm. I got dropped off at the babysitter. I had to be up and ready."

"So you're actually one of those morning people?"

"Probably. I feel exhilarated first thing in the morning. That's why I prefer running before breakfast. It's my way of starting off my day with energy."

Harrie frowned. "That's a deeply disturbing attitude. I'd rather ease into my day. It's always been my opinion that running is for cheetahs and pronghorn antelope."

DJ grinned. "Those two animals can outrun a lion any day."

Harrie drank the last of her coffee. "I make it a point to stay away from lions for that very reason."

DJ set his cup in the sink and turned to her. "Something else is going on with you."

She sighed. "It's no big deal."

He took the coffee mug from her hands. "Big enough to make you lose sleep."

She said, "I had the dream again last night. It's nagging at me. There's something I should remember."

He leaned in and kissed her forehead. "I'll wash the cups. You go finish getting ready. Maybe we can get your mind off all that—at least for this morning."

Harrie walked back to the bedroom and her thoughts turned again to the dreams. She picked up her brush and ran it through her hair.

In the moments before the alarm brought her out of the dream, she'd seen something. Why couldn't she remember what it was?

She pulled her hair into a ponytail and secured it with a scrunchie.

It's right here. So close I can almost see it. She stared at her face in the mirror, hoping for answers.

Unfortunately, the reflection staring back at her was as clueless as Harrie.

57

Saturday At The Air Field

Nick Ellis pulled into the parking lot at the George Maloof Airfield. He chided himself for skipping breakfast and opened his Thermos. He took a long swig of hot coffee, and surveyed the parking lot.

It was still early—barely 7:00 AM. Still, he saw one compact car and two trucks parked on the opposite side of the lot. He didn't see any people, but assumed they were close by.

He hadn't slept well last night. After the incident at Flying Star, his apprehension about the stalker filled his brain. Nick tried to convince himself it was a coincidence. But this was now the third—no, the fourth time he'd found himself in the same place as this strange man. And Sgt. Paiz seemed to believe it was real.

There had to be some reason, and the only thing he could think of—the thing that had occupied most of his thoughts since he discovered the body—was it had something to do with that body.

But why? All Nick did was find a corpse at his workplace. It had nothing to do with him. Yet since that night, he felt something was amiss. Somebody, for whatever reason, was watching him.

He checked the time. 7:05 AM.

His stomach growled, reminding him of his missed breakfast. It occurred to him there might still be a couple of granola bars in his glove box. He rummaged around among the maps, fast food receipts, and a pair of cracked sunglasses he thought he'd thrown out months ago. He frowned. His mother would have a hissy fit if she could see this mess.

One beat-up granola bar peeked from beneath an old lottery ticket. He hoped it wasn't as old as the rest of this junk. One bite shattered that idea. But hey. Beggars can't be choosers, right?

How many times had he heard his mom say that? He chuckled and took another swig of coffee to wash down the petrified snack bar.

He almost choked at the sound of a sudden knock on his car

window. His heart beat so fast he couldn't breathe. The ancient granola bar landed in his lap, as did the last of his coffee.

His neck made a loud "cracking" sound as he turned too sharply to see who had crept up on him.

His drone buddy, Mark Goodrum, stood on the other side of the glass, a big grin on his face. Mark made a cranking motion with his hand. Nick sighed and lowered the window.

Mark said, "What are you waiting for, man? We have drones to fly this morning."

Nick shook his head and grabbed an old napkin. "Can you wait while I change my pants?"

58

Later Saturday Morning

Steve Vaughn and his twin sons, Rob and Chris, had taken several turns launching the drone. The love affair between men and their model airplanes had been updated. Drones were clearly replacing model airplanes for a large group of people these days.

Seeing the crowd of fans standing around watching them, Harrie couldn't stifle a giggle.

"What are you laughing at, Red?" Steve gave her an indulgent grin. "You think you could do better?"

Harrie held up her hands in a surrendering gesture. "Not even close, my friend. I'd be so afraid of crashing that beauty of yours. I'm just enjoying the spectacle of a bunch of grown men having a great time with all these amazing flying machines."

The group initially consisted of Steve, Ginger, Rob and Chris, Harrie, DJ, Caroline, and Swannie. But after Steve sent the drone up for its first flight, Cabrini Paiz, husband Jason, and young son Jay had joined them.

When Harrie spotted Cabrini talking to Nick Ellis, she was tempted to question her about the case. But she realized this wasn't the time or place to do so.

Harrie, Ginger, and Caroline drifted over to a nearby picnic bench. It was a typically beautiful, sunny day in early May. A light breeze tempered the heat of the sun.

Ginger broke the silence. "It's a shame there aren't any trees here."

Harrie removed her sunglasses and looked at Ginger. "Uh, hello. I think the lack of trees is deliberate. They would hamper flight. This is a facility for flying model planes, which obviously needs open space."

Ginger nodded. "I know that. But I don't plan on coming out to this wind-blown prairie every time Steve or the boys decide to fly their new toy."

Caroline grinned. "I understand how you feel. But don't rush to judgement. They might all run out of enthusiasm after the newness wears off."

Harrie turned to her mother-in-law. "Okay. What do you know that we don't?"

"Just this," Caroline said. "When DJ was growing up, he had a very short attention span for activities that required him to show up early in the morning"

Harrie said, "You have to be kidding me. Your son gets up almost every morning at 5:30 AM and goes for a run. He told me this morning that as a kid he was always a morning person."

Caroline laughed. "Yeah, well, he wasn't. He complained bitterly about getting up so early when I started working at the law firm. I had to drag him out of bed for weeks before he adjusted. Eventually he got used to it, and after that he seemed to enjoy the peacefulness of early morning."

"So," Harrie said. "He played me with his story of loving to run early in the morning."

"No," Caroline said. "He simply misremembers reality. The early morning running started when he went to the FBI Academy in Quantico. It was drilled into him, and it took very well. He realizes he needs to keep in shape as long as he's an agent. Running seemed to grow on him. It helped him concentrate, and it was the best way he found to stay in shape."

Ginger said, "I don't get it. If he's now hooked on early morning runs, why wouldn't he be just as willing to rise early on the weekend to go out droning?"

Harrie grinned. "I think I can answer that question." She turned to Caroline. "It's because the running is connected with the FBI. He'll do whatever he needs to do to be the best agent he can be."

Caroline nodded. "Very astute, Harrie."

"But he has expressed an interest in the drones," Harrie said. "Didn't you see him this morning? He could hardly restrain himself. I could tell he really wanted to fly Steve's drone."

"That's because he loves to try new things. But I predict this won't last much longer than a month—if that long." Caroline leaned back against the picnic table and stretched her legs out in front of her.

Harrie tilted her head. "Why do you say that?"

"In the time you've been married, how often has he spent a Saturday away from the office?"

"Well—" Harrie paused and tried to remember. "I guess I'd have to say not often. Maybe twice a month? He's usually home before noon."

Caroline smiled. "Exactly. If he doesn't go in, he probably calls to see what's going on. Am I right?"

"That's true. Come to think of it, I'm a bit surprised he managed to be here today."

"Don't look now but that may have changed," Ginger said, as she looked back at their group of droners. "Your husband just walked away from the rest of the group. He's heading our way."

Harrie swiveled around. She shaded her eyes with her hand. "Swell. And he doesn't look happy."

When DJ reached them, Harrie saw his clenched jaw. This did not bode well.

"Ladies, could you please take Harrie home with you. I have two situations which need my attention." He leaned in and kissed her.

She held on to his arm. "What's happened? You don't look like your normal, calm self."

He shook his head. "Even if I knew the whole story I couldn't tell you. I'll check in with you in a couple of hours. I should know something by then."

Harrie started to say more, but caught the look on Caroline's face. "Okay," she said to her husband. "I'll talk to you when you have a chance."

She watched him as he walked to his car. The weary smile he'd given her as he turned to leave clutched at her heart. He was clearly upset, and it made Harrie feel so helpless. Much as she struggled, she'd never found a way to make things easier for DJ when it came to the burdens he carried with his job.

"I guess we should rejoin the group," Ginger said. "And I suppose I should try to show *some* enthusiasm for the new hobby."

They walked toward the drones and their pilots. Harrie noticed both Swannie and Cabrini heading for Swannie's car.

"Caroline, do you see what I see?" Harrie caught up with Caroline.

"I just noticed. It appears something big is happening."

Harrie frowned. "What do you suppose it is?"

Caroline sighed. "I couldn't even guess. Swannie already had something going on this morning he couldn't discuss. That's why I drove myself and met him here."

Ginger grinned. "Great. Then you can take both Harrie and me home."

Harrie sighed. "I knew I should have brought my own car."

59

Saturday Morning

DJ Scott adjusted his rearview mirror. He saw Swannie and Cabrini turn left, headed for their crime scene.

As soon as Swannie arrived at the airfield this morning, he told DJ he had something important to tell him.

Unfortunately two messages, arriving simultaneously on DJ's phone, cut short any time to talk. The first message was an urgent summons from Colin Crider. DJ was on his way now to meet the CIA operative.

The man's cryptic message left DJ on edge.

"Things going to hell. Need your help. Meet me at the Petroglyphs."

Since it was close to the airfield, DJ made the decision to head there first. Now he felt uneasy. All the intrigue and B-movie tactics had worn thin.

He pulled into the parking lot and slid into a spot close to the Visitor Center. DJ looked around the area, thinking the Petroglyphs covered a massive amount of ground, and he'd be challenged to pick the spot Crider intended for their meeting. Immediately following that thought, he spied Crider heading toward the amphitheater.

By the time DJ reached him, Crider had seated himself on the top row. It provided a full view of the rest of the seating and the stage at the bottom. DJ took a deep breath, girding himself for whatever crazy issue had captured Crider's attention. He sat on the stone slab next to Mr. Pain-in-the-Butt CIA.

As usual, Crider looked straight ahead, seemingly without interest in the tall FBI agent seated beside him. DJ silently counted to ten before Crider spoke.

"My operative's in trouble."

DJ blew out a breath. "And . . . this is important to me . . . why?"

Crider shook his head and looked at the ground between his feet. "Feeling put upon today, are we Scott?"

DJ leaned back slightly. "Can you get to the point quickly? I have a crime scene to visit."

Crider nodded and also leaned back. "I thought my operative was safe when you told me about the note he sent your wife. I felt confident things were on track, and that I'd hear from him soon."

"I take it you didn't."

"No. But worse than that, I discovered someone else has inserted himself into my situation."

"Do I have to guess who this someone is or can you shorten the process and just spit it out?"

"Tsk, tsk," Crider said. "And here I was planning to help you out. Why so snarky, Scott?"

DJ felt himself relax. Crider's style was to always keep his "prey" off guard. DJ had let his own irritation and anxiety set the tone here. Time to reverse course.

"It just occurred to me, Crider. You're always needing my help. Should I put in a bill for consulting services to your bosses at CIA?"

Crider stiffened slightly, turned his head, and focused his icy blue eyes on DJ. But he didn't try to hide the amusement in them. "Well played," he said.

"Thanks. Can we please get to the point? Crime never sleeps, and I have someplace to be."

Crider actually chuckled. "Okay, fair enough. Tell me what you know about Ted Gunderson."

"What's he to you?"

"Well, at the very least, he's the trouble stalking my operative. And I understand he paid your wife a visit yesterday."

"That's true. So what's your trouble with the man?"

Crider sighed. "He's possibly the only person who might know where my missing operative is."

60

Saturday

DJ arrived at the crime scene and walked into the middle of a jurisdictional dispute. At least a dozen people stood beside an Albuquerque Fire and Rescue vehicle in the parking lot of one of the large banks in town.

He spotted Swannie and pushed his way through. "What's going on?"

Swannie shook his head. "About what you'd expect. A State Police officer is down. They already took him to UNMH. Two bank robbers were wounded, and transported. A private citizen with a concealed carry permit wounded the robber who shot the State Police officer. A third robber escaped, and has been cornered in the South Valley, which is in Bernalillo County jurisdiction."

DJ frowned. "Who's here from the FBI?"

Swannie shrugged. "Your supervisor, but I've been so busy since we arrived I haven't had time to look for him."

Before DJ could speak, Swannie held up a restraining hand. "You and I have to talk. It's important, but I think it'll keep."

"Sounds ominous," DJ said. "Want to give me a clue?"

Swannie rubbed his chin. He seemed more tired than anything. "It's about the guy following Nick Ellis. It will definitely keep until tomorrow. Think we can get together a few minutes then?"

"Sure. I don't think Harrie and I have any plans for tomorrow. Give me a call, and we'll work out a time."

Swannie patted DJ's shoulder. "Thanks. See you tomorrow sometime." Then he walked over to one of the detectives talking to a customer.

DJ turned to survey the scene. People milled around. Cars had parked on the side streets, and a large news van, complete with antennas and satellite feed sat at the edge of the parking lot. The cameraman struggled with his equipment, while the high-heeled, sleek blonde in a tight, short skirt, clutched her microphone. She tugged at her skirt and licked her lips—ready for a closeup.

DJ shook his head and walked inside. It was much quieter here.

Several of the employees were sitting apart from each other. Local police and detectives were individually questioning three women—most likely the tellers. A man paced the floor inside a glass enclosure labeled "Manager," and the young guard, hired from a company supplying them to financial institutions, sat in a chair by the door. His bent posture and lowered head telegraphed his misery. It was his weapon that had wounded the other robber.

DJ's immediate supervisor, John O'Leary, walked over to him. "I think we're good here. You don't need to stay. What happened with your CIA contact?"

DJ related his encounter with Colin Crider. His boss nodded, and said, "I think it's time you focus on this fellow you told me about yesterday. Can you get a photo of him?"

DJ nodded. "If he really is an employee at the Hyatt, that shouldn't be an issue."

"Any reason to think he's not?"

DJ hesitated. "After talking to Crider, I'm not sure. It's just a hunch. I'll let you know when I find out."

"Do that," O'Leary said. "How's your wife? Does she have any helpful information?"

"I don't think so, but I'll see what she says. If I ask too many questions, she'll want to insert herself into the investigation more than she already has. I'm trying to make sure that doesn't happen, but it's a challenge."

O'Leary chuckled. "I don't know your wife all that well, but I must say, she seems like a lady who could keep you on your toes. She won't be easily 'managed' if I know women."

DJ grinned. "Now you see my dilemma."

"I do, my friend. I wish you luck."

They parted, and DJ returned to his car. He looked down at his clothes. When he got dressed this morning, his focus was on appropriate attire for drone activity. If he went home, Harrie would want details, and he wasn't prepared to give her any. He had a change of clothes in his locker at the office.

DJ started his car and pointed it toward the local FBI office.

61

Saturday

After DJ left the airfield, Ginger cheered on the twins, while Harrie and Caroline focused on Mark Goodrum and Nick Ellis. They maneuvered their drones in graceful flight.

"You really should try this, Harrie." Mark motioned to her and offered his handheld drone controller.

"Hey, I'm still learning how to use my radio. I don't need new challenges at the moment."

Mark grinned. "Okay." He shrugged his shoulders. "But it's not every day I offer someone the opportunity to fly this baby."

Harrie reddened. "Oh, Mark. I didn't mean to insult you . . ."

"I'm kidding, Harrie. I remember the first time I took the controls on one of these things. They can be intimidating."

She said, "Maybe when I feel more comfortable with the technology."

Mark patted her shoulder. "I suspect you'll be a whiz at it before you know it."

From behind Harrie, Ginger said, "That's right."

Harrie jumped at the sound of her voice. "Geeze Louise! Sneak up on a person, why don't you?"

Ginger giggled. "I'm sorry. Truly I am. It was just so tempting. The little devil who sometimes sits on my left shoulder egged me on, and I couldn't resist."

"Where have you been?" Harrie frowned at her friend.

"Surveying the crowd. I'm surprised you weren't doing the same."

"I thought you and Caroline were watching the twins fly."

"We were, and Caroline still is. I saw something I needed to investigate."

Harrie couldn't believe she heard right. "You, who always chastises me for doing that? You were investigating?"

Ginger leaned in and whispered. "Not so loud. Come with me." She grabbed Harrie's arm and pulled her along.

Harrie thought better of objecting or commenting. She hurried to keep up and spotted a group of men several yards away. Ginger stopped and turned to face her.

"Do you see the big, tall guy with his back to us?"

Harrie casually edged to the left so she could see around Ginger. "What about him?"

"Right next to Mr. Big is a short guy with a red cap."

"Okay. So?"

Ginger sighed. She stood next to Harrie, without looking at the group. "The short guy is somebody you should recognize."

Harrie's heartbeat increased. She squinted and stared at the man. When it hit her, she stopped breathing for a few seconds.

This time she grabbed Ginger's arm. "That's the man who came to the office yesterday and demanded to see the manuscript."

"Congratulations," Ginger said. "You win the booby prize."

Harrie's brain whirred. She looked back at the group. "Did you see the man on the other side of Mr. Big?"

Ginger's eyes grew large. She stole a furtive look. "You mean the guy dressed all in black?"

"Yes."

"I'm drawing a blank. Am I supposed to know him?"

Harrie turned to leave and pulled Ginger along this time. "Let's get out of here."

Ginger stopped and disengaged herself from Harrie's grip. "Not until you tell me why this sudden urgency to leave."

Harrie's breathing normalized. Her back was still the men. "Do you remember when we met Nick for lunch on Monday?"

"Of course. I'm not that forgetful."

"Do you also remember the weirdo who watched us as we went in?"

Ginger frowned. "As usual, I didn't notice. But I remember afterward you said something about it. You said a guy watched us in a creepy way."

"Creepy is an understatement. Don't look now, but the guy standing next to Mr. Big on the other side is the same weirdo."

Ginger lifted her sunglasses ever so slightly. "Well, don't you look, because Mr. Creepy has now turned to stare at us." She grabbed Harrie's arm.

"Come on Short Stuff, get those legs moving. We're outta here."

62

Saturday Afternoon

DJ walked into the lobby of the Hyatt Regency Hotel downtown and observed the scene. People milled around in small groups. Some clustered in the gift shop and others seemed pulled to the bar. A sign just off the lobby welcomed a national group of insurance executives.

He chuckled to himself. Nothing like being away from home on a convention trip to bring out the adventurous side in a group of weary insurance salesmen. Everyone was too busy trying to impress each other to pay attention to him.

A young man at the front desk wore a vest with the words "Desk Clerk" inscribed on it.

"I need to speak to your manager," DJ said.

The young man frowned. "I'm sure I can handle any problem, sir. How may I help you?"

DJ pulled out his FBI credentials, flipped open the cover, and held it up for the desk clerk to see. "You can help me by getting the manager out here—now."

The clerk's eyes looked much larger than they had when DJ approached. "Yes, sir. Right away, sir."

DJ drummed his fingers lightly on the counter until he caught himself. Out of the corner of his eye, he glimpsed the desk clerk he'd been talking with, followed by an older, taller man, who wore a vest identifying him as "Manager." They approached DJ.

Pinned to the manager's vest was a plastic name tag. It said, "Mr. Wallace." The man had a bemused smile on his face as he stretched out his right hand.

"Always happy to assist the FBI. How may I help you, Mr . . ."

"Special Agent Scott," DJ said. He returned the hand shake while holding up his creds with his left hand.

The young desk clerk, obviously hoping to be included in the conversation, stood close. The manager turned to him and nodded toward the end of the counter. "There's a customer waiting over there. You need to take care of him. I'll handle this."

The young man's expectant grin faded. He walked to the end of the check-in desk, threw one last, disappointed look at his boss, and engaged with the impatient customer in front of him.

DJ put his credentials away and took out his notebook and pen. "I spoke with you on the phone yesterday about your employee, Ted Gunderson. I'd like to get a bit more information about him."

Mr. Wallace frowned. "I beg your pardon?"

DJ squinted at him. "Is there more than one manager for the check-in desk?"

Wallace rubbed his eyebrow. "Ah, no. I'm the day manager. But we do have a night manager."

"So," DJ said. "Do you remember talking to me by phone yesterday about Ted Gunderson?"

The man looked puzzled. Then he brightened. "Yes, of course. I didn't realize I was talking to the same person. Sorry. What is it you want to know?"

"How long has Mr. Gunderson worked here?"

Wallace scratched his chin. "No more than a month or two. He worked nights at first. He came on the day shift just last week. Why? Is something wrong?"

DJ ignored the question for the moment. "Would it be possible for me to see his employment application?"

Wallace's expression changed. He rubbed the back of his neck. "If there's a problem—if Ted's in any trouble—I need to know. We can't have someone with a criminal record working with our customers' money and credit cards."

DJ shook his head. "No, I'm not aware of a problem. I simply need to verify his identification. I've tried to reach him by phone, and he didn't respond."

Wallace tilted his head to one side. "Then why didn't you talk to him earlier?"

Now it was DJ's turn to be confused. "Sorry? I don't understand."

Wallace shook his head. "If you wanted to talk to the boy, why bring me out here?"

"Are you saying— " DJ stopped in mid-sentence.

Wallace grinned. "The guy you sent to fetch me is Ted Gunderson."

63

Saturday Afternoon

Harrie, Ginger, and Caroline sat around Harrie's kitchen table. They'd been discussing the adventures of the morning when Harrie's cell phone rang.

"Okay," She said. Her shoulders slumped. "Do the best you can. I'll see you when you're finished."

Caroline smiled "So, is DJ doing okay?"

Harrie frowned. "I'm not sure. He sounded kind of strange. I think he's found out something, but he's not ready to tell me."

Ginger let out an un-ladylike snort. "When are you gonna catch on? DJ can't tell you everything he finds out. Geeze Louise, he'd be thrown out of the club if he did."

Harrie crossed her arms. "And what club would that be?"

Ginger threw her hands up in disgust. "I don't know. The club of secrecy or something. They'd probably have to kill you if he told you secret stuff."

Caroline chuckled. "I'd say best not to be too inquisitive."

Harrie said, "Come on, ladies. I'm not that bad—am I?"

"Let's change the subject." Caroline turned to Ginger. "Tell me more about these strange men you saw this morning."

Ginger described the men. Caroline thought about it and didn't say anything for a minute or two. She seemed to be pondering something.

"Are you absolutely sure the short guy was Ted Gunderson?"

Ginger leaned in. "Absolutely. I'd know that little squirt anywhere." She shook her head and blew out a breath. "What an obnoxious blob of a man."

Caroline narrowed her eyes. "Did either of you ever see him before yesterday?"

Harrie and Ginger looked at each other. Harrie said, "I'm pretty certain I've never seen him before." She turned to Ginger.

Ginger hesitated, then frowned. "I didn't think so yesterday. But today, I'm not so sure."

"What does that mean?" Harrie looked at her friend in

amazement.

Ginger shrugged. "If I'm not badly mistaken, I think I noticed him last week at the drone field."

"You never said anything about that." Harrie's eyes had taken on a look of alarm.

"Sorry," Ginger said. "I'll try to keep better track in the future."

"I have an idea," Caroline said.

Harrie's eyes lit up. "Wonderful. Let's have it."

Caroline stood and took her coffee cup to the sink. "Not quite yet. I need to check on something first. I don't want to get your hopes up."

She picked up her purse. "I'll call you tomorrow. I have to do some research. It's worth waiting for, believe me."

And with that, she was gone.

Harrie and Ginger hadn't moved, and when the front door closed, they looked at each other.

"Do you have a clue what she has up her sleeve?" Ginger asked.

Harrie shook her head. "No idea at all. But I know one thing for sure."

Ginger said, "Oh?"

Harrie picked up the other two coffee cups and put them in the sink.

"Caroline has been hanging around us too long. I think she's picking up some of my bad behavior."

64

Saturday Evening

By 2:00 PM, Caroline and Ginger were gone. Harrie decided to do some grocery shopping. DJ's favorite dinner—steak, baked potato, and a green salad—would be the menu for tonight.

By the time DJ arrived at 4:00 PM, Harrie had everything ready, except grilling the steaks. She was about to pour him a glass of wine when he surprised her.

"Let's go for a walk."

"Wouldn't you rather wait until after dinner?"

He shook his head. "No, I need to clear my head. I think walking might help."

"Okay." She reached over to turn off the oven. The potatoes would keep.

The afternoon had been balmy and still—overall, a lovely day in May.

Harrie put on her sunglasses and followed DJ out the front door. They turned east and walked up to the end of their block. He reached for her hand.

"Are you okay?" Harrie said.

"I'm tired. It's been a really long day."

"That's why I'm a little surprised you wanted to walk before dinner."

"I guess I'm more mentally tired. I thought walking might give my brain a chance to rest. It needs it."

"Sounds like you've been inundated with problems today. Anything you can talk about?"

"Well," he said, "funny you should ask. There might be one thing you can help me with."

"What's that?"

"Tell me what happened at the drone field after I left."

Harrie stopped in her tracks. It was the last question she'd expected.

DJ looked at her. "What's wrong?"

She shook her head. "Nothing. You surprised me, that's all."

She resumed walking, and so did he.

"Can I assume by your reaction that something did occur after I left?"

Harrie sighed. "Nothing 'occurred' if you mean some sort of action."

She took a deep breath. "Ginger wandered away for a few minutes. When she returned, she insisted I come with her to see something."

"Oh?"

Harrie's nervous laugh gave her away. "She pointed out a guy who we believe is Ted Gunderson."

DJ stopped again. "Are you sure?"

Harrie remained quiet and nodded.

He reached into his pocket and pulled out his smartphone. He held up a photo for her to see. "Is this Ted Gunderson?"

Harrie frowned as she studied the photo. "No. That's a young guy. Ted Gunderson has to be at least 50 if he's a day."

DJ let out his breath. "This is the Ted Gunderson who works as a desk clerk at the Hyatt downtown. I met him today, and his boss verified his identity."

Harrie said, "But that's crazy. Why would this old guy pretend to be someone he's not?"

DJ stopped walking. "Let's go back. I think we need more privacy for this discussion."

Harrie's shoulders slumped. "Now we'll never know who he was."

He grinned. "Don't give up so quickly. That's not like you at all."

On the short walk back, Harrie's brain did summersaults. Should she tell him about the other man at the drone field? She ran several scenarios through her head. Her unusual silence seemed to trigger DJ's attention.

"Why are you so quiet? Is there something else going on I should know?"

Harrie shook her head and shrugged.

DJ sighed and gave up.

But Harrie knew that would change the minute they walked in their front door. Her normal attitude was to withhold any information that could, a) get her in trouble, or b) get her in bigger trouble.

When they walked up to the front door, DJ opened it, and Harrie had a mind-boggling thought. She could simply skip that step. Hiding the truth always ended up in disappointment. Plus, when it was all over, she got into trouble anyway, and then felt awful about holding back the truth.

As soon as they were inside, with the door closed behind them, Harrie said something she never expected to say.

"I need to tell you the entire story of what happened today. I want you to know everything."

The look on DJ's face was worth it. It clearly conveyed she must be ill.

Or that he was pondering the possibility that her body had been taken over by an extraterrestrial.

65

Saturday Night - Harrie & DJ

They decided to have dinner before any heavy-duty discussions. DJ made the suggestion, and Harrie felt giddy with relief. It gave her time to plan how to tell her story.

It had taken two glasses of wine after dinner to get through the entire thing. DJ had lots of questions—most of which Harrie couldn't answer. She felt certain he had as much to tell her but didn't think he would. Full disclosure was *her* new thing. She couldn't expect the same from her tight-lipped husband.

Harrie set her wine glass on the end table. She slipped off her shoes and tucked her feet under her. "Where does all this leave us?"

DJ drained his wine glass and put it next to Harrie's. "I have a few things to tell you. But remember, you need to keep it confidential."

Harrie knew her face must have reflected how stunned she felt. "Are you sure you want to take me into your confidence?"

DJ let out a long breath. "I think you'll understand why this is a delicate situation. I happen to know you actually can keep things to yourself when you are motivated."

Harrie swallowed hard. "I'm touched. I promise I won't let you down."

"I'm counting on it."

"Okay," she said. "Let's have it."

"First is this fellow who calls himself Ted Gunderson. Obviously that isn't his name, and I'll be working to discover who he really is. For now, I need more information."

Harrie shrugged. "I don't know what else I can tell you."

DJ said, "You know those security cameras you have at Southwest Editing?"

"Sure."

"Have you thought about looking at the footage?"

Harrie felt like slapping herself upside the head. "No, and I'm absolutely furious I didn't."

"Don't berate yourself. It only occurred to me when I was at the Hyatt. I realized these days most businesses have cameras. We usually ignore them. That made me think of your cameras. I want to get a look at this fellow pretending to be Ted Gunderson."

"I'll ask Caroline tomorrow. She deals with the cameras. I think they record directly to the computer in the vault. We must have a lot of footage filed away."

DJ nodded. "All we need is the recent stuff for my purposes."

Harrie had a sudden thought. "There's something else I'd like to see on that footage. I wonder if we could pinpoint the date when Richard Tracy brought in his manuscript?"

DJ frowned. "Why would you need to see him?"

"Curiosity, I guess. Wouldn't you like to see him too?"

"Not particularly. I don't want to get pulled in . . . ." He stopped, took a breath, and looked at Harrie for a long moment.

"What's wrong?" she said.

He sighed. "I wasn't going to share this with you, at least not yet, but I think it's time you should know. I had another meeting with our old friend Colin Crider this morning."

Harrie felt momentarily speechless. She found her voice and said, "Why?"

DJ laid his head back against the couch. "Okay. Hold on to your hat. I don't think you're gonna like this."

Harrie felt a shot of adrenaline. "What's going on?"

DJ momentarily closed his eyes. When he opened them, he said, "As you've guessed, your mysterious manuscript was written by a CIA operative. He works for Colin Crider."

Harrie frowned. "I already figured that out. No big secret at this point."

"Now, Crider is looking for information about Ted Gunderson."

Harrie's eyes narrowed. "How does he know about Ted Gunderson?"

DJ shrugged. "I'm guessing, because you have the manuscript, he's keeping an eye on your office. I suppose he's worried someone will try to steal it."

Harrie knew her face must show her confusion. "It was a lousy manuscript. Why would anybody want it—much less steal it?"

"That, my dear, is the very question I intend to ask Colin Crider. After what you've told me about events today, he and I will have a long conversation."

"And when will you have this conversation?"

"As soon as I dangle the bait in front of him."

Harrie squinted her eyes. "I hesitate to ask, but what bait?"

"That, my Love, is where you come in."

66

Sunday - Swannie

Sundays had always been special to Swannie. As a kid, he loved them because the entire family spent the day together. First there was Sunday breakfast, followed by the usual rush to get all the kids ready for church. His mom was the organist and his dad served as head usher. His brothers and sisters (all six of them) took turns helping out the various Sunday School classes.

But the best part was Sunday dinner.

For as long as he lived at home, his mom served pot roast one Sunday, and fried chicken the next. For many years, his grandparents, aunts and uncles often attended. He loved those meals and looked forward to Sunday dinner each week. When he looked back on it, he couldn't decide if it was the food or the family togetherness that he loved most.

When he met Caroline Johnson, and they began spending a lot of time together, he'd felt that same sense of "family" he'd enjoyed as a child and young man. Their Sundays together reminded him of those long-ago days back in Nebraska with his own family.

He didn't like giving up this Sunday's dinner plans with Caroline. But it was imperative he talk to DJ about Cabrini's meeting with Nick Ellis on Friday.

When Caroline answered her phone she seemed out of breath. "Hello?"

Swannie frowned. "Did I catch you at a bad time?"

"No, no. It's fine. I just walked in the door and put my purse down."

Swannie didn't want to ask where she'd been. He felt it would be rude. But he couldn't help being curious.

"I need to postpone our plans. It's important I meet with DJ, and I'm not sure how long I'll be. May I call you when we're finished? Then, if it isn't too late for you, I'll take you to dinner."

He heard Caroline's soft chuckle.

"I'm glad you called. I've invited Harrie and DJ over for dinner this afternoon. I thought you'd like to join us. I'm sure Harrie won't mind if you two fellows retire to the study and have your discussion. She and I will be getting dinner ready."

Swannie's mood improved immediately. Leave it to Caroline to solve a problem she didn't even know he had. "That's a wonderful suggestion. What time is all this to take place?"

"Well," Caroline said, "it's almost noon now. I suggested they come about 1:00 PM. You're welcome to arrive any time you're ready."

Swannie felt a big grin spreading across his face. "I'll see you in half an hour."

He spent the next few minutes finishing up some paperwork. He gathered the notes he'd taken about Cabrini's encounter on Friday evening.

The notebook he habitually carried in his jacket pocket was a battered relic from his first days as a detective. He shook his head as he stuck his current notes inside the book. Time to break down and buy a new one.

With that thought, he picked up his keys and headed for his car.

When he backed out of his garage, he absently noted a black sedan parked across the street from his house. By the time he'd used his remote to shut the door, a stray thought had seeped its way into his head.

Normally he would have backed out of his driveway and headed west, the same direction as the parked car. But this new thought, now growing larger in his brain, caused him to turn left instead, heading east toward Tramway Boulevard.

Within three minutes the black sedan had performed a U-turn and was on Swannie's tail. He took a deep breath.

"Fasten your seatbelt, creep. It's gonna be a bumpy ride."

67

Sunday Morning - DJ & Crider

Since DJ had initiated this meeting, he arrived well in advance of the agreed-upon time. He also picked the spot—one he hoped Crider would remember.

He tried to recall the reason he had picked Hidden Park for that first meeting with Colin Crider. It was only a couple of years ago. Still, a lot of cases and investigations were behind him since then.

DJ rarely encountered people who knew about Hidden Park. It had always been an unadvertised wonder in Albuquerque. He knew its actual name was McDuffie Park. But locals "in the know" had always called it Hidden Park because a person would have to know where the hidden access paths were located.

He walked up the path on the south side of the green oasis. With his first glimpse of the mature trees and thick grass, he felt a welcome peace settle around him. He took in a deep, full breath, and let all tension flow out of his body.

Now he remembered exactly why he'd chosen this place. He recalled Crider's reaction to the park's serenity that first time they'd met here. While DJ felt calm and peaceful, it seemed to make Crider jumpy.

DJ felt a grin coming on, and he stifled it immediately. No amount of planning could ever guarantee Crider wouldn't have already out-maneuvered him by arriving even earlier than DJ.

As soon as that thought passed through DJ's brain, Crider spoke softly from behind him. "What is it with you and this creepy park? There are at least a hundred windows surrounding this place, from which someone could observe us. Doesn't the FBI teach you guys anything about covert operations?"

DJ made sure his heart was back in his chest before he spoke. "I have nothing to hide, my friend. I can't answer for you, of course."

Crider sat beside him. "What do you have for me, and it better be good. I'm missing Sunday School."

DJ kept his jaw from dropping, and quickly recovered his wit.

He stretched his legs out and leaned back. A Mountain Scrub Jay flew down from a tree and angrily scolded them. DJ reached in his pocket and pulled out a handful of peanuts in their shells. He tossed them on the grass, and the Scrub Jay greedily snapped up the first peanut and flew off with it.

Without looking at Crider, DJ said, "I'm pretty sure I'll have some good information for you by tomorrow. Something has come up—several things, in fact—and I believe by tomorrow I'll be able to give you a lead on your operative. Is that good enough for you?"

Crider, for once, looked directly at DJ as he spoke. "I appreciate your help. I'll be eager to hear the details of this mysterious information." He turned his head forward to gaze out across the park.

After a couple of minutes of silence, he said, "I suppose there are worse places to meet."

To DJ, that almost sounded like an attempt at friendly banter. He realized all semblances of normal friendliness were probably washed out of Crider by his CIA training. What a life that must be. It occurred to DJ he certainly wouldn't want to trade jobs with the man.

The silence stretched and DJ said, "Why do you want information on Ted Gunderson?"

Crider sat up straight. "I should think that would be obvious. I need to know why he's interested in the manuscript?"

DJ frowned. "That's the other thing. How did you even know about Gunderson and his interest in the manuscript?"

A rare grin crossed Crider's stoic face. "Perhaps you have eyes watching us through the many windows looking out upon this park. Maybe that's why you like to meet here. I, too, have many eyes. They help me do my job and stay alive."

DJ watched the Scrub Jay zero in on another peanut and fly off with it. "That's not the way I work," he said. "I'm sorry you have to do it like that. But I still need to know how you knew about Gunderson."

Crider shook his head. "When we meet again, and you tell me these wonderful things you've discovered, I'll share that information with you."

"You drive a hard bargain."

Crider stood and adjusted his sleeves. "Not even close, my

friend, not even close."

DJ sat and watched Crider as he left the park. The CIA man looked neither to his right nor his left as he took the long way out through the northernmost path. It occurred to DJ the man was making a silent statement of some significance.

If Crider actually believed there were people posted behind any of those windows surrounding the park, he seemed to be thumbing his nose at them.

68

Sunday Early Afternoon

Swannie pulled up to the security gate at Canyon Estates and waited his turn behind a small red car. The black sedan sat two cars behind him in line.

When Swannie's turn came, the guard flashed him a smile. Clem often greeted him at the gate. Clem waved him through, but Swannie stopped and nodded at him.

"Hey, Clem. Can I talk to you a second?"

Clem shot a quick glance at the line of cars waiting behind Swannie, then walked over and leaned down. "What's up Lieutenant? You're cleared to go through."

"Clem," Swannie said, "do NOT look back at the cars while I'm talking to you."

Clem nodded. "Okay."

"There's a black sedan two cars back. When it gets here, delay the driver as long as you can. He's been following me since I left my house. I've called some of my people, and I'm hoping they got here ahead of me."

Clem smiled. "You're in luck. Two of your detectives arrived about five minutes ago. They told me there was a problem, and you'd be here soon. They're waiting for you at the first stop sign. I'll give you as much time as I can."

Swannie nodded. "Thanks, Clem. I need time to talk to my guys without this creep seeing me."

"Sure thing, Lieutenant. Just promise me you'll fill us in when this is over."

Swannie grinned. "Will do. You take care. And thanks again."

Clem straightened up and motioned Swannie to proceed.

As promised, he saw two unmarked police cars up ahead. They had turned into the adjoining street. He pulled up beside the closest one.

Swannie lowered his passenger-side window and leaned over.

"He was two cars behind me in line just now. The guard agreed to delay him as long as possible. I'll go ahead and get out of the way. I want you to follow this creep at a discreet distance and see what he's up to. I want cars outside both gates. Tell them I want to know which gate this guy is leaving by. Then I want him followed."

"You got it, Lieutenant," the driver said. "We'll run his license plate and see what's up. We'll call you when we have anything."

"Okay," Swannie said. "Don't lose him."

They nodded. Swannie did a "U" turn and got back on the main street through Canyon Estates. There were several stop signs along the way to Caroline's house, and he watched in his rearview mirror hoping not to see the black sedan.

The speed limit within the complex was 25 miles per hour, so Swannie hoped Clem was able to detain the black sedan long enough. He parked three houses down from Caroline's, and walked back. He hurried inside. Now it was up to his team.

With any luck at all, they would have answers soon. But Swannie had one gnawing worry. If this had anything to do with the murder at the Petroglyphs, it might not be that simple.

69

Sunday Afternoon

Harrie and DJ arrived promptly at 1:00 PM, and Swannie met them at the door.

"Do you mind if I sidetrack DJ for a moment? We have a couple of things to discuss."

"Be my guest. You can keep DJ entertained, while Caroline and I put the finishing touches on dinner."

"Thanks. We won't be long." Swannie led the way down the hall to Caroline's study. He closed the door and turned to DJ.

"I'm really sorry we couldn't talk yesterday. I've so much to tell you." He ran his hand through his hair.

DJ frowned. "What's going on? You look frazzled."

Swannie leaned back in the desk chair he'd chosen. "I'm not sure where to start. There's so much you need to know."

"Then let me go first. I have an eye opener for you," DJ said. "The man who went to Southwest Editing on Friday isn't Ted Gunderson."

"Then who is he?"

DJ shrugged. "I don't have a clue yet. But Harrie and I talked about it, and we think there's a way to find out."

"Maybe he's the one following Nick Ellis."

DJ's eyes narrowed. "What makes you think that?"

Now it was Swannie's turn to be confused. "Let's start over. First, I'll tell you about my meeting with Cabrini yesterday morning. Then I need to get into the issue of who's been following me today."

"Hold on," DJ said, and leaned forward. "Let's start first with your being followed."

Swannie sighed. He knew impatience tinged his face. "I'm waiting on a report from some of my guys. Right now there's nothing definitive to tell."

"Then tell me what you know at this moment."

So Swannie explained about the black sedan parked in front of his house, and the subsequent trip to Caroline's house.

"I expect a call any minute, but I have no idea what's going on with this black sedan."

"Okay. Then tell me about the meeting with Cabrini."

Swannie filled him in on the details of the incident at Flying Star on Friday evening.

"Other than the fact the guy claims to be a federal agent, we have no clues."

DJ remained quiet for a few seconds. Then he said, "Colin Crider told me yesterday morning that he can't locate his operative. He thought the note sent to Harrie meant the guy was safe. Now it seems otherwise."

"Maybe the guy Cabrini saw Friday night is Crider's operative."

"Maybe," DJ said. "But I doubt it. Crider would know if his guy is in town. This man Cabrini told you about. Do you think she could give us a description?"

"Oh, I imagine she can, but maybe we'd be better off to just have her talk to Crider."

DJ shook his head. "I don't know. Crider plays it close to the chest. He never gives up anything unless he thinks he's on top, or it's to his advantage."

Swannie's cell phone rang, and he took the call.

DJ listened while Swannie mostly asked questions, followed by long periods of silence. When the call ended, he turned back to DJ.

"They have the man in custody. He's a two-bit hood with a record for everything from burglary to check kiting. But he has very little to say."

"Did he admit to following you?"

Swannie nodded. "He admitted it readily. But he has no idea why. He received a phone call from someone who told him what to do. They told him where to pick up his payment for the job. I gather it was a substantial amount. He simply had to follow me and email them my destination. Rather odd, wouldn't you say?"

"So he has no clue who his benefactor is."

"None at all."

"Can you get me a photo of this guy?"

Swannie frowned. "Sure, but why?"

"Harrie told me about three men she and Ginger saw at Maloof Airfield yesterday. I'd like to show them the picture and see if they recognize him."

"Good idea," Swannie said. "I should show it to some people too."

A knock on the study door interrupted the discussion.

Caroline said, "Dinner's ready, fellows."

"On our way."

Swannie stood and turned to DJ. "Don't say anything about this to the ladies. Caroline will worry."

DJ grinned at his friend. "You need to get over this idea you have that my mother is some fragile flower. I guarantee you she's stronger than you can imagine."

Swannie opened the door. "You're probably right. Maybe I'm the one who needs protecting."

70

Still Sunday

The conversation throughout dinner remained light. Everyone seemed to skirt around the events bedeviling the group. When they finished dessert, Caroline suggested serving coffee in the den.

She couldn't resist. "You may be wondering why I called this meeting."

Harrie laughed, and DJ grinned. Swannie looked puzzled.

Caroline said, "I'm sorry. I've always waited for the right occasion to say that. Thanks for letting me get it off my bucket list."

She turned to Harrie. "Remember our conversation yesterday afternoon?"

"The one about the three guys Ginger and I saw?"

"That's it," Caroline said. "I had an idea how we might identify them."

Swannie frowned. "Wait a minute. You're not thinking about getting involved in all this are you?"

Caroline crossed her arms. "I'm not sure exactly what you mean by 'getting involved.' I had what I thought was a good idea. So, to that extent, yes, I'm involved."

Swannie looked sheepish. "Um, I didn't mean that the way it came out. I think I'll just shut up and listen."

DJ laughed. "Good plan, my friend. You're learning."

Harrie leaned over and patted his arm. "You know, Swannie, women love the idea of a strong, protective male in our lives. We simply don't like being smothered by them."

"I think I'm figuring that out. But thanks for the tip."

Caroline grinned. "As I was saying, it occurred to me there might be a way to identify at least one off these strange men at the airfield. So, after I left your house yesterday, I went to the office and checked the video feed on our security cameras."

Harrie clapped her hands. "That's so weird. DJ and I were talking about the same thing last night. I told him you were in charge of all that, and I would mention it to you. I should have known you'd be ten steps ahead of me."

Caroline said, "I'd planned to show it to you and Ginger tomorrow at work, but then it occurred to me DJ and Swannie might have something to add. So, I made a copy, stuck it on a thumb drive, and brought it home. Wanna see it?"

"Absolutely," everyone said in unison.

"I'll need the computer so let's adjourn to my study."

The three of them followed Caroline down the hall.

She sat at the desk, turned on her Mac desktop, and plugged in the thumb drive. Next she opened the movie program and enlarged the video to fit the entire 27" screen. Harrie pulled up another chair and sat beside Caroline. DJ and Swannie stood behind them.

Caroline said, "I went through all this yesterday. The recordings went back almost a year, so I took snippets I thought might be applicable. That's why we're seeing what appear to be little short movies. If you see someone who interests you, sing out. I can stop and go back."

Harrie said, "Did you see anyone who stood out?"

Caroline hesitated. "I saw several interesting people, but I'd rather wait to see if anyone captures your attention."

The recordings had no sound, but this audience remained quiet, as though they expected to hear something anyway.

After about ten minutes, Harrie said, "How much footage did you bring us?"

"Roughly 40 minutes. It took me quite a while to put together."

DJ said, "What made you settle on these particular images. There must have been some criteria you used in your choices."

Caroline gave him a look that would be familiar to any son or daughter.

DJ held up a hand. "Never mind. I trust your hunches. Always have. Just wondered."

Caroline looked at Harrie and shook her head. "You'd think they'd learn eventually, wouldn't you?"

Harrie chuckled. "Never mind, Caroline. I have great faith in your instincts about such things."

Another ten minutes went by. Occasionally one of the group would ask to repeat a segment. But nothing stood out.

Harrie realized she'd been focusing on the videos so intently she wasn't aware she'd been nervously running her tongue back and forth against the back of her bottom teeth. It was a bad habit she'd developed in childhood when she focused intensely on a project. Sometimes the tip of her tongue became almost raw before she caught herself.

At the same time something else dawned on her. This habit was also a precursor to those occasions she uncovered a forgotten memory or remembered a dream. In this case, it was last week's memory of the man following her in the black Prius with the dented door.

"Go back," Harrie said. "I think I've seen that guy before."

71

Later Sunday Afternoon

When Harrie recognized a man in the video, she realized things would get awkward immediately. She had only told Ginger about her adventure on Friday. Now she'd have to 'fess up' to the three people standing over her with questioning looks.

"Caroline," Harrie said. "I have something to confess, but I think it would go down easier with a glass of wine."

Caroline grinned, but Swannie and DJ simply looked confused.

"Absolutely, Sweetie. I'll get the wine."

When the wine had been poured for all, the other three turned to Harrie. She took a long sip and set the glass on the desk.

"I always intended to tell you all, but so much has happened."

She paused to "feel" the mood of the group. She sensed interest and acceptance from Caroline, confusion from Swannie, and quiet analysis from DJ.

After another long breath, Harrie explained about how she'd deliberately sought out a potential stalker last Friday. Swannie asked several questions, but Caroline and DJ watched and listened.

When Harrie got to the part about seeing the black Prius parked next to their house on Sagebrush Lane, Caroline smiled broadly.

"The fellow on the video you asked me to rewind and show again, is that the individual you saw in the black Prius?"

DJ finally spoke up. "Hold on a minute, Mother. I'm curious about a couple of things."

Harrie opened her mouth, but DJ said, "I've waited patiently through your remarks. Now it's my turn to ask questions."

Swannie interrupted. "Why didn't you call the police?"

Harrie picked up her wine glass and downed the rest of the liquid. She looked at the two men.

"What part of this explanation did you not understand? I already said I wanted to see if I could catch someone following me. What would have been the point of calling the police?"

"Swannie's right," DJ said. "You should have reported it. I don't suppose you got a license plate number."

Harrie looked beseechingly at Caroline. She didn't have the words to respond.

Caroline said, "DJ, I'm guessing these aren't the tactics you use when conducting an FBI interview."

DJ frowned. "Mother, this is my wife—the woman I worry about pretty much on a daily basis. She frequently gets herself in trouble. Naturally I worry about her—especially when I've asked her to be extremely careful."

Harrie sat quietly, enjoying the back and forth between her mother-in-law and her husband.

"I still think you could do away with the 'attitude' while you ask your questions." Caroline crossed her arms, stood up taller, and leaned back, ever so slightly, chin tilted in a defiant stance. She could be intimidating.

DJ sighed. "You know, Mom, next time I have a particularly difficult suspect to interrogate, could I get you to give him what for. He'd be putty in my hands after you got through with him."

Caroline shook her head and laughed. "That's right, turn on the charm. But I'm still asking you to not browbeat Harrie. Let her tell her story and give her some respect. She's not a reckless teenager."

DJ turned to Swannie. "Are you still under the delusion that my mother can't take care of herself?"

Swannie held up his hands in surrender. "I'm convinced you were right. She's a power house. But I've always known that." He smiled at Caroline, and she laughed.

Harrie sat quietly through all this back and forth. "Would it be okay if I finish my story now?"

DJ and Swannie looked at her. Then they nodded.

Harrie said, "I'm telling you the man in the video is the man who followed me in the Prius last Friday morning." She turned to Caroline. "Do we know his name?"

"As a matter of fact," Caroline said, "I do." She picked up her glass of wine. "I did some detective work to discover the date of the video and made some comparisons."

"Good job, Mom." DJ held up his glass in a toast.

"Come on, Caroline," Harrie said. "Don't hold out on us. Who is it?" she joined DJ and Swannie on the sofa.

Caroline's huge smile was wonderful to see. "I'm betting it's Richard Tracy."

72

Later Sunday Afternoon—Still

Caroline's identification of the male subject in the video called for action. DJ immediately excused himself to meet with Colin Crider. Swannie decided to go downtown to the station and speak with the suspect who'd been following him.

That left Caroline and Harrie to clean up the dinner debris. Harrie worked on the various pots and pans while Caroline loaded the dishwasher. It gave them the perfect atmosphere to talk.

"I'll call Ginger when I get home. She'll be so torqued she wasn't here to see all this."

Caroline closed the dishwasher and took off her apron. "I'm sure Ginger's been busy dealing with the boys today. She said they planned to sit down as a family and discuss Chris's desire to attend the Air Force Academy. Did you know Steve's already secured a recommendation for the boy from one of our senators?"

"No, but I'm not surprised. I'm glad it's a real possibility for Chris."

Caroline filled two coffee mugs and set them on the kitchen table. She and Harrie sat and relaxed.

Caroline said, "Speaking of possibilities, would you mind if I ask you a personal question?"

"Of course not. You've become my other-best friend. Ask me anything."

"Okay. I've never heard how you came to have these prophetic dreams. I hoped some day we could discuss it, but the time never seemed right."

"I'm sorry. It never occurred to me you didn't know. I assumed DJ told you about it. I don't give it much thought unless I've had one that needs solving."

"When did you first experience one?"

"Well, they aren't always prophetic. The very first 'other worldly dream' I had happened when I was about 15. It was more like a lucid dream with a twist. Then a few years ago I had a huge one."

Harrie related the dream she experienced after the death of her husband, Mark. She explained it was so uplifting she was able to shake the mind-numbing grief she'd felt for more than a year.

"In this dream, Mark was sitting at my kitchen table, sipping coffee from a cup. He had been a huge cream user, but I hadn't kept cream in the refrigerator since his death. Nevertheless, he was sipping creamed coffee.

"I woke up next morning feeling better than I had since he died. When I went into the kitchen, there on the table sat an almost empty coffee cup. In the bottom of the cup were the dregs of creamed coffee."

Caroline shivered. "Didn't that freak you out?"

Harrie shrugged. "Strangely enough, it didn't. It gave me a feeling of relief and hope. In the dream, he told me he'd always watch over me. I found it comforting."

"From what I'm seeing now, you don't seem to find them comforting. I can tell they cause you distress."

Harrie nodded. "That's true. But I accept it as part of my heritage."

Caroline's eyes opened wider. "You believe you inherited this ability? From whom?"

"My maternal grandmother. She had the same thing. In fact, she had all sorts of abilities."

"Why do you think this particular 'ability' manifested itself in you when it did?"

"I'm guessing because it was when I needed it most. She passed away less than a year before my fifteenth birthday. She was so dear to me, and right after my birthday, she came to me in a dream. I'd been grieving her loss and wasn't doing well."

"What do you think triggered it at that time?"

"It must have been grandmother's doing. She wasn't shy about using her abilities around me when I was a kid. I spent lots of summers with her and my grandfather on their farm just outside Fort Worth. I believe she was trying to prepare me to accept the gift."

Caroline frowned. "You say you accept the gift, and yet, you still experience bad reactions when you have the dreams."

Harrie nodded. "The thing is, I always dread letting people down. I have to be careful talking about these things. I've discovered many people reject the idea of information from the beyond, or prophetic dreams. I'm also afraid if I don't figure them out, more bad things will happen to people. When I have a dream for the first time, it bothers me that I don't understand what I'll be required to do."

Caroline slowly stood her head. "Well, you certainly have my admiration. I think I now understand why you're so driven when you've have one. I salute your courage and determination to solve the puzzle."

Harrie sighed. "Thanks. I wish my mother had been as understanding as you are."

"You mean your own mother doesn't accept your gift?"

Harrie laughed. "My mother didn't even approve of her own mother's abilities. She certainly didn't want me being part of that world. She said so—many times. I've never told her about all this, so please don't mention it the next time you see her."

Caroline patted Harrie's arm. "Mum's the word."

73

Late Sunday Afternoon - DJ and Crider

Crider chose a surprising meeting place this time. DJ couldn't help smiling. He shook his head as he approached the man.

"I hope you didn't think this would be open on Sunday afternoon," DJ said. He took his place next to Crider. The CIA operative sat on the low concrete wall of a planter at the Cherry Hills Library in the Northeast Heights. He wore his usual dark glasses. This time, so did DJ.

Crider said, "I thought it would be closer for you."

"Closer than what?"

Crider shot DJ an annoyed look and removed his sunglasses. "Who's wasting time now?"

DJ stifled a grin and removed his own shades. "Sorry to bother you twice in one day, but I thought you'd be glad. You should know that as of this past Friday, your operative was alive and well."

"And you know this how?"

"Because my wife identified him as the man who followed her that day."

"How did she recognize him?"

"My mother showed us a video compilation of people who've been in and out of Southwest Editing Services over the past year."

Crider looked at DJ. "This is what you do on a beautiful Sunday afternoon?"

DJ said, "We were looking for a photo of this fellow who claims to be Ted Gunderson. In the process, we saw Richard Tracy. Harrie recognized him as the man in a black Prius who followed her last Friday."

Crider took a deep breath. "Well, well. Harrie McKinsey is quite the magnet for trouble, isn't she?"

"I believe the question should be, why was a CIA operative following her in the first place?"

"I imagine to protect the manuscript."

DJ leaned forward, elbows resting on his legs, hands clasped.

"That's lame, and you know it."

Crider remained silent a few seconds, then shrugged. "Sometimes we need to check on things. You know how it is."

"Actually, I don't. Your Mr. Richard Tracy left the manuscript in the capable hands of Harrie's business. If he was concerned, all he had to do was contact their office. Since he didn't, he must have some other objective."

Crider's eyes had narrowed when he turned to look at DJ. "What are you suggesting?"

DJ straightened up. "Not suggesting anything. I'm saying something else is going on, and I want to know what that is. Why is the CIA interested in my wife?"

Crider said, "The CIA is not interested in your wife, per se. We're interested in other people who *are* interested in your wife."

"What other people?"

Crider stood and put on his sunglasses.

"How about we start with Viktor Ivanovitch?"

DJ also stood. He liked the fact he was at least two inches taller than Crider. He said, "Remember that day we met at Coronado Mall? If you'll recall, I told you we had it on good authority the victim at the Petroglyphs was Viktor Ivanovitch."

"I was there, and I heard what you said. You must know that I have ways to verify such things."

"And you're now saying the information I gave you was wrong?"

"Let's walk a bit," Crider said. "I don't like staying in one place too long."

"I've noticed. But let's get back to the subject. Is Ivanovitch our victim or not?"

The two men walked leisurely toward the nearly empty parking lot. In that moment, DJ realized his was the only car there. It occurred to him he'd never seen how Crider arrived at any of their meetings. For all he knew, the CIA agent was teleported. He should ask Tim Burns if the FBI had one of those devices.

DJ said, "You obviously have more recent information than I do. Will you share, or is this now a one-way street?"

"Tsk, tsk, Scott. I can't help it if the CIA has better sources of information. Just be grateful we do."

"I'll pass that judgement on after I hear this new information.

And don't forget my original question. Who is following Harrie and why?"

Crider stopped, pulled off his sunglasses again, and turned to face DJ.

"It's possible I mentioned to some of my bosses that Harrie McKinsey had a nose for trouble. I also may have said something about her gift of prophecy."

DJ felt anger bubbling up but stifled it before responding. He counted to three—mentally—and smiled. "Since when do you, or for that matter, the CIA, put any stock in strange dreams?"

Crider fixed DJ with his icy stare. "Since we discovered over the past several years, she has accurately predicted sketchy details of several crimes that she could not have known about at the time. It's something the CIA is intensely interested in."

DJ stopped. "Wait. Is this about the CIA Remote Viewing project?" He shook his head. "I thought that was dead years ago."

Crider turned to look at DJ before he spoke. "What you don't know about the CIA would fill a library."

DJ took a moment to brace himself, then looked at the ground. He felt a cold, hard determination settle around him. He fixed his gaze on Crider, projecting—he hoped—everything he felt at that moment. It boiled down to barely concealed rage.

He turned back to Crider. "This is not up for discussion. You will call off anyone you are aware of—including the CIA—who might be stalking my wife. If you don't, I'll have all of you up on charges. You got that?"

Crider looked away, breaking eye contact. "Calm down before you stroke out. I have no intention of allowing anyone to 'stalk' Harrie. I'm simply telling you what I'm up against. I'll get back to you as soon as I find my operative. He has lots of explaining to do."

"You'd better mean that." DJ controlled, with great difficulty, the shaking which invaded his body during the ultimatum. The emotions flooding through him at that moment astounded him. He now understood how someone could do bodily harm to a person threatening a loved one.

And he didn't like that feeling.

74

Monday Morning

DJ was always early for the job. Today, he arrived earlier—6:30. He couldn't shake the thought he'd missed something important.

Yesterday's early evening meeting with Crider shook him. He was more determined than ever to get to the bottom of things. He made a check list and recorded it on his computer. Now he prepared for the first task.

In Albuquerque, it was 7:00 AM. In Quantico it was the more decent hour of 9:00 AM. He dialed a number. The familiar voice he needed to hear answered.

"You must've hit another snag and require my expertise. What's up Dude?"

Tim Burn's cheerful voice penetrated DJ's dark mood, but not as much as it usually did.

He tried to sound cheerful. "Up to my ears, Buddy, and yes, I do need your help. Tell me, oh wise one, has the FBI obtained a transporter?"

There was a slight pause on the line. "Say what?"

In all seriousness, DJ said, "You know, that gizmo they have on Star Trek. It scrambles everybody's molecules and deposits them, reassembled, in a distant place."

"Dude, it's too early in the morning to be drinking the hard stuff. What's up?"

DJ sighed. "Do you remember our phone call just last week when you told me our victim at the Petroglyphs was Viktor Ivanovitch?"

Another, longer pause. Now the voice sounded cautious. "Um, yeah, sure. So?"

"So—I discovered last evening, that's not true."

DJ heard a heavy sigh. "I told 'em this wouldn't go down. I told 'em you'd figure it out." Another sigh. "What happened?"

As succinctly as possible, DJ described the events of the past week, ending with the Colin Crider meeting Sunday evening.

"Do you know how annoying it is to be outwitted by the

freaking CIA? I looked like a junior Mouseketeer with big round ears and a clueless look on my face."

"I'm sorry, DJ. Really. It wasn't my doing, I swear."

"Are you prepared to tell me the truth now?"

Another big sigh. "Yes, and no. I can verify the body is not Viktor Ivanovitch. No, I cannot tell you what happened—at least not yet. It's time I took another beating from the brass."

"That bad, huh?"

"Don't even ask. But I'm pretty steamed myself. Of course I'll have to be judicious about showing it, but this just isn't right. I'm sorta glad it happened, though. They're gonna to be P.O.'d when I tell them what Crider did."

"Okay," DJ said, "I'll let you get to it. I trust you'll call me as soon as you can?"

"Believe me, DJ, this time you'll get the straight scoop."

"I'd better. Because at the moment, I'm left hanging here. The Bureau looks really bad if we don't fix this."

"I'll fix it with Flex-Seal tape. You know how strong that stuff is."

"Yeah, right. Just do it."

75

Monday Morning - Harrie

Harrie seemed to be pulling herself up a steep cliff. She noticed she had no climbing equipment, but the bottoms of her feet had developed suction cups. *What an odd way to travel.* The sound of a machine edged closer. It brought to mind an electric lawn mower, or maybe a chain saw.

Harrie woke suddenly. Tuptim, the purring Siamese cat who had been snuffling her mistress's ear, jumped straight off the bed. She shot a stern look at Harrie.

"I'm sorry, okay? How would you like it if I purred in your ear while you slept?"

The offended cat busied herself grooming her hindquarters, ignoring this human who so often didn't appreciate a good tongue bath.

When she looked at the clock beside the bed, Harrie let out a yelp. "Yikes!"

She grabbed her robe and headed for the kitchen. Destination—coffee pot. The cat sensed food would be offered and quickly ran ahead.

Harrie groaned. "Okay, Your Highness. Got the message. Cat gets fed before Harrie gets coffee."

Tuptim attacked the dish of food with dainty gusto. Harrie shook her head and filled her mug with still hot—but slightly stale—coffee.

She read the note DJ had left on the counter. It made her smile.

"Couldn't bring myself to wake you. You were zonked. Hope you slept well. See you tonight. Love, DJ"

Harrie took the coffee to her home office. She turned on the computer and sipped while waiting for the machine to boot.

The previous afternoon while DJ had another meeting with Colin Crider, Harrie used the time to catch up on work. She composed a letter she'd been dreading. The person receiving it would be disappointed, and Harrie disliked this aspect of the job. She needed to tell the young, eager writer that the manuscript she'd spent the last two years creating needed massive revision. Because Harrie was no stranger to disappointment herself, she hated to dish it out to her clients. She knew how difficult this message would be for the inexperienced writer, so Harrie worked hard to frame it in the most helpful, yet honest way possible. She hadn't yet printed it out.

She did so now and read it aloud for the first time. That always helped her catch trite phrases and redundant language. It also helped jog her memory.

Something had nagged at her for days. With all the suspicious people she'd encountered in the past couple of weeks, her attention became scattered. She'd had trouble focusing on work. A little voice in the back of her head tried to get through.

Harrie took another sip of coffee and the nascent thought, swirling there for a week, popped through.

She drew in a breath. It was so obvious. This same sort of letter must have been written by Harrie, Ginger, or Caroline, to the elusive Keyser Söze, aka, Richard Tracy. Who had written that letter, what did it say, and how did Tracy respond?

Harrie grabbed her coffee mug and hurried to shower. A very annoyed Tuptim scrambled to safety just in time.

It took Harrie only twenty minutes to shower, dress, and apply minimal makeup. Her brain functioned at almost full capacity.

When leaving Canyon Estates, she'd already calculated the likely location of the letter. Her focus was less on her driving than on the success of the mission.

Later on, she'd realize that was probably why, for once in a long time, she hadn't checked her rearview mirror after leaving the gated community.

76

At Harrie's Office

Harrie arrived at Southwest Editing Services as both Caroline and Ginger pulled into the parking lot. She sighed with relief. Harrie needed both of them. Their simultaneous appearance gave her a much-needed shot of hope.

"What are the odds?" Ginger waited for Caroline to catch up with her.

Caroline said, "And here I thought I'd arrive early enough to start the coffee before either one of you turned up."

They grinned at Harrie when she gallantly held the door open. Once inside, each woman tended to one of the necessary entry chores: Harrie headed for the security panel and turned off the alarm. Caroline went to the kitchenette to start the coffee, and Ginger stopped at the reception desk to return the phone system to workday status.

The three congregated in the small kitchen/break room to have an impromptu staff meeting.

Caroline brought her coffee to the table and joined them. "Okay, I give up. What brought you both out at this hour?"

Harrie grinned. "Wow, Ginger. I can see we've slipped into executive behavior." She glanced at her watch. "Gracious, it's only 8:00 AM and we're both here."

"Well I know why I'm early," Ginger said. She sat and sipped her first of many cups of coffee for the day.

Harrie tilted her head and grinned. "And why would that be?"

"I'm behind on the gross receipts tax report. I've been a slacker with that stuff."

Caroline set her coffee down. "I've told you both, I'd be happy to take some of the administrative stuff off your hands."

Harrie sighed. "I know you did, and we'll probably take you up on that offer soon. I, for one, thoroughly dislike that aspect of owning a business."

Ginger sipped. "The thing is, Caroline, we both worry that you're stuck with all the personnel issues, the training, the counseling, the discipline. We feel guilty."

Caroline laughed and shook her head. "Need I remind you how easy this job is compared to working at the law firm all that time?" She turned to Ginger. "Steve must have told you over the years what a zoo it was with more than a hundred employees scuttling around. This is child's play compared to that."

"Maybe we should give her a raise," Harrie said. Her big grin made the other two women laugh.

Harrie heard the front door being unlocked. She grabbed her mug and said, "I think that's Azalea. I need to talk to both of you in my office. Come in as soon as you can."

Caroline and Ginger looked at each other and shrugged.

Ginger said, "You got it, Boss."

As Harrie hurried to her own office, she saw Azalea heading for the ladies room. The girl was nice, and she was certainly attractive. But Harrie considered her a bit of a 'ditz.'

By the time the young woman exited from the ladies room, put her purse under the desk, and turned on her computer, both Caroline and Ginger had vacated the break room and joined Harrie in her office.

"What's up?" Caroline sat at the round conference table in Harrie's office.

"Yeah," Ginger said. "You seem a bit hyper this morning."

Harrie shrugged. "I suppose I am. I woke up later than I intended. Then I had this amazing revelation. I couldn't wait to get here and discuss it with you."

Caroline held up her hand. "Hold on. I'd like to fill Ginger in on what we discovered yesterday afternoon."

Ginger frowned. "Okay. Now I feel left out. What were you up to yesterday?"

Harrie and Caroline took turns filling her in on the events of Sunday. Occasionally Ginger stopped one of them and asked a question, but she was amazingly quiet during their recitation.

When they finished, Ginger shook her head. "This begins to sound eerily familiar. Now's about when we start looking for criminals behind every bush."

Harrie said, "But don't you think it would be great to get to the bottom of this soon? It would be nice to get back to our regular business. I know I'll be delighted to stop having this stupid dream every night."

"So what's the plan? I assume you have one." Ginger sat back in her chair.

"That's where you guys come in," Harrie said and grinned.

Ginger shook her head. "And she's off and running."

Caroline smiled at Harrie and patted her hand. "What can we do to help, Sweetheart?"

Harrie pulled out the letter she'd been working on to send their not-quite-ready writer. "When I printed this out, it struck me we must have sent a letter like this to Richard Tracy. I mean, the manuscript was so bad, we wouldn't have done anything else, right?"

Caroline took the letter. "Now we're getting somewhere." She handed it to Ginger.

Ginger read it, and a big grin blossomed on her face. "You're right. I don't know why we didn't think of this earlier."

Caroline picked up the letter. "I'll make a copy of this. Then I'll have one of the typists put it on letterhead and get it ready for signature. Meanwhile, Ginger and I can go through the correspondence file to see what we can locate."

"Right," Ginger said. "Let's order in lunch about 11:30 AM and see what we can come up with in the meantime."

"Good idea," Harrie said. "But if you can avoid it, don't say anything about this to Azalea, will you?"

Ginger narrowed her eyes. "Any particular reason?"

Harrie shook her head. "I don't really know. It's just an odd feeling I got this morning when I saw her coming into the building." She sighed. "I know that sounds weird."

"Not really," Caroline said. "Besides, it would be pointless. Azalea's only been here a few weeks. The manuscript came in at least six months ago. She doesn't seem able to find even the stuff she filed. I can't imagine her ability to research would be up to the task."

Ginger picked up her coffee mug and drained it. "I don't know. I think you're both underestimating her."

"You do?" Caroline stopped at the door, her hand on the knob. "Why?"

Ginger grinned. "Because, I think she's figured out if she acts dumb, somebody else will bail her out. Then she has less to do and can't mess up. You guys have fallen into her clever trap."

Caroline laughed as she turned the knob on Harrie's office door. "You may be right. I never thought of her as Machiavellian. But stranger things have happened around here."

When her office door opened, Harrie felt a little chill wash over her. She froze in place.

Standing there, arm raised as if prepared to knock on the now opened door, was the Machiavellian Azalea.

77

Monday Noon - DJ & Swannie

Swannie took another bite of his green chile cheeseburger. DJ Scott noticed the look of pure contentment on his friend's face.

He shook his head as he bit into his own burger. "I feel almost obscene watching you eat that thing."

DJ had called Swannie after talking to Tim Burns. They agreed to meet at the Blake's Lotaburger on San Antonio Boulevard, not far from I-25.

Swannie laid his burger on the bag and wiped his fingers. "People in glass houses shouldn't throw stones. Have you ever watched yourself chow down on one?"

DJ grinned. "Well said. I defer to the master in all things."

Swannie snorted. "Yeah, sure. So why the impromptu lunch date?"

"I ended up having two meetings with Crider yesterday. Then I talked to my buddy in Quantico this morning. I'm not happy."

DJ related the gist of his conversations and the things he'd learned.

Swannie listened intently and finished his meal as DJ outlined the problems.

"Has it occurred to you somebody is playing you?" Swannie put the last of his fries in his mouth and put his trash in the burger bag.

DJ chewed on an onion ring. He frowned at Swannie. "I think you know the answer to that. What I'm more fichotted about is that they have someone following Harrie."

Swannie's face took on a confused, questioning look. "Where did you pick up a word like that? What does 'fa-chot-ted mean?"

DJ picked up another onion ring. He couldn't help grinning. "That's a really good question." He shook his head. "It's a word I hadn't even thought of in years until recently. Mom's best friend used to say it when she became annoyed. I asked her one time what it meant. She said, 'What do you THINK it means?'

"I was confused, and she started laughing. Then she said,

'Sweet boy, listen to words in context. You learn how words fit with feelings if you pay attention to the context in which they are used.'

"I realized that's how most kids learn to speak a language. In her case, 'Aunt' Joan used that word when she was annoyed."

Swannie leaned back. "Your Aunt Joan sounds a lot like your mother."

DJ grinned again. "They're sisters from another mother."

"So," Swannie said. "Back to the gnarly question of exactly 'who' is following your lovely wife."

DJ said, "Before we get to that, did you remember to bring me a photo of the guy following you yesterday?"

"Ah, yes," Swannie said. He reached in his pocket and pulled out a copy of the mug shot. "One Johnny Reynolds. Often arrested, most often convicted. A real sweetheart."

DJ took the photo and studied it. "Okay. I'll pass it by Harrie and Ginger. I'll let you know if they recognize him from the drone field on Saturday."

"Are you saying my being followed by this guy on Sunday is tied in with the Petroglyph thing?"

DJ shook his head. "No. But you must admit, it's odd."

Swannie shrugged. "I can't deny it. But the same thing applies to most aspects of this case. Which brings up the subject of your friend in Quantico. You seemed upset about him earlier."

"It's not him. It's that I dislike being 'played,' and that's exactly what's happening. Brace yourself. The identity of our Petroglyph victim is once again an unknown."

Swannie leaned on the table and scratched his head. "How in the hell—excuse me, DJ. What in blazes is going on at the FBI?"

DJ leaned back and took a deep breath. "I feel certain it's not the FBI who's running this show. I believe it's the CIA. As you know, we are now encouraged to cooperate with other federal agencies. This thing has been botched from the beginning. I think our people are left holding the bag."

"What can you do about it?"

"I'm working on that, and I may need your help."

Swannie grinned and rubbed his hands together. "I thought you'd never ask."

78

Monday Lunchtime - Harrie, Ginger & Caroline

It had been a weird morning. Harrie convinced Caroline and Ginger they should stick with their plan of having lunch brought in. Besides, no one really wanted to go out today.

Caroline unpacked the lunch order. A new food delivery company in Albuquerque brought them salads from Flying Star Cafe. Caroline had also ordered a carrot cake to top off the meal. She asked if they could eat in her office.

"I'm expecting a couple of phone calls, and it would be easier for me."

They agreed and gathered around Caroline's conference table.

Harrie opened the box containing her salad and closed her eyes. "This is such a treat."

Caroline said, "Since I'd never tried one of these salads, I decided today was the time to be adventurous. I hope it's as good as you and Ginger seem to think."

"Trust me," Ginger said. "I think you'll love it." She speared one of the deep fried feta cheese balls. When she bit into it, a huge smile appeared.

Harrie grinned. "Your look of pure delight is the best recommendation this dish could have. You could have a career in commercials."

Caroline sipped her tea. "Let's talk about the elephant in the room."

Harrie took a bite of avocado before she spoke. "What can I say? Someone left a spooky message for me on our answering machine. It certainly isn't the first time."

"I believe it's a bit more than that," Ginger said. "It's downright threatening. You know DJ will have a fit when he hears it."

Harrie put down her fork. "With any luck, he won't hear it. And I don't want either one of you telling him about it, either."

Ginger's mouth dropped open. "You must be kidding. I can't let you do that."

Harrie started to reply, but Caroline stopped her. "Harrie, you know I love you like a daughter, but you can't ignore this. You have to tell DJ. In fact, I'll tell Swannie."

Harrie blew out a breath. Her nerves were stretched so tight, she thought they might snap. "You know how DJ is. He sees trouble following me around all the time. He's overprotective and treats me like a little kid. If he hears this tape, he'll probably have me confined to a monastery somewhere to keep me safe."

Ginger shook her head. "I think the word you're searching for is a nunnery."

Harrie opened her mouth, but Ginger moved to stand directly in front of her. "I don't know why you think you're Wonder Woman. You don't have any of those bulletproof bracelet things she wears, and you weren't raised on a mystic island with Amazonian women." Ginger started to turn away.

Harrie's mouth still hung open, but Ginger apparently wasn't finished. She turned back and said, "And maybe a nunnery is exactly where DJ *should* put you."

Harrie swallowed the large lump in her throat. She turned to Caroline.

"Do I deliberately court trouble? Wait—don't answer that."

Caroline said, "I don't think you 'deliberately' court trouble. You're simply an amazing magnet for it. Maybe it's because of your dreams, or maybe people see your curiosity as something to fear."

Ginger held up her hand. "I hate to be a nag, ladies, but let's get back to the tape. Did either one of you recognize the voice?"

Caroline frowned. "It sounded to me like one of those computer generated voices. It didn't sound human."

Harrie left the table and stood gazing out the window. Her shoulders slumped.

Ginger went to her friend and hugged her. "Sweetie, you know what you have to do. Caroline and I will stand behind you. You've gotta give DJ a chance to help. We can't do this on our own."

As Harrie turned to speak, they heard a soft tap on the door. Her heart skipped a beat as the door opened, and DJ walked in.

"Hey, what's going on in here?" When he spied the carrot cake in the middle of the table, he said, "That looks good. May I join you?"

Caroline hooked her arm in her son's. She led him to the table, pulled out a chair, and indicated he should sit. "We'd love to have you join us. But first, we have something you need to hear." She turned to Harrie. "Don't we, Harrie?"

Harrie sighed. "Yes, we do." Then she slid the small recording machine toward DJ.

79

Monday Afternoon - The Tape

DJ listened to the tape numerous times. To Harrie's amazement, he didn't go ballistic.

She had enough sense to remain silent, but the effort made her twitchy. There were so many questions. If he didn't say something soon, she wouldn't be able to stop herself.

At last DJ registered his wife waiting beside him. He gave her a tired smile. "Sweetie, would you mind if I take this tape to be analyzed?"

Relief flooded her body. Maybe this wouldn't be as bad as she'd feared.

"Sure. That's fine," she said.

"May I borrow this little machine to play it?"

Harrie nodded. "Absolutely. I seldom use it anymore. Don't know why I even keep it around."

His face relaxed. "Thanks. The first people who need to hear this are Swannie and Cabrini. If I have the opportunity, I'll play it for Crider."

"Do you really think he'll give you anything?"

"I don't know. But I'd like to watch his reaction. That could tell me a lot." He put the tape in an envelope pulled from his pocket. He stuck the little player in his other pocket.

Harrie smiled. "Do you always carry evidence envelopes in your jacket pocket?"

"Of course. You never know when you might need one. Be prepared."

Caroline re-entered the room, carrying a long knife. "Will we eventually get that back?"

DJ's eyes grew large. "Geeze, Mom. You don't need to threaten me. I promise I'll return it. Are these little tapes that expensive?"

Caroline lifted her face toward the ceiling. "Lord, why did you give me a comedian for a son?" She moved to the table, uncovered the carrot cake, and cut slices for everyone.

Ginger picked up two paper plates laden with cake. "I'll take these out to the ladies, and make sure Azalea gets a really big slice."

DJ said, "Is Azalea the one who discovered the threatening message?"

"Yes," Harrie said. "She can be a bit ditzy, but she often surprises us."

"When did she give it to you?"

Harrie squinted at him. "You mean what time?"

He shook his head. "No, I mean how soon after you arrived this morning did she bring it to you?"

Harrie searched her memory. "Well, we arrived before Azalea or any of the other girls. The three of us were in the break room, talking about the excitement yesterday. Caroline and I filled Ginger in about the videos, and discovering the guy who'd been following me. I guess Azalea showed up about 8:30."

"Did she hear you talking about that stuff?"

Harrie frowned. "No. Why?"

He shrugged. "Just curious. What happened next?"

"I asked Caroline and Ginger to meet me in my office. We needed to discuss the situation more, and I wanted privacy."

"Do you recall what time Azalea brought in the tape?"

Harrie's eyes narrowed. What's this about? You never question me this thoroughly about my day."

He rubbed his chin. "Wouldn't you say today's events are not the usual routine around here?"

"I suppose that's true, but why ask me about the exact time she brought it? What difference does it make?"

"Okay," he said. "How long have your employees been with you? I know my mother was your first employee, but how many editors and others do you have working here?"

"You know as well as I do the answer to those questions."

"Humor me."

Harrie felt a mild irritation beginning. Then it dawned on her, and she realized DJ's inference.

"Are you thinking Azalea is some sort of spy?"

A smile slowly covered his face. "That's my girl. Now you're thinking."

80

Later Monday Afternoon

By the time DJ arrived at Swannie's office, Cabrini had been summoned.

"What's up Agent Scott?" She sat in one of the chairs around Swannie's conference table.

DJ said, "Has Swannie filled you in on anything yet?"

Swannie shook his head. "No time. She got here just before you walked in."

"Okay," DJ said. "Hang on to your hat. You'd better take notes."

DJ took his seat, and Swannie started the debriefing. He began by bringing Cabrini up to speed on his adventures Sunday.

By the time they'd finished, almost 45 minutes had passed.

DJ took over. "Here's the latest on my meetings with Colin Crider."

They spent another 15 minutes on that subject. Then DJ said, "Now for what happened at Harrie's office this morning."

Cabrini groaned. "Oh, please don't tell me Harrie is still in the middle of this."

"Sorry," DJ said. "You know the drill."

He explained about the disturbing tape. Then he pulled out the small player, popped in the tape, and played it.

Cabrini and Swannie both leaned in to hear the odd, mechanical voice.

"This message is for Harrie McKinsey. We are watching you and know what you are doing. Do not interfere with our program. Stop asking questions, and do not try to find or identify us. If you continue your meddling, someone will die."

DJ switched it off, and Cabrini turned and looked at the two men. "What sort of idiot pulls a lunkhead stunt like this?"

DJ shrugged. "I'm guessing someone who is NOT a friend of Colin Crider."

"Are you sure?" Swannie had his left elbow propped on the table, chin resting in his hand. With his right hand, he drew doodles around a string of words on the pad in front of him.

DJ sat back and stretched out his long legs. "You have a different angle on this?"

Swannie stopped doodling. "Does it strike you that 'someone' is having quite a lot of fun at our expense?"

"Such as?" DJ leaned forward.

Swannie shook his head. "You'll have to forgive me, because I've only met Colin Crider that one time he came to our big dinner party a couple of years ago. You have far more knowledge of him and more time spent in his presence. Is he capable of using us for his own purposes?"

DJ frowned, then realized where Swannie was going with this. "In a New York minute. If you think about it, those guys are used to doing what's necessary in order to survive. You can bet if there's a good enough reason, they would use whoever they needed."

Swannie grinned. "That's what I thought. It's time we used them."

Cabrini spoke up. "I'm listening to you guys, and I still don't know what's up, Care to share? In English this time?"

Swannie rose from his chair at the table and headed for his desk as he spoke. "Early this morning, I was looking for something in my desk drawer—I've forgotten now what—but you'll understand when I show you."

DJ and Cabrini left the table and joined Swannie at his desk. He reached in and pulled out a 3 by 5 index card. He grinned as he held it up.

Cabrini looked at DJ and shrugged. DJ nodded. "I hope that's something more than it appears to be."

"Take a seat, my fellow conspirators. Let the old man explain a thing or two."

They all sat, Swannie behind his desk, the other two in front of his desk. Swannie leaned in and moved his lamp to the center. They now saw the 3 by 5 card featured a gold foil sticker affixed in the middle of the card.

Swannie said, "Remember last week right after this mess got started? I told you about finding one of Harrie's old business cards."

DJ nodded. "You said it was in our victim's sneaker, under the insole."

"That's odd, isn't it?" Cabrini looked perplexed.

"Of course," said Swannie, "but I didn't follow up on it. After I lifted this gold foil sticker off the card, I recognized the business card as Harrie's. I carefully placed the gold sticker on this clean 3 by 5 index card and stuck it in my desk to follow up later. With all that happened after that, I forgot until I found it again this morning."

"I don't get it," Cabrini said. "What's so special about a gold foil sticker?"

Swannie grinned. "Exactly what I thought until I examined it under my detective scope."

Cabrini frowned and sat back. "Now you're making stuff up."

Swannie held up his jeweler's tool with the magnifying glass and high intensity light. "Oh, ye of little faith." He handed the tool and the sticker to DJ. "Put this on and take a look."

DJ put on the headband, adjusted the magnifying glass, and peered at the sticker. He shrugged.

Swannie handed him some tweezers, and light dawned in DJ's eyes. He took the tweezers and carefully lifted the gold sticker from the card. Underneath was a minuscule black dot.

DJ looked up. "Well I'll be damned."

Cabrini frowned. "What's so important about a little black dot?"

DJ nodded toward Swannie. "Sergeant Paiz, you should buy your boss a big lunch and salute him. We may have a clue after all. This little black dot is what they call a 'microdot' in the spy business."

Cabrini looked puzzled. "Well, I congratulate you both. But if you can't read it, what good is it?"

DJ grinned. "I don't think that's going to be a problem. You see, I know a guy in Quantico who owes me."

81

Monday Still

Harrie had worked on the same paragraph for the past hour. Her editing focus was shot, but she tried to ignore the problem. No use. Her brain would not cooperate. She considered the wisdom of getting Caroline and Ginger back in her office so they could discuss the events of the day. Thankfully, she remembered what DJ said to them before he left.

He had casually walked over to her credenza, turned on her FM Radio, and twisted the volume knob much higher than usual. Then he came back, leaned in, and whispered to them.

"Whatever you do, be natural. Go about your business as usual."

Now, remembering the conversation, Harrie shook her head in annoyance. *Sure, easy for you to say.*

She tossed her pen on the desk and got a water bottle. Her irritation level escalated a notch when she discovered it empty. She started to pick up the phone and dial Ginger's extension. She stopped when she remembered the rest of DJ's warning.

"There could be recording devices hidden in here. Until we can check it out, don't talk about any of this inside the building."

Damn! This is impossible. I can't think straight, and I can't work. I have to get out of here.

She took her purse from the credenza and opened the office door. The reception area was clear at the moment. She straightened her shoulders and walked confidently to Ginger's office. She rapped on the door, opened it, and said, "Get your purse. We're going to be late for our meeting."

Ginger looked up from her laptop and frowned. Harrie could see her friend starting to form words, but cut her off, holding up her hand like a traffic cop. She hoped the look she shot Ginger conveyed her desperation.

Ginger hesitated only two seconds. "Oh, right. Thanks for reminding me. Let's go." She closed her laptop, opened her handbag, and stuck the laptop inside. She hurried to join Harrie.

The two women stopped at Caroline's office door. Harrie said, "Caroline, we're heading off to meet with that new client you told us about. We'll fill you in later."

Caroline looked only slightly puzzled before she apparently realized they were improvising. "Good. I hope it works out for us."

As they walked toward their cars, Harrie said, "You drive. I'm too distracted."

Ginger nodded and unlocked the doors. "Get in, tell me where to go, and why we're going there."

"I'm tempted to say head for the nearest bar, but that's not a good idea right now. Pick a place where we can get decent coffee and sit in a corner to talk."

Ginger's eyes lit up. "There's a McDonald's up the road. At this time of day it should be relatively peaceful. The coffee's not bad, either."

"Fine," Harrie said. "It's not really the coffee I need anyway—just the ability to talk in private."

They found a parking space in the shade, up next to the building. Once inside, Harrie pointed to a table for two in the far corner. "If you'll grab that table, I'll get us some coffee."

When she returned with the coffee, Harrie noted Ginger had brought out her laptop. She pulled the second chair around so she could view the computer screen with Ginger.

"What did you find?" Harrie sipped the hot coffee and felt herself relaxing.

"Another puzzle. I did find the letter we sent to 'Richard Tracy' regarding the 'need for improvement' in his work. I have a copy of it here. Then I found something else."

She clicked on another folder in the directory and brought up another document.

"What's this?" Harrie peered at the screen, puzzled.

Ginger grinned. "That, my friend, is another one of Caroline's innovations. I swear, I never realized how helpful it would be having a legal secretary set up our files and procedures. Did you know she scans in returned mail?"

"No, I didn't. But why?"

"Fortunately, for cases such as ours. You'll notice this is a scanned-in copy of the envelope we used to mail the letter. It has a stamped message: No Such Address—Return to Sender."

"So, Richard Tracy never even saw our letter critiquing his manuscript? Bummer."

Ginger sighed. "No, not bummer. Good thing. We now have the postmarked date of our letter, and we know he never intended for us to actually work on the manuscript."

Harrie massaged the back of her neck. "I'm getting one of those headaches. It must be impacting my ability to think and reason. I guess I should have caught on to that as soon as we uncovered the identity of the writer and knew it had something to do with Colin Crider."

"Don't berate yourself. I know those dreams of yours take a toll. You become tense and distracted."

"You never told me that before."

"I didn't notice at first. I didn't understand the connection between having one of the dreams and your becoming distracted and uptight. It dawned on me one day, and I felt really thick I hadn't figured it out before."

Harrie took another slug of coffee. "I think the coffee's helping. And getting away from the office is a relief. I feel uncomfortable talking about anything while we're there."

"Do you really think Azalea is some sort of spy? I mean, she doesn't seem the type."

Harrie snorted. "So who is the type? Marlene Dietrich? Wouldn't it be self-defeating to hire a 'spy type' to be a spy?"

Ginger shrugged. "Well, now that you put it that way. What can we do about it?"

Harrie drained the rest of her coffee and blotted her lips. "DJ promised to bring home some sort of 'detecting' equipment tonight. He'll sweep the office to see what we find."

Ginger rubbed her hands together. "Cool. Can I watch?"

Harrie shook her head and grinned. "And here I thought you didn't want anything to do with all these 'detecting' messes I get into."

"Oh, get real. You know I live vicariously through you."

"Okay, then, Nancy Drew. We'd better get back to the scene of the crime. We need to continue pretending we don't know anything."

Ginger drained her own cup. "Who's pretending?"

82

Monday Evening

DJ handed the box to the FedEx clerk, verified the address and account number, and smiled at the helpful man. His name tag said "Jerry," but DJ had never inquired any further into the man's identity. He was an efficient professional and didn't ask questions, which in DJ's opinion made Jerry perfect for the job.

DJ looked at his watch as he left the Fed-Ex facility. Tim Burns would have the package by the time he got to the lab in the morning. With any kind of luck, they would have an answer sometime tomorrow.

Swannie and DJ had discussed the job of sweeping the Southwest Editing Services offices for concealed listening devices.

Swannie said, "I'm guessing the FBI has more advanced, snappier equipment available than we do,"

"Probably," DJ had said. "But I don't want to stir the hornets' nest until I have to. If your equipment will do the job, I'd rather go that route."

So it had been decided they would meet at Southwest Editing around 6 PM. It was exactly 6 PM when DJ entered their parking lot. Swannie and Caroline sat in Swannie's car, and DJ parked next to them. He rolled down his window.

"Are Harrie and Ginger still inside?"

Caroline said, "Yes. Ginger's reading a manuscript aloud so Harrie can do the line editing. They'll be able to drone on for the next two hours if needed."

DJ said, "Are all the employees gone?"

Swannie said, "Don't worry. Harrie made sure everyone was gone before I got here."

DJ said, "How did she do that?"

Caroline grinned. "She invented a project. She told them my tenth anniversary as Office Manager was coming up this Friday. She sent the whole bunch on a shopping trip to buy me a present, pick out a cake, and arrange to have everything delivered here on Friday as a surprise for me."

DJ frowned at his mother. "You haven't been here ten years. It's only been six."

Swannie said, "Yes, but none of them know that—especially Azalea—so they were happy as clams to be given this project."

DJ got out of his car and locked the door. "Have you worked out how we get in there undetected?"

Caroline and Swannie exited the car. Caroline said, "I'll unlock the door and go tell Harrie and Ginger I'm back from my 'errand' and ready to help them. They'll be in the conference room."

DJ nodded. "Great. We'll follow you inside and start the sweep. If you need to say something to me or Swannie, write it down and hand it to me."

Caroline grinned at her son. "I think I can handle that."

She unlocked the door. The two men followed, with Caroline holding it open for them and the equipment they carried.

She gave a thumbs up as she relocked the door and headed for the conference room.

DJ heard her greet Harrie and Ginger, and he nodded to Swannie, pointing toward the break room.

It took less than ten minutes to cover the break room, finding nothing that set off their equipment. Next they tackled Ginger's and Caroline's offices. Again, nothing. When they entered Harrie's workspace, their stealthy machine lit up with a dim yellow light. Swannie motioned toward the headphones he wore and gave DJ a thumbs up.

DJ knew the sound Swannie heard grew stronger as the light intensified.

He nodded his understanding. Swannie moved toward Harrie's desk, and the yellow detection light changed to pale orange. DJ picked up the telephone set on Harrie's desk and turned it over to reveal the bottom of the unit. His anger welled up so fast it startled him. He motioned to Swannie, who leaned in with the machine's wand.

The wand hovered over the base of the phone set, and the now bright orange indicator light turned a vivid red. DJ's jaw tightened. He forced himself to take a deep breath.

Someone will pay for this.

83

Monday Night

"I still don't see why you didn't remove the stupid thing."

Harrie was more than a little upset upon finding out her office telephone had been bugged. Now, while DJ and Swannie tried to explain their next move, she continued her angry tirade at any and all who would listen. Fortunately, they had reconvened at Caroline's house, so whoever planted the wire didn't have the benefit of Harrie's own private plans for their demise.

Harrie missed Ginger. She'd understand how Harrie felt. But tonight was a big event at school for the twins, and Ginger and Steve needed to be there.

She stopped pacing the floor when another thought occurred to her. Tomorrow she'd need to get Ginger out of the office to tell her what they found. She felt sure her friend would be just as angry as Harrie.

A sudden tiredness flowed over her. She plopped back into the easy chair she'd occupied when DJ and Swannie revealed the results of their investigation.

Swannie turned to DJ. "Do you suppose she can handle the rest of our report?"

Harrie, whose heart still thudded at the initial revelation, felt that same organ beat faster. "There's more?"

She knew her voice had risen so high most humans wouldn't recognize it as anything but a bird-like screech. Fortunately her husband's ears were attuned.

DJ appeared with a glass of wine. He handed it to his flustered wife. "Take a sip of this. You need to calm down."

"Calm down? How do you expect me to calm down? I'm surprised you're not more upset about this." She looked at the glass but didn't sip from it.

DJ shook his head. "Been there, done that, bought the T-Shirt." He sat on the wide, plush arm of the chair. "Look, I know this is annoying—"

He stopped as she opened her mouth again, and started to push up out of the chair. He gently shoved her back, took the glass from her hand and held it up to her lips.

"No more from you until you calm down. You promised me you'd be able to handle the result of our search, no matter how it turned out."

Harrie felt herself deflate. One moment her anger swirled through her, bouncing off every nerve in her body. Then DJ's calming voice and concern—not to mention the glass of wine he held to her lips—got through to her brain.

"You're right," she said. She sipped her wine and thought about the possible repercussions of their discovery. "Are we sure Azalea is the one who planted it?"

DJ threw a look at Swannie. Swannie looked down at his feet, and took a sip of wine before he replied. "We don't know. Further investigation may reveal who and why."

Harrie felt her nerves settling down, and her brain beginning to function again. She looked up at DJ. "What's your take on this? What's our next move?"

A tiny smile passed across DJ's handsome face before he spoke. He set his glass on the end table beside her.

"I'm going to talk to Crider again. With luck, he won't know that we know—yet."

Caroline spoke up from across the room. "Will you tell him?"

"At the appropriate time." He looked at Swannie. "Want to explain the rest?"

Swannie shrugged. "Sure. Brace yourself, Harrie. We also found a bug hidden under the conference room phone."

Harrie frowned. "Why would they bug the conference room?"

Caroline said, "Look how many times we use it—just the three of us—to discuss office management, clients, employees, you name it."

"I see your point," Harrie said. Then something occurred to her. "Okay, I get that the bug is transmitting what we've been talking about in those rooms. But where is that transmission going? Is there someone sitting outside our building listening to us?"

DJ and Swannie looked at each other. DJ sighed. "Not likely, but we aren't dismissing anything yet."

"Wait," Harrie said, her voice tense. "Do you think someone besides the office staff managed to gain entrance? Would that be possible?"

"Anything is possible," DJ said. "But for now, let's stick with the most obvious."

Harrie nodded. Even as she did, a weird tingling sensation moved through her body. Things were moving in a dangerous direction.

84

Tuesday Morning

When Harrie opened her eyes, she realized the giant headache she'd been dreaming about was real. She shut her eyes again to gather her wits and decide on a course of action.

First order of business would be a large mug of coffee and two ibuprofen. Following that, she would climb into the hottest shower she could manage. The combination of caffeine, ibuprofen, and hot steam would likely break through most of the pain. She opened her eyes and groaned.

Harrie sat up in bed. She'd expected to see Tuptim, but the cat was nowhere in sight. She put on her robe and padded down the hall. From the kitchen came the sounds of an electric can opener. Obviously Tuptim had used her famous cat-like charm on DJ.

She entered the kitchen and saw her husband, in his running clothes, crouched down with an open can of cat food. He spooned some of it into Tuptim's food dish, all the while crooning softly to the purring cat.

"I see you've been chosen as her servant today."

DJ stood, leaned over and kissed her. "She knew you weren't up for it. You okay? You tossed and turned all night. I didn't want to wake you."

Harrie took a sip of the hot coffee she'd just poured. "I must have kept you awake. I'm so sorry."

"It's all right. I slept most of the night anyway. Another dream?"

Harrie sat at the kitchen table. "Another version of the same one. Really weird. I saw the amphitheater at the Petroglyphs first. Then, suddenly, I was standing on a downtown street where a bunch of homeless people had set up a tent city."

DJ frowned. "Any ideas about that?"

Harrie shook her head and winced in pain. She went to the cabinet where she kept a bottle of ibuprofen, shook out two tablets, and brought them back to the table. She gratefully accepted the glass of water DJ handed her.

"When I tame this headache, I'll give it some serious thought. For now, it's just another one of those strange mysteries of life."

DJ capped the remaining cat food and stuck it in the refrigerator. "Okay then, feel better. I need to get showered and be on my way. When you figure it out, call me."

"You'll be the first I call I make."

"I know that's not true, but I'll settle for being the second." He leaned in and kissed her.

After DJ left for work, Harrie took her own shower. She felt much better. Her three-pronged attack had worked.

As she dressed and arranged her hair and makeup, stray explanations waltzed through her brain. She deliberately avoided trying to 'force' the answer, or stress over this new wrinkle. She knew a particular part of her brain would sift through all the new aspects of her dream.

At some point, an answer would appear. For now, all she need do was remain observant, open to suggestions, and have patience. If only it were that simple.

And, if only she actually *had* that elusive patience.

85

Tuesday Morning Too

DJ decided to use his cell phone to place the call to Tim Burns in Quantico. It was a 'gut' decision. If anyone had asked, he wouldn't have been able to say why. He couldn't explain it, even to himself.

When he heard Tim's voice, he could tell his friend was stressed. He braced himself for what must lay ahead.

"Timmy, my boy. What's the good word?"

"Hey, DJ. Thought you'd be calling later."

DJ's brain went into hyper alert mode. Tim Burns rarely called him 'DJ.' It was always 'Scott,' Dude,' or 'Bro.'

"Sorry. Don't mean to hurry the process. But we need some answers about that tape before we can go much further."

The silence seemed unusually long before Tim responded. "It's okay, Dude. I couldn't talk right then. What's up?"

"Did you receive my package this morning?"

"Yes, I did, and it's very interesting, I must say."

"Really? In what way."

Tim chuckled. "In every way. Somebody's pulling your leg, Dude."

"Explain," DJ said.

"Well, to begin with, you indicated this tape came from an answering machine. It didn't."

"How can you tell?"

"It's close to the same style as the tapes for one of a dozen old answering machines. But it doesn't fit. This tape is for a small-sized, personal taping device. People used to take them to meetings. They hold an hour or two of conversation. Most of the answering machine tapes were segmented for 30 second messages. Plus, those tapes were never that long. Who wants to encourage a long-winded message?"

"How do you know all this stuff?"

"Before I answer that, I have a question. Who owns this 'answering' machine?"

"It's from Harrie's office. It's what they use to take messages."

"Dude, you do realize this is the 21st Century, don't you? Everything is digital now. Nobody uses a stinkin' answering machine anymore."

DJ sighed. "What can I tell you? My mother is cheap. She bought the darned thing at a garage sale and brought it to Harrie's office. They've never complained."

Tim said, "Well, they're more patient than I am. But you should know. You've been punked."

DJ's brain took in that information and set it aside for the moment. "Let's move on to something more 'thorny' if you don't mind. I'm still waiting for my explanation about our Petroglyphs victim. Anything you can tell me about that?"

DJ heard a huge sigh on the other end of the line. "Bro, you need to go see your SAC immediately. That info has been released to him. I'm not allowed to discuss it."

"Tim, you've always been straight with me. What's going on up there?"

"All I can tell you, my friend, is that I'm as much in the dark as you are about the identity of that body. There are apparently so many levels of security on this thing, it's beyond both of us. But I can tell you two things."

DJ perked up. "Let me have it."

"Okay," Tim said. "Number one is I'm really glad you called me on your cell and mine. Otherwise I couldn't have told you anything at all."

"What's the other thing?"

"If you don't already have a CIA contact you can depend on, you'd better get one quick."

86

Tuesday Morning Later

It had been a busy morning. About the only bright spot for Harrie had been the success of the three-pronged attack on her headache. Things had gone downhill about the time she arrived at the office.

Caroline greeted her at the front door. She pantomimed they should talk outside the building. The bugs were still in place.

"What's up?" Harrie shifted her shoulder bag.

Caroline said, "None of our employees are here today."

Harrie frowned. "Where is everybody?"

Caroline shook her head. "Down with food poisoning."

Harrie blew out a breath. "I thought I'd erased all the negative stuff this morning." She rubbed her neck. "Now I think I need to call the chiropractor. It's possible I've displaced a rib or two."

"Maybe it's just as well. You should call him right now."

Harrie narrowed her eyes. "I don't think so. Explain to me how our entire team is down with food poisoning."

Caroline sighed. "After they finished shopping for my phony 10th anniversary party, they decided to all go to dinner. Apparently there's a new restaurant close to the mall. I've already forgotten the name. It was something weird."

Ginger drove up and headed toward her two workmates.

"Why are you standing out here? Did they evacuate the building?" She looked toward the front door as she spoke.

"Earth to Ginger," Harrie said. "Remember the bugs? They're still there, per orders of DJ and Swannie."

"Ah," Ginger said. "Makes sense. So, what were you two talking about?"

Caroline filled in Ginger about the situation with the staff.

Ginger seemed to listen with increasing alarm. Her face displayed a progression of emotions. "I smell a rat."

Caroline and Harrie looked at each other. Harrie said, "Explain."

"Well, Short Stuff, I'm surprised you didn't pick up on it. This is the sort of thing you're so good at."

"In my defense," Harrie said, "I had a rotten headache this morning—which I believe is paying me another visit. Were it not for that, perhaps I could have foreseen the trouble we're discussing."

"We look deeply suspicious standing out here like we're plotting an insurrection," Ginger said. She sat on the edge of the planter gracing the front of their building and turned to look at Harrie. "We need to rip out those bugs,"

"I'd agree with you," Harrie said, "except we both know that's a bad idea. We have to ride this roller coaster all the way to the end."

Harrie's cell phone rang. "It's DJ," she said to her two companions. "Hi, there," she greeted him. "What's going on?"

She listened intently. Then she said. "It's okay. Caroline, Ginger, and I are standing out in front of the office." She related the story about the food poisoning of their staff.

"No," she said in response to his question. Then she brightened. "Well, since there's nobody here but us, lunch for all sounds great. Where should we meet you?"

She listened a few more seconds before she said, "Good. We'll see you in about an hour."

Caroline sat beside Ginger on the edge of the planter. "I hadn't quite finished telling you the whole story when Ginger arrived. You both need to hear it."

Harrie and Ginger looked at each other, and Harrie nodded.

Caroline said, "Initially, all the ladies went to the restaurant together. But just as they were ordering, one of them received an emergency phone call. She excused herself, saying she was needed at home, but would see them this morning."

Ginger said, "So, why is this one, poison-free employee, not here as promised?"

The nerves along Harrie's spine came alive. A tingling sensation started in her lower back, then shot up her spine to the base of her skull.

Harrie looked at Caroline. "Who left the dinner last night, thus avoiding food poisoning?"

Caroline stood and brushed a bit of planter debris from her skirt. But even before Caroline spoke, Harrie knew the answer.

"Azalea."

87

Tuesday Noon

DJ reserved one of the small conference rooms at the FBI field office and ordered a couple of pizzas. The SAC wanted to speak in person to Harrie, Ginger, Swannie, and Caroline.

Now, when DJ heard about the food poisoning of the staff, it raised a flag in his mind. If Azalea was involved, she could be more dangerous than he'd thought. He sent an email to SAC Williams explaining this latest wrinkle.

Swannie arrived first. One of the administrative staff escorted him up to the conference room, and he and DJ had a few minutes to talk before the ladies arrived.

"What did Crider say when you talked to him?" Swannie picked up a bottle of water and unscrewed the cap.

DJ shook his head, "Nothing. I haven't been able to get hold of him. And you know? That's odd. I don't remember any time I've called him that he didn't pick up."

Swannie shrugged. "First time for everything, I guess."

DJ filled Swannie in about the happenings at Southwest Editing. He ended by saying, "It seems obvious to me that 'Azalea' is not who she pretends to be."

SAC Williams joined them before Swannie could comment. He'd already met the SAC on several occasions. The two men were chatting when DJ's Bureau cell phone buzzed. "SA Scott," DJ said, then, "I'll come down to escort them."

"The ladies are here, as is the pizza," DJ said. He left the two men talking and hurried down to the lobby.

When DJ retrieved his visitors from the outer lobby, they passed through the security area and then into the atrium.

"Wow," Ginger said as she looked around. "This is an interesting building you work in." Both Harrie and Caroline had been here before, but it was a first for Ginger.

When they arrived in the conference room, Swannie had already set places at the table and distributed napkins and bottles of water.

Light conversation accompanied their lunch, but soon a pregnant silence settled over the group.

DJ cleared his throat. "SAC Williams is concerned enough about the situation developing in this case that he wants to personally brief you. Please understand, what you hear in this room is not to be shared with anyone. Can we rely on your discretion?"

There was a chorus of 'yes' and 'of course' responses.

SAC Williams smiled and leaned forward in his chair. "All of you are familiar with the constraints of security issues. I won't bore you with a lecture, except to say this is a highly unusual meeting with civilians. Lieutenant Swanson, I am, for the moment, excluding you in that statement. I'm sure you've worked under the same kinds of constraint most of your police career."

Swannie nodded. "Yes sir, I certainly understand. And several of my detectives have worked on your combined Task Force Initiative."

"Good," Williams said. "To Ms. McKinsey, Mrs. Johnson, and Mrs. Vaughn, I want to be clear on the importance of discretion with this information."

Harrie, Caroline, and Ginger exchanged looks, and mutely nodded.

"I know you hear a lot of things about the FBI in newspapers, magazines, and the 24-hour news cycle on television. But because all of you in this room have day-to-day exchanges with one of our agents, you probably realize things aren't always as they seem."

Everyone nodded in agreement. Williams continued.

"Before '9/11,' communication and coordination between federal agencies—and even some local and state agencies—was a bit different. After 9/11 things changed radically. We now make sure other agencies are brought in when appropriate, and the FBI responds in kind when situations warrant it.

"We maintain relationships with contacts in other agencies—oftentimes at a much higher position level than Special Agent Scott. Of course, he's not necessarily privy to some information. That's where we find ourselves in this current situation.

"There's an on-going operation which, for a variety of reasons, must be allowed to play out. Some people, who must remain in the background, need protection. Invariably an unexpected player will wander into a scenario and, shall we say, 'muck it up' a bit? That's the situation we're in now. There's a time factor involved, which needs to be met. All of you have a role to play—one way or another. Can we count on your help?"

Harrie held up her hand. Williams nodded at her. "You have a question, Ms. McKinsey?"

"Yes sir, I do. DJ must have told you about our offices being bugged. He insisted we leave them in place. It makes working there a bit awkward. What is it, exactly, you think we can do to help?"

Williams took a long breath, looked at DJ, then back to Harrie.

"For now," he said, "we hope you will ignore the bugs and go about business as usual—with one tiny exception."

She tilted her head. "What's the exception?"

His smile seemed strained. "We'd like you to help us trap some very bad people."

88

Tuesday Afternoon-Southwest Editing Services

Harrie, Ginger, and Caroline took a collective deep breath before Harrie unlocked the front door to Southwest Editing. Caroline turned off the alarm. They looked at each other, and Harrie belatedly realized how unnaturally quiet their entrance had been.

"Come on Ladies. We've got to cheer up."

Ginger's eyes grew unnaturally large until she apparently grasped exactly what Harrie was doing.

Caroline spoke next. "I'm worried about our staff. Food poisoning can be very nasty. Don't you think we should check on them?"

"Good idea," Harrie said. She nodded at Caroline.

Ginger said, "I need to finish the manuscript I worked on yesterday. Keep me posted on the staff."

She gestured frantically to Harrie, pantomiming that the two of them should go into Ginger's office. Harrie nodded and followed her.

After closing the door, Ginger walked over to the window and motioned for Harrie to join her.

She stood close to Harrie and whispered, "I don't think I can pull this off."

Harrie said, "Sure you can. Just act natural."

"I don't know . . . " Ginger sat behind her desk and picked up the manuscript.

Harrie shook her head, opened Ginger's door, and went to her own office.

Several minutes later, Caroline entered Harrie's office. "I checked on all the ladies. From what I gather, they ordered an appetizer and shared it. It had a cream sauce base. The bad effects are worse on the ones who ate the most of it."

"Did anyone think they could be here tomorrow?"

"Oh, sure," Caroline said. "Cynthia said she could come in this afternoon if we needed her. I told her not to bother. Her discomfort was confined to only a couple of hours this morning. She said by noon she felt fine."

"What about everyone else?"

"Well, Becky seemed to be the hardest hit. She said she feels better than she did early this morning, but she's still a bit shaky. She spent the entire morning at the hospital. But her husband took her home a little while ago."

"That's good news, I guess." Harrie took a deep breath. "Why don't you go ahead and leave. If you have something you want to work on, take it home and relax."

"I think I'll do just that," Caroline said as she stood. "I'd recommend you do the same."

"I'll think about it, but I believe I'd be more productive if I just hang out here and tackle this pile on my desk."

"Okay," Caroline said. "I'll say goodbye to Ginger, then be on my way." She grinned and gave Harrie a thumbs up sign.

Harrie grinned and mouthed the words, 'call me later.'

Caroline nodded and left.

Harrie let about half an hour pass before she initiated the rest of their plan. At that point, she picked up her phone and dialed Ginger's office extension. Ginger let it ring twice before picking up.

"What's up?"

"Not much. Did Caroline fill you in on the condition of the girls?"

"Yeah, she stopped by before she left. She suggested I leave, and I think I will if you don't mind."

Harrie grinned to herself. Ginger was much better at this than her earlier nervousness would have indicated.

"Good idea. I'm sure Steve would be happy to have you home early for a change."

"Ok," Ginger said. "I'll lock the door on my way out."

"Thanks," Harrie said. "See you tomorrow."

Just before going out the door, Ginger came to Harrie's doorway and gave her a questioning look? Harrie grinned at her and silently mouthed the words, "You did great."

Ginger sighed in apparent relief and saluted her friend before she turned and left the building. Harrie heard the door lock.

She settled in to wait. If SAC Williams was right, something should happen before long.

She edited two chapters before she heard the front door unlock. She leaned back in her chair and waited. Within two minutes the young woman stood in Harrie's office doorway.

"Good afternoon, Azalea."

89

Still Tuesday Afternoon-DJ & Crider

After Caroline, Harrie and Ginger left the FBI, DJ found a message from Colin Crider. He returned the call, and Crider picked up immediately.

"We need to talk."

"I agree," DJ said. "Where?"

"How about the lobby of Presbyterian Hospital on Central?"

DJ frowned. "I'm afraid to ask, but why there?" He heard a long sigh from the other end of the line.

"I'm visiting a friend, okay?"

"I'll be there in half an hour," DJ said and disconnected the call.

He stopped by the SAC's office and brought him up to speed.

Williams said, "See if you can get him to give you any new information. I'd like to see what his version of the story is."

DJ nodded. "Will do, Sir."

DJ arrived at Presbyterian, and found a spot in the parking garage adjacent to the building. He walked into the lobby and spied Crider sitting on a bench against one wall, well away from other people. It occurred to DJ this was likely the first time Crider hadn't waited to make a late appearance.

Crider leaned over in what DJ recognized as a habit of the CIA Operative—his knees and thighs supporting his arms. DJ joined him on the bench and adopted the same posture.

"You must know all hell is breaking loose." He looked straight ahead, waiting for a reply from Crider.

The wait took about ten seconds. "I've withheld a few things from you." Crider looked at the ground.

DJ turned his head to study Crider. "I must say, you're a master of understatement."

The hint of a grin appeared on Crider's face. He sat up straight. "Give me the short version."

"The victim at the Petroglyphs is NOT Viktor Ivanovitch—and nice touch acting all surprised when I initially told you it was."

"Thanks, what else?"

"You've been bugging my wife's offices."

Crider shook his head. "Standard procedure. You know that."

"Then why introduce a human spy into the mix? Didn't you get what you wanted out of the bugging?"

Crider leaned back against the wall. "You are well aware listening devices only give you a one dimensional picture. Having eyes on the scene creates depth and context."

"Or, you could have talked to me at the beginning and asked for my help."

Crider expelled a small grunting sound. "Yeah, right. The CIA is always so eager to bring in the FBI on one of our operations."

"Even so," DJ said. "It would have saved all of us a lot of stress and strain. Next time, you need a better trained operative to infiltrate a group of women. Harrie and her partners were sharp enough to figure it out and alert us."

Crider shrugged. "She's one of our best. I'm just glad they were able to pump her stomach."

DJ had stood while Crider spoke. Now he sat back on the bench. "What do you mean? I understood Azalea wasn't affected by the food poisoning. In fact, my boss worked out a trap for her. My mother indicated Azalea would be back in the office this afternoon. We sent Harrie back there to lure her into trying to steal the manuscript. Then our agents will move in."

Crider's face turned ashen as DJ spoke. He stood, and the look on his face alarmed DJ.

"Are you okay? You look like you've seen a ghost?"

"You need to call 9-1-1. The operative we sent to infiltrate your wife's group is using the name Becky."

90

Later Tuesday Afternoon

Harrie's hand touched the comforting steel of her concealed carry pistol. She had removed it from her purse and secreted it in the second side drawer to her right. It was small but effective. She reminded herself to thank DJ for giving it to her for Christmas. Concealing this one, on her person or anywhere else, was easier than her first weapon, 'Mrs. Peal,' had been.

Azalea sat at the reception desk, going through the daily mail. The two women had talked only briefly when Azalea appeared right after lunch. She reiterated what a lucky thing it was she'd been called home before consuming any of the tainted food.

Harrie stood and paced. The plan couldn't proceed until Azalea asked about the manuscript. Harrie had even mentioned it, but the woman ignored the opportunity. Harrie's thoughts were interrupted by the ringing of the phone. She started to pick it up, but Azalea got there first.

She went to the door of her office, thinking she might discover the caller's identity. Azalea seemed to be taking a message. Harrie sighed and went back to her desk. Her nerves were stretched tight, and she did some deep breathing. Maybe her composure would return.

Why, oh why, had she accepted her part in this little deception?

Harrie sat back at her desk when she heard Azalea end the call. Time was running out, so what now? She picked up the bogus manuscript they'd prepared, and settle in to read it again.

Harrie checked her watch. She'd been back from lunch no more than an hour. It seemed much longer.

A small sound, then a tiny change in the air pressure got her attention. It felt like the front door had been opened. But when she walked out of her office, she saw no evidence of it. Azalea was nowhere in sight.

She looked in the break room, no Azalea. Had she stepped out the side door? They used it only when they had large deliveries. Harrie checked that door. Unlocked. Why? She opened it and peered outside. Nothing out of the ordinary.

She closed the door and turned around. Azalea stood perhaps five feet away, with a quizzical look on her face. Harrie wondered why, until her gaze moved lower.

Azalea's right hand held a steely gray pistol. It looked exactly like the one Harrie had left in her middle desk drawer.

91

Tuesday Still

Without saying a word, Colin Crider followed DJ to his car.

Once DJ heard the news that Azalea was not the CIA operative they thought she was, he had been on the phone with SAC Williams and Swannie.

As he walked to his car, he focused on his conversations. He disconnected from his last call and turned when he heard footsteps behind him.

"Whoa, what do you think you're doing?"

Crider scowled. "I'm going with you, lunkhead. What does it look like?"

DJ huffed, but unlocked the car. Crider got in on the passenger side.

While still inside the parking garage, DJ restrained himself from breaking the 15 mile per hour speed limit. When he was clear, he gunned the big SUV.

DJ's jaw was so tight it ached. He consciously flexed it several times to relieve the pain.

"Sorry about this, Scott." Crider's normal control seemed to have slipped a bit.

"Did your operative tumble to the fact that Azalea was also a spy?"

"Not until early this morning. Then it all fell into place. By the time Becky stopped heaving, she realized what she'd missed. Her husband called me shortly after that from the hospital. I rushed down, but they wouldn't let me see her until just before noon. I called you as soon as I knew the whole story."

"You should have called me as soon as you knew your operative had been compromised."

"That's what I'm telling you. Her husband told me it was food poisoning, and I bought it—until this afternoon, when I finally talked to her."

"When did Azalea catch on to Becky?"

Crider sighed. "Apparently not until sometime yesterday."

DJ wheeled into Southwest Editing's parking lot. A police car and two Bureau vehicles sat out of sight near Harrie's building. Then he caught a glimpse of Swannie.

He took his cue from the others and parked out of view of anyone peering out the windows of Southwest Office Services.

DJ and Crider quietly exited the car and joined Swannie.

DJ said, "What's happening?" That's when he noticed a newcomer he didn't recognize.

The stranger responded. "We're monitoring the situation. Thank God we have Harrie wired. She's talking to Azalea right now. As soon as we hear the secret word, the team goes in."

DJ frown. "I'm sorry," he said "I don't think we've been introduced."

The stranger stood only a couple of inches shorter than DJ. He seemed like someone who worked out regularly, and could handle most any situation. A tiny smile inched across the stranger's face.

Crider stepped forward. "DJ, I'd like you to meet my operative, Richard Tracy, also known as Keyser Söze."

92

Tuesday, Dragging On

Harrie forced her focus on the current dilemma, rather than mentally berating herself for leaving the pistol in a desk drawer.

"I'm still not clear what you want, Azalea. Can't you just tell me?"

Azalea's true personality fascinated Harrie. Before knowing the woman was an imposter, Harrie considered her a little dense and flighty. This same woman now nonchalantly held Harrie's very own concealed carry pistol—keeping it trained on her. Far from ditzy. More cold, calculating, and dangerous than anything.

Azalea tilted her head. She looked at Harrie the way she would a precocious, but annoying, child. "Really, Harrie. I believe you're much smarter than that. You know perfectly well I need that manuscript."

"I gave it to you. That's what you asked for, and here it is." Harrie reached over and retrieved the manuscript Azalea had tossed in anger back onto the conference table.

"Nice try," Azalea said. "Copies don't help us one bit. I need that original you so carefully guard. I believe it's in the vault. My first day on the job, you told me you stored all originals in the vault."

Harrie's brain whirred. Azalea had said, "us." There was a partner involved in this mess. But who?

Harrie stalled for time. "I thought you knew we removed the original from the vault. All I have left is this copy."

Azalea's eyes blazed. Harrie could almost feel the heat of the woman's anger rolling off her. "You and I both know that isn't true. The morning you found it, I personally saw you take the original and make copies of it. Then you returned the original to the vault. When your husband arrived, you obviously gave him a copy. That's what he went away with."

Harrie felt her heart thud hard against her chest. She never dreamed anyone, much less Azalea, had seen her swap out the original for a copy. Even DJ didn't know that.

"Ok," Harrie said. "You're much more clever than I realized." She felt a stirring of hope when she saw Azalea's reaction to the perceived compliment.

"Enough chit-chat. Move it. I have things to do and people to see." The pistol gripped in Azalea's hand swung in an arc as she turned toward the vault.

"Ok, ok, but first tell me something." Harrie stopped, still inside the conference room.

Azalea sighed. "You're a real pain-in-the ass, you know that?"

Harrie worked up a barrage of tears and let loose. "I'm sorry," she sobbed. "I just need some help here."

A loud crash sounded from the side door, and Harrie dropped to the floor. She crawled as fast as she could until she was under the big conference table. Meanwhile, Azalea had whipped around, pistol aimed for the head of anyone who might walk through the conference room door.

Each of the conference room chairs had a five-wheeled base. Harrie had selected them because they moved so easily. She grabbed for the one in front of her and gave it a mighty shove. It sailed straight for Azalea and made contact with her backside. She lurched forward, dropping the pistol in the process.

Before Azalea recovered her balance, a team of FBI agents and APD officers swarmed the room, secured the pistol, and grabbed her arms. When the handcuffs clicked shut around her wrists, DJ brushed past and grabbed Harrie's arm. She struggled to crawl out from under the conference table, and he helped her complete the journey.

He wrapped her in his arms so hard she squealed. "DJ I can't breathe."

"What took you so long to say the magic word?"

"I wanted to make sure everybody was here."

"The plan was to say it as soon as Azalea demanded the manuscript."

"Yes, but with the gun pointed at me, I thought I'd better try to disarm her first."

"That wasn't part of the plan, and you know it."

She grinned at him. "All's well that ends well."

He grabbed her again, hugging her hard.

Swannie stepped into the room. "Everything okay in here?"

"It will be once I stop shaking," Harrie said. "That was a real rush"

"You don't know how much," DJ said.

Harrie felt a familiar tingle in her spine. "That sounds ominous."

"My sweet wife, when we laid out this plan today, we were missing an important piece of information."

Harrie frowned up at him. "Like what?"

DJ blew out a breath. "Like the fact that Azalea wasn't spying for the CIA. Becky had that assignment."

"Becky? So what's Azalea's story?"

DJ shook his head. "That's what I'm on my way to discover. Meanwhile, I'm taking you home. My mother is waiting for you there."

"Wait," Harrie said, and pulled away from DJ. "There's something I need to show you first."

He frowned but followed her into the vault. "What's so important it can't wait?"

Harrie unlocked one of the large filing cabinets and reached inside. She removed a large envelope and handed it to DJ. "This. I should have told you at the time, but I couldn't see what difference it would make."

He opened the envelope and pulled out the manuscript written by Keyser Söze, aka, Richard Tracy. He lifted his left eyebrow. "Uh, how many copies of this thing do you have?"

Harrie chewed on her bottom lip. "That isn't a copy. It's the original. You have one of the only paper copies we made."

"Why didn't you tell me you still had the original?"

Harrie shrugged. "I didn't think it would matter, but after Azalea made such a thing about wanting the original, I realized there must be something more to it."

Harrie could almost see his brain working—flipping through possibilities.

He looked off into the distance. "Come on. I have to get you home. We still have more work ahead of us this afternoon."

When DJ and Harrie reached the front door of the building, Crider blocked DJ. He reached for the manuscript.

Crider frowned. "Where do you think you're going with this?"

DJ opened his mouth, but Crider shook his head. "Wait. After all we've been through, the least I can do is explain something. I should have told you at the beginning."

DJ's jaw clinched in that position she knew only too well. She noticed Crider's jaw was similarly rigid. DJ let go.

Crider said, "This isn't what it appears to be."

DJ shrugged. "I gathered that a long time ago. Please, enlighten us. Why is this valuable-but-terribly-written manuscript wanted by so many people?"

Crider's eyes wavered. First he looked at Harrie, then back at DJ. He shook his head.

"It's a report gained at the cost of several lives. The microdots concealed in these pages are vital to our national security."

93

Wednesday Evening

Harrie took one final look in her mirror. Not too bad, considering.

She checked her watch. Her guests would arrive within the hour. She made a final inspection of her dinner table. The day had been a busy one.

After the excitement of yesterday, Harrie, Ginger, and Caroline decided to close the office for today. Harrie felt sure her poor staff could use the time to finish recovering from their bout of 'food poisoning.'

Besides that, Harrie and her two friends were putting on a dinner party for the Gang of Six (or seven, or eight—depending on who attended.) They needed time to prepare.

Caroline suggested a grocery shopping trip in the morning and an afternoon of food preparation by all three. They agreed, and tonight's feast was worth the time and effort they'd contributed all day.

Ginger showed up first. Harrie let her in and they both headed for the kitchen.

"Steve working late?" Harrie asked.

"A little, but he promised to be on time." Ginger poured herself a cup of coffee and sat at the table.

"It's odd. I never knew how much fun it could be, with the three of us in the kitchen, putting together a big dinner party. I don't think I've ever done that."

Harrie chuckled. "My mom did it all the time. She came from a large family, and her sisters would descend on us to spend half the day cooking a feast. It was memorable."

"Well, thanks for introducing me to the ritual. It'll take me a month to recover, but it was exhilarating."

Caroline arrived next. "What's the word on Azalea? Have you heard anything?"

"I spoke to DJ about an hour ago. He said Crider would reveal all he could at dinner tonight."

The other guests arrived one by one. When they sat down to

dinner, the regular group, plus some new faces, graced the table. DJ brought out two bottles of Gruet Rosé and poured.

There were the regulars: Harrie, DJ, Ginger, Steve, Caroline, and Swannie. The new guests were Colin Crider, Becky from Southwest Editing Services, and Richard Tracy. Sgt. Cabrini Paiz would arrive a bit later due to a previous commitment.

When Harrie served coffee and dessert, DJ stood to get everyone's attention.

"Thank you for being here. It seemed the best way to get everyone on the same page, settle any confusion, and come up with a story that answers questions, but doesn't hamper national security. The news media hasn't gotten wind of this mess, but they still could."

Harrie looked around the table. "Would you mind if I asked the first question?"

DJ said, "Go for it."

She nodded at her former employee. "I'm sorry you became so ill, Becky. I must say, you never gave us a clue you were a spy. Why was that necessary?"

Becky grinned. "Harrie, I apologize for lying to you." She gestured to the others. "You've all been so kind and accepting. But as much as I liked you, I had a job to do."

Colin Crider added, "We wanted to make sure you were safe."

Ginger looked over at Richard Tracy. "Is your name really Richard Tracy?"

The man in question said, "My first confession is that my name isn't Richard Tracy—but I'm sure most of you guessed that anyway. You can call me 'Dick' because I can't tell you my real name any way. I think all of you know that Colin and I have been working on reeling in an important informant for several years. About a year ago we succeeded. At that time, we made a record of information from our new asset. We created a series of microdots. Those dots needed a logical place for concealment. We decided on creating a manuscript."

Ginger held up her hand. "Why did you send it to Southwest Editing Services?"

Crider took over. "My idea, I'm afraid. After I met you two years ago, I knew you fine ladies had an outstanding reputation. Obviously our literary attempt was far from acceptable—we were in a desperate hurry after all—but we also knew you had a rule about keeping all originals in your extra convenient vault."

He turned to Harrie. "By the way, how does an editing service justify the cost of installing a bank vault on the premises?"

Harrie leaned back and crossed her arms. "By having the good luck to lease a building which, prior to our occupation of it, had actually been the branch office of a bank—complete with its own vault."

Crider grinned. "Good answer. Anyway, we knew you would make copies of the manuscript to work on and secure the original in your vault. It was the next best thing to getting it into Fort Knox."

Caroline had the next question. "Why put Becky in our midst to spy on us?"

"Actually," Crider said, "she wasn't there to 'spy' on you. Her job was to guard you and the manuscript. And, just for the record, her name isn't really Becky." He turned to his operative.

"What name are you currently using in other places?"

Becky grinned. "Tess—Tess Trueheart."

Harrie frowned. "That's Dick Tracy's girlfriend's name."

Becky-Tess blushed. "Yes, we know. That's why I chose it."

Harrie turned to Dick. "How clever of you."

'Dick' grinned. "That's the way we roll. Few of us ever know the other guy's real name. But Tess and I are married and usually work as a team. So . . . ."

Swannie had been unusually quiet through all this. He said, "What is the real identity of our murder victim at the Petroglyph National Monument?"

Colin looked at his operatives before he spoke. "We don't actually know. He's an unidentified homeless man with no information on file anywhere."

Swannie said, "How in the hell did you manage that—and why?"

Crider sighed. "Necessity is the mother of invention—or so I've been told. We needed a body to be identified as that of one Viktor Ivanovitch. This poor, unfortunate corpse was languishing at OMI for a few days. They were backed up with autopsies. Another operative, who had recently secured a position at OMI for just such an occasion, dressed the body, snuck it out of OMI and spirited it to the amphitheater at the Petroglyphs. And by the way, don't ask me how because we're not at liberty to explain. Anyway, once it was found, autopsied, and the phony identification made, he returned it to the coolers. No one was the wiser."

Caroline said, "It was a nice touch, hiding one of Harrie's old business cards in the sneaker of the deceased. Why go to that trouble?"

Dick said, "We needed a way to connect the body to your company. We believed it would ensure your help when discovered."

Swannie frowned. "I think I found one of your microdots on that business card, under a gold foil sticker. But why?"

Crider smiled. "Another clue to get the right people involved, in case you hadn't already."

Steve, who among all of them had the least connection to the current events, asked a question. "Why was it important to have the body discovered where it was, and why identify it as Viktor Ivanovitch?"

Crider shrugged. "I wanted to be sure the FBI would be at least peripherally involved, because our higher levels were coordinating the operation. Having it discovered at a National Monument gave credibility to having the FBI called in.

"And the reason for the ruse is simple. We needed to get the real Viktor Ivanovitch safely out of the country, with a new identity, in an out-of-the-way place. He helped us in return for witness protection."

Harrie's mind churned. "Who is Azalea working for? You said it wasn't the CIA."

Crider said, "She's involved with a foreign government. We can't be specific who that is, but they spend a lot of their time spying on the United States."

DJ said, "It must be the government of former citizen, Viktor Ivanovitch."

"Good guess," Crider said.

The doorbell rang, and Harrie looked at her watch. "That must be Sgt. Paiz. Ginger? Would you mind getting her dessert and coffee?"

Ginger nodded and went to the kitchen. Harrie went to the front door to greet Sgt. Cabrini Paiz.

"Sorry I'm so late. I thought I'd be here at least 45 minutes ago."

Harrie shook her head. "No worries. We've been questioning the CIA. We'll fill you in later."

They entered the dining room, where Ginger had just set a place for Cabrini with a cup of coffee and dessert.

Harrie said, "Everyone, this is Detective Sgt. Cabrini Paiz."

Cabrini stopped in her tracks and stared.

Harrie frowned. "Is something wrong?"

Cabrini shook her head. "Not unless you think there's something strange about having dinner with the man who's been following our park ranger—Nick Ellis."

Eyes shifted from Cabrini to the object of her attention. What they saw was the surprised look on the face of Dick Tracy.

94

Wednesday Evening - Still

Harrie broke the sudden, awkward silence.

"Have a seat Cabrini. I saved you some dessert and coffee. We're just getting to the nitty gritty."

Cabrini sat, and Caroline brought in the coffee pot to offer the others. Caroline said, "Cabrini, I don't think most of us know what you're talking about."

Dick Tracy spoke up. "I'd like to discuss that, if you don't mind." He looked around the table at his audience. "I think the three of us owe you as much information as possible."

Cabrini said, "I agree with you. Let's hear it."

Tracy took a breath. "We've explained to your friends that Colin and I were in desperate need of a place to hide our quickly-thrown-together manuscript. With its microdot content, we worried it would get into the wrong hands."

Swannie said, "I'd like to hear, if you can tell us, who these people are. Have we met any of them?"

Tracy spread his hands. "I know most of you have met Azalea. She's been working in tandem with a man. We had them under surveillance most of the time. The man's name would mean nothing to you, even if I could tell you. But some of you might know him under a recently used name—Ted Gunderson."

Harrie's mouth fell open, and she saw Ginger's stunned look. "You know about Ted Gunderson? He came to our office and tried to gain control of the manuscript."

Tracy looked at Tess and smiled. "Yes, thanks to Tess, we knew all about that. And by the way, we were impressed with the way you handled him."

"Glad you approve," Harrie said. She tried to keep the sarcasm out of her voice.

Tracy grinned. "Now that Azalea is in jail for going after you with a gun, he's probably left the country."

DJ turned to Crider. "Harrie thought she saw him at the George Maloof Airpark last Saturday. There were two other men with him.

Do you know why he was there?"

"I have a pretty good idea," Crider said. "Gunderson has been trying to verify the death of Viktor Ivanovitch. Perhaps he thought he could find out from Nick Ellis. We weren't ready to let him have that information until this week. We know he was tasked with assassinating Ivanovitch. They considered him a traitor and wanted to make sure he didn't defect."

"So," DJ said, "once you do a press release, or cause the information to be leaked some way, you believe Gunderson will be happy and leave the U.S.?"

Crider smiled, but looked uncomfortable doing it. "That's a good way to describe it. The two men Harrie and Ginger saw him with are, as we speak, 'discovering' information we've fed them. We feel sure they'll waste no time telling Gunderson."

Cabrini said, "You still haven't explained why you were following Nick Ellis. The poor kid was scared to death. He thought whoever killed the victim at the Petroglyphs was out to get him too."

Tracy shook his head. "I'm sorry to hear that. I tried to be invisible. He was so jumpy all the time, I began to wonder if he was hiding something."

"So that line you fed me about working for the government and making sure Ellis was okay, wasn't true." Cabrini tilted her head and waited.

"No," Tracy said, "I was truthful with you. I do work for the government, and I was attempting to protect Nick Ellis. I simply didn't understand how frightened he would be."

A question occurred to Harrie. "Why did you mail me that note from Greece, telling me to destroy your manuscript?"

Crider and Tracy looked at each other. Crider said, "That was actually my doing. At the time, we thought the op had been compromised. If you had destroyed it, the microdots couldn't get into the wrong hands."

"But you sent it to our old address."

Crider scratched his chin. "I know that now. Back then, I didn't. That's one reason I had to bring DJ in on some things. Also, 'Becky' could have stepped in and, if necessary, destroyed it."

Ginger raised her hand to speak. "Why did you bug our offices? And why did you only bug Harrie's and the conference room?"

"Same reason I assigned Tess to become 'Becky' and work there. Keeping an eye on our manuscript, but also keeping track of the information you, Harrie, and Caroline were uncovering."

Harrie said, "Can you come take the damned things out now? We're stressing out, big time, knowing somebody's listening to everything we say." She received confirming nods from Caroline and Ginger.

Colin Crider spoke up. "They're already gone. We're done here. The bad guys didn't get what they wanted, and our witness has safely landed in his new home country."

DJ held up his wine glass. "I'd like to propose a toast."

Harrie grabbed another bottle of wine and handed it to him. He applied the corkscrew and filled each person's glass.

"Now for the toast," he said. "To our core Gang of Six, thank you, once again, for helping us solve another puzzle."

Everyone took a sip of wine. DJ raised his glass again. "Thanks to Colin Crider for coming back into our lives with another adventure. What would we do without him?"

Laughter rippled around the room. Crider turned slightly pink and took his sip of wine.

"And finally," DJ said, "thanks to my beautiful and nosey wife for keeping us all on the edge of disaster with her prophetic dreams."

Harrie opened her mouth to say something snarky. But the look on DJ's face, plus the faces of Caroline, Ginger, and the rest of her friends, stopped her. These people, even the CIA personnel who started all this, brought such wonderful things into her life.

She reflected that her prophetic dreams had taken on a different flavor since her teen years. They showed her scary things, but no longer caused the intense fear of the past. Instead, she felt they were a gift to help answer questions or point the way to solutions. She hadn't realized until that moment how lucky she really was.

She felt a big grin spreading across her face. Her eyes filled with tears as she held up her wine glass.

"I toast all of you. Without you and your acceptance of my weird dreams, life wouldn't be nearly as wonderful."

When they'd finished their wine, Swannie stood.

"I have something to say." He looked around the room.

Caroline looked down at her lap, fidgeting with her napkin.

Swannie had poured another small amount of wine into his glass. Now he held it up.

Harrie felt a huge surge of electrical energy—instantly sensing what was coming. The Ancient Ones had appeared in her last dream and gave her a message. She held her breath and waited to hear what she already knew.

Swannie said, "I'd like to propose another toast tonight. I decided to take a leap of faith. I asked Caroline to marry me, and she said 'yes'."

Everyone looked at Caroline, who smiled broadly. She stood next to Swannie and held up her own wine glass.

"Thanks to Harrie for bringing us together."

Ginger squealed, and Steve shook his friend's hand. The rest of the assembled guests gathered around the beaming couple.

Harrie smiled to herself and took a sip of wine.

Should I let them know the spirits came to me in my dreams, and they told me this would happen tonight? Would they even believe me?

Is there any possibility they could understand the honor I feel to be contacted by the Ancient Ones who roam the Petroglyphs?

Maybe someday.

But not just yet.

Acknowledgements

This might be the most difficult piece of the book to get down on paper. There's much to say, but limited space to do it.

I don't want to overlook anyone, and that's always the fear. When I finished this book, I realized there were so many people who had a part in making it happen. I'll do my best to include everyone. Please forgive me if I've left anyone out!

My first gratitude, as always, goes to my amazing husband. Don is very supportive, to the point of taking over dinner preparations when I'm working on a project. But this time, he also supplied me with the setting and theme for the story. Thanks for that, Sweetheart. You have good ideas.

The next thanks go to my writers critique group. The membership there has changed over the sixteen years I've been part of it. As we've lost old friends, we've brought in new ones to keep us going. Thanks to all of you current members: Margaret Tessler, Charlene Dietz, Diane Flaherty, Paula High-Young, Rita Herther, Babs Langner, and Ruthie Francis. Since I started the book back in 2017, a few people who heard parts of it then are no longer with the group. So thanks to Joan Taitte, Mary Bergen Blanchard, Linda Triegel, and Gloria Casale for their ideas and support while they were here. Having a group such as this giving feedback and advice is invaluable.

Once the first draft was finished, I distributed it to my Beta Readers. These people helped in so many ways, and I depended heavily on them for catching typos and "holes" in the story. Thanks to Joann Hunter, Margaret Tessler, Ruthie Francis, Joan Taitte, and Stephan Marshall. Your suggestions and sharp eyes are priceless.

And thanks to my ham radio friends for their continued support and kick-in-the-pants motivation to keep the books coming. I hope you are pleased.

It's time to jump into the void again and see what I can find. Wish me luck.

You'll also enjoy these other Harrie McKinsey Mysteries

The Easter Egg Murder
Harrie McKinsey Mystery 1

The Easter Egg Murder is loosely based on the real-life murder of Cricket Coogler in 1949 in southern New Mexico. Patricia Smith Wood's fictional account of this event and her equally fictional ending create a captivating mystery that spans more than fifty years and winds in and out of the lives of a diverse cast of New Mexicans on its way to a surprising ending.

Murder on Sagebrush Lane
Harrie McKinsey Mystery 2

Harrie finds a small child sitting in the flower bed, her pajamas smeared with blood. Harrie's search for the parents involves her in a grisly murder investigation, a second murder, an attempted kidnapping, stolen top secret data, and a killer who intends to make her his final victim.

Murder on Frequency
Harrie McKinsey Mystery 3

There's nothing unusual about a ham operator contacting other radio enthusiasts. Unless he's been dead for five years. When Harrie McKinsey and Ginger Vaughn decide to study for their ham radio licenses, they get pulled into this mystery and find a trail leading to a long-lost treasure somewhere in New Mexico. Before it's over, there's another murder, an abduction, and a showdown with an aging Mafia don who values treasure more than human life. Harrie, Ginger, and their merry band of FBI, APD, and private detectives have to be on their toes to prevent another murder and save a family.